The Dymchurch Reckoning

Emma Batten

*To Denise!
Happy reading,
Emma*

First published in the UK by Emma Batten 2023.

Printed and bound in the UK

A catalogue record of this book can be found in the British library.

ISBN 978-1-7399854-2-4

Edited by Debbie Rigden

Cover painting by Kean Farrelly

www.emmabattenauthor.com

To Kean,
with thanks for your enthusiasm for my
writing and unfailing support for my
unpredictable author life.

About the Book

In this sequel to *But First Maintain the Wall* and *The Whitsun Gallop*, I follow the lives of Harry and Phoebe Farrers, moving forward three years to 1765.

The opening chapters were inspired by the true story of Rye butcher, John Breads, who planned to murder the town mayor in the churchyard, but mistakenly killed the wrong man. Other than the influence of that event, my Dymchurch version, all other storylines and all characters are entirely fictional.

The role of the jury was different in the 18th century. They were expected to gather evidence as well as deciding whether the accused person was guilty or innocent under the guidance of the judge. In a small, court the accused had no one acting on their behalf.

As always, I try to make the area recognisable and to be accurate in descriptions of Romney Marsh.

This book features Rothschild Farm, Burmarsh, renamed by my fictional character as Rothschild Manor. Also in Burmarsh, the pub is mentioned but I am aware the building was not used for that purpose until 1801. In Dymchurch, the present New Hall courtroom dates from 1739, and is occasionally open to the public. The gaol dates from 1797, but I cannot resist including it in these Dymchurch novels.

I hope you enjoy following the lives of familiar characters as well as meeting new ones and trying to work out 'whodunnit'.

Emma Batten 2023

With Thanks

Many thanks to Kean Farrelly for creating a painting of Dymchurch church in the 18th century and for the beautiful rural scene on the back cover.

Thank you to Maud Matley your encouragement and enthusiasm for my author plans, drafting the French and checking the novel before print.

Many thanks to Michael Golding for the first edit. I know I complain about your exuberant reworking of my writing, but I do appreciate everything you do.

Debbie Rigden – thank you for another fabulous edit. I love working with you and always look forward to seeing your thoughts and comments.

Huge thanks to Liz Hopkin for the thorough comma check and for spotting sneaky typos, and to Beverley Adams for the final checks.

Last, but not least, many thanks to my readers who continue to buy my books, comment on social media, visit me at craft fairs and come to my workshops.

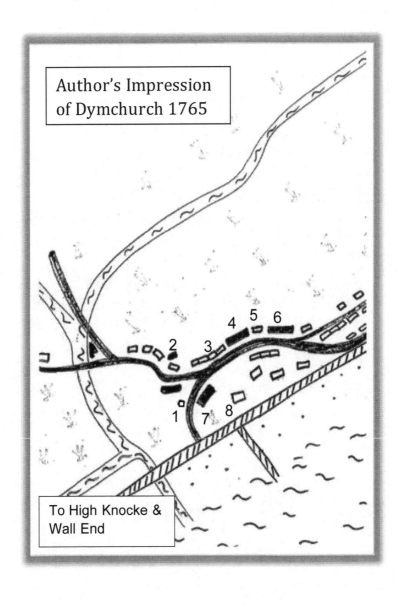

Author's Impression of Dymchurch 1765

To High Knocke & Wall End

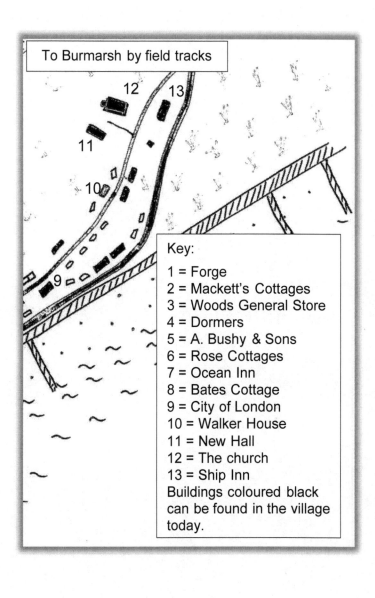

To Burmarsh by field tracks

12 13

11

10

9

Key:

1 = Forge
2 = Mackett's Cottages
3 = Woods General Store
4 = Dormers
5 = A. Bushy & Sons
6 = Rose Cottages
7 = Ocean Inn
8 = Bates Cottage
9 = City of London
10 = Walker House
11 = New Hall
12 = The church
13 = Ship Inn
Buildings coloured black
can be found in the village
today.

Chapter One
Harry
Dymchurch
September 1765

Sir Rupert Bannerman, Leveller of the Marsh Scotts and magistrate, stood, raising himself to full height, while his gaze remained firmly on the man standing in the dock. When he spoke, his tone told of an authority undisputed within the Corporation of Romney Marsh.

"Anthony Bushy, it seems that I have been too lenient with you in the past. This is the third time you have appeared in court in the last eighteen months. Your guilt is unquestionable, as proven by the weights and measures overseer. To fine you again would make a mockery of my justice system. From this moment onwards, I forbid you to serve customers either in your own shop or in any other butcher's premises on Romney Marsh. This ruling will run for two years. Within the next day, I expect the person who plans to take your role to make themselves known to my clerk."

The clerk, seated at a desk before the magistrates' bench, gave a short nod without looking up from his ledger.

"I can't trade in my own shop?" the accused questioned, despite the meaning of Sir Rupert's words being perfectly clear. "I've a pig to be slaughtered and a pen of chickens."

1

"You may butcher the animals as you see fit, but the selling of meat is to be dealt with by someone who can balance a pound of beef against a weight of the same value. Whoever is chosen to substitute you, I suggest they have enough wit about them to realise that myself and my jurats will be keeping a sharp eye on your business. Any more trouble and I shall be forced to evict you from the premises."

"I don't understand…"

"Then I do you a favour in removing you from the responsibility of conforming to weights and measures laws!" Sir Rupert retorted. A snigger ran around those who had gathered in the New Hall courtroom merely for the sport of witnessing the crimes to be judged that afternoon. "Enough of this," the Leveller of the Marsh Scotts barked. He waved his hand in the direction of the butcher and the small rabble of spectators leaning against the hessian-clad walls of the courtroom. "I am done with this session. Leave the court now, and you, Mr Bushy, do not neglect to give my clerk the details of your replacement. Two days."

The accused man appeared to accept his punishment, and although he shot a scowl in the direction of the magistrates' bench, no more words were uttered. He sauntered out the best he could, giving the impression that he was by no means cowed by being called to the court that day.

Sir Rupert slumped back in his chair as the lofty room emptied, leaving just himself, the jurats and clerk. Harry stood, stretching his limbs and straightening his jacket. He looked towards William Payne, still seated on the other side of Sir Rupert, and said, "No troubles in court this afternoon, thankfully. How's Marianne? And the children?"

"They are keeping well, thank you," William responded as he reached into his jacket and retrieved

2

a slim envelope, sealed with a pool of wax. "She was hoping to visit Phoebe and the children tomorrow afternoon and asked me to give you this."

"I'm sure Phoebe will be delighted!" Harry smiled as he accepted the note. "Young James took his first steps last week – he has finally caught up with Clara who was a full ten days ahead of him! And you know how Esther adores your girls – they are so good with her." Harry spoke of his three adopted children: The eldest had been with them from four days after her birth, whereas the twins had arrived at two months old, making the family complete.

"They can all marvel at the twins walking, and if Marianne can help at all then you both know the offer is there..." William stood and stepped off the raised platform where they had been seated throughout the court proceedings.

"I know Phoebe was grateful for the gowns and little chemises." Harry recalled the neatly pressed bundle that had arrived in the care of Marianne Payne's maid two weeks beforehand.

"Blazes!" Sir Rupert Bannerman let out a guffaw, which bounced off the vaulted ceiling. He roused himself from the chair and stepped off the dais where all three had been seated. Then he strode through the courtroom, his jacket brushing against the oak benches and tables. "Are these my worthy jurats or a pair of spinster aunts?" he asked while passing through the doorway. "My head was already aching and now it pounds to hear of swaddling cloths, wet nurses and... and... muslins! Any more of this and I shall have to take up knitting so we can speak of it at the supper following the Michaelmas meeting."

Harry grinned, following Sir Rupert onto the landing at the top of the stairs. "If William or I indulge in knitting, or indeed crochet, then I fear we will have to step aside to allow you to fill our positions with candidates more worthy of the honour."

However, the Leveller of the Marsh Scotts now spotted his manservant in the hallway and his attention turned to other matters. "Brown!" he called, "A brandy in my study, please. I am feeling chilled through. An hour in front of the fire should have me back on form." He spoke to Harry again while descending the stairs, "I pray I shall not be forced to part with either of you!"

The jurats, men who upheld the law and attended the day-to-day running of Romney Marsh Proper, left by the back door of New Hall. Harry waited for William to collect his horse from a groom, then they strolled along the road, with the bay gelding walking beside them on a slack rein. It was still mid-afternoon and the early autumn sunshine bathed Dymchurch in warmth, leading William to observe, "How odd Sir Rupert felt the need for a fire. I hope he isn't sickening for anything."

"I hope not," Harry responded. "We have the Michaelmas meeting in two days. He wouldn't want to miss it."

They approached Walker House, and any thoughts of Sir Rupert were put aside as the men spoke more of domestic matters before parting. Then William mounted his horse with ease and set off. At the far end of the High Street, he would turn inland, riding through the countryside to the village of St Mary in the Marsh.

Harry turned the brass handle, pushed on the panelled front door and stepped inside. Once in the hallway, he had a moment to appreciate its tranquillity, with the steady rhythm of the grandfather clock, and muted light settling on the beautifully turned elm banister. While he removed his coat, a set of small fingers could be seen curling around the lower edge of the parlour door. Smiling, Harry crouched a little and waited.

4

"Papa!" Esther cried. "Papa!" Then turning back to the room, she announced Harry's arrival, "Mama, James, Clara... Mary – Papa is home!" The battle with the heavy door was won and she tumbled into the hallway, then into Harry's arms, squealing as he lifted her and planted a firm kiss on her soft cheek.

"Hello! How's my little girl?" Harry ran his fingers through Esther's chestnut waves and looked into her big brown eyes.

"I'm bigger than Clara," she declared.

"But smaller than Georgina and Joanna who are to visit tomorrow if Mama is free!" Harry popped Esther down on the parlour rug amidst a pile of wooden bricks. He knelt to greet the twins and spoke to Phoebe, "Marianne Payne sent a note. She is hoping to visit."

"That would be wonderful," Phoebe responded, her face lighting up. Marianne and her daughters were always welcome, with the girls becoming small mothers to Harry and Phoebe's children and providing hours of entertainment.

Six years before, not long after their marriage, Walker House was built and had boasted an elegant parlour. While remaining a charming space with graceful sash windows and classical panelling, this room was not destined to remain a place to entertain genteel company, where the children would only be permitted to enter in an evening to enjoy a story upon their doting mother's lap. It became the heart of the home with laughter and chatter, punctuated with the inevitable tantrums, resonating throughout the day. The central rug became a spot to gallop naively carved horses, tend cloth dolls and create towers of wooden bricks. Meanwhile, the polished planks made an impressive sound when bashed with rattles and were the perfect surface for a spinning top.

Harry managed to balance six bricks before James tottered along, felled them and promptly dropped to the floor. "Help me build it again?" he asked his young son.

If Harry was unique in his determination not to be a distant father figure, and Phoebe exceptional in encouraging the children to play freely in the best room, then perhaps it would come as no surprise that the relationship with their staff was unusual. Janey the housekeeper and Mary the maid were also aunt and sister to the little girl, Esther. Born in the hospital for infectious diseases, Esther was rejected at birth. Her mother had passed the age where she felt any joy to be bearing a child and, already in poor health, feared not many years would follow before her new baby would be left motherless. A suggestion was made that the infant be adopted by Harry and Phoebe who were losing hope of having children of their own. Sadly, Esther's birth mother had been right in her prediction – she died before the little girl's second birthday.

Leaving the jumble of bricks on the rug and her young siblings by adoption, Esther picked up her rag doll and headed towards Mary. Alerted by the childish babble accompanying Esther as she toddled about the house, Mary turned towards the little girl whom she had not seen since those first days after the birth. Smallpox had been cruel to this young woman, for although she had escaped the worst of the disfiguring scars so commonly found in those who survived the disease, the infection was then at work in her eyes. Blisters formed around the delicate tissues, and on leaving hospital Mary was blind.

The doll was placed in Mary's lap, and she exclaimed, "Thank you, Esther! Shall we wrap her in a shawl? I think I have it here." Reaching into a basket at her feet, Mary extracted a small woollen blanket and deftly swaddled the doll. "Mr Farrers, I'm going to the kitchen now. Would you like tea? I can ask Janey…"

"No, I'm off to the forge," Harry replied. He watched as Mary picked up a cane, using it to alert her to any toys or small children that may be littering the path to the parlour door. He and Phoebe resisted helping or offering advice about potential hazards, knowing Mary preferred to be as independent as possible.

"Were there any incidents in court?" Phoebe asked once they were alone with the children.

"Three separate cases and none of them serious," Harry told her while restacking the bricks. "You'll not be served by Anthony Bushy at his shop anymore. Three times he's been caught for giving incorrect measures, and Sir Rupert won't allow this to happen again. One of his sons or his brother will have to tend the shop from now on. He is to let the clerk know who he chooses to replace him."

"There is something about that man…" Phoebe considered her next words while running her fingers through Clara's fair curls. "I get the impression that he will do as he wishes and pay little heed to the law."

"I am certain Sir Rupert will not hesitate to take the lease of the shop away if Mr Bushy disobeys him in this matter." Harry stood, allowing James to use his leg as a support so the child could pull himself to his feet. "I must change and make haste to the forge. It is not fair to leave Matthew, although he is quite capable. I'll see you all later."

Harry wasted no more time, running up the stairs while loosening his jacket. In the bedroom he replaced his linen shirt with one of hemp and pulled on a rough tweed waistcoat. His breeches he changed for older ones, repaired many times over the years. He left home through the back door, after pausing to pull on sturdy boots. Walking briskly along the village street, Harry gave the occasional greeting, a wave or nod to those he passed. Determined to make good use of the afternoon, he was not going to be waylaid on route to the forge.

The village of Dymchurch lay behind the long curve of a seawall. From atop this great bank of strong oak stakes, whippy blackthorn bundles and lashings of sticky clay-soil, a path led towards Everden Groyne in the east, and to Wall End in the west. On the seaward side, the sands were vast and golden at low tide, and at high tide the English Channel swept against the Wall.

On the landward side, the settlement was mainly a humble collection of simple cottages, traditional trades, shops and inns. Plots of land had been cultivated for vegetables, enclosures constructed for pigs and coops for chickens. Upright two-story houses of red brick and tiled roofs created an air of dignity in the vicinity of the church, including Sir Rupert's home – New Hall – the vicarage, a manor house and Walker House where Harry and Phoebe lived. These larger properties were now behind Harry as he passed the terraces of cottages and shops in the village centre. On the outskirts of Dymchurch, the forge squatted low on the roadside, opposite a tavern called Ocean Inn.

The door of the forge was open, and Harry called a greeting to his employee, "Good afternoon! I trust all is well?"

"Here between the fire, workbench and anvil, all is well," Matthew Alder replied, his tone cheery. "But I can't help noticing there's someone at the Ocean with something to gripe over. He's been holding court on the bench out the front for the past half hour."

"Oh?" Harry looked back over his shoulder and towards the tavern. "There's no one about now."

Matthew glanced up, squinting as he attempted to look through the thick glass at the window. "Must have moved on or gone inside. It was Anthony Bushy, unless I'm mistaken." Then he grinned at Harry and continued, "I've got these hinges to finish and no time to be worrying about what others are up to over there, but it's early in the day to be making a fuss and taking to the rum, or whatever he fancies."

"Anthony Bushy?" Harry repeated as he donned a leather apron. "I don't like the sound of that. He was in court this afternoon for cheating with his weights. Sir Rupert Bannerman has forbidden him to serve in his shop, or any other, for two years."

"Fair enough!" Matthew stated. "He deserves it."

Harry was pleased with the assistant he had taken on three years beforehand, finding him to be a hard worker who produced good quality metalwork. Matthew's attention returned to the iron hinges while Harry worked on the decorative hooks he had been crafting earlier. They busied themselves with little conversation for the next hour before being interrupted by a lone figure who left the bar of the Ocean and wended his unsteady way across the road.

Anthony Bushy, butcher from the High Street, made himself known when he was midway across the road: "Hey! Mr Jurat. Mr Blacksmith… Let's talk like men about this bother."

Harry sighed, placed his tools on the bench, and moved to the doorway. Matthew, sensing trouble, stood behind him.

"What is there to talk about?" Harry asked.

"This weights and measures nonsense." The butcher now stood within an arm's length of Harry. As he gesticulated wildly, the stench of ale and tobacco wafted about. "I'm as honest as the next man. Who doesn't try their luck on occasion?"

"No one who doesn't want to stand in the courtroom before Sir Rupert Bannerman," Harry retorted. "That's the chance you took. You were treated fairly and perhaps if you go home and sleep on it, then you'll realise that."

"He's just sniffing around looking to cause trouble for us hardworking men of Dymchurch," Anthony Bushy continued. "Sending someone into the shops to check on us. You should look out – he'll be here next, watching what you're up to with all your metalwork. Then he'll be off to see Giles and Peggy, them who are your wife's family, he'll be... he'll be..."

Now the trail of words petered out. The alcohol had induced confusion. Harry turned away, not inclined to indulge the butcher with any more attention. "Let's get back to work," he said to Matthew.

The last they heard from the drunken man were his final assertions as he ambled away, before half-turning and hollering, "I can still do the slaughtering. That's what he said. He said I could still go butchering."

Chapter Two
Harry

"Gentlemen!" Aaron Chapman of Rothschild Manor, Burmarsh, rose to his feet. He looked every part the Lord of the Manor that evening - donning a wig of luxurious brown waves upon his own prematurely thinning locks, a beauty spot on his cheekbone, and a circlet of stiff material around his neck. His appearance was overdone for a night at the Ship, and everyone knew it, except Aaron himself. Brushing down his waistcoat, he tapped upon the table with a silver-topped cane, there to serve no purpose other than to accentuate his supposed grandeur. "Gentlemen, I bid you a good evening. I must deliver an important document to New Hall before the servants are all in bed, then I shall ride home."

Those who gathered at the long table bid exuberant farewells. The Chapman family were universally disliked locally, but it had been an enjoyable evening with much good wine and brandy from the cellars of the Ship. Besides, Aaron had provided a fair amount of entertainment – to dress as a London dandy was extravagant, and no matter how many times he referred to his home as 'The Manor', it would always be Rothschild Farm to those who knew the area well.

"He fancies himself as Leveller of the Marsh Scotts!" William Payne said as Aaron left. It was a right that none of the jurats could aspire to. Lord of the Levels was a hereditary title, whereas a jurat earned his position.

Harry smiled, used to his friend's foolish comments. "It's been a good evening, but I must head home now."

"Home?" William grinned. "You only need to amble along the road. Have another brandy."

"The babies..." Harry began. "It's their teeth."

"Understood! I'm glad mine are past waking us through the night."

Pushing back his stool, Harry stood to give his own parting words, "Thank you everyone for your company but I must go now."

At this he faced some banter about the hour still being early and there being no need to break up the party yet. However, these words flew about without rancour, and Harry merely laughed them off as he left the Ship within minutes of Aaron.

Standing beneath the ornate portico, Harry stopped for a moment to appreciate the clean, cool night air. He took a few steps away from the inn and paused once more, breathing deeply while listening to the slap of the tide on the seawall. Not far away a fox screeched, and nearby a horse shuffled about in its stable. Home beckoned, and he began to pick his way across the rough, stony ground – as alcohol ran through his veins, the crescent moon made a poor companion. With his gait unsteady, Harry hesitated at the midway point between the Ship, church and New Hall. At once, he was alerted to something being out of place.

The small Norman church was partly concealed by trees that had not yet shed their leaves, and knowing it well, Harry barely glanced at the low, pointed steeple and tiled roof bathed in the muted moonlight. However, he did sense movement within the churchyard and assumed Aaron had paused at the inn to alert the stablehand that his horse would need preparing for the ride home, meaning that he was only a few paces ahead of Harry. *What papers does he have that are so important that the staff must be bothered this late in the evening?* These thoughts merely fluttered in and out of his mind. Aaron's plans were of no consequence to Harry, although he remained wary of his old rival and knew the other man would take any opportunity to cause difficulties for him.

Life is peaceful now… Harry reflected as he moved on. An image of his three children entered his mind – *perhaps not peaceful, but good.* However, he had meandered no further than the empty gallows between the church and New Hall, when his ponderings were interrupted by the sound of footsteps pounding on the path not so far away.

"Take your hands off me! How dare you!" Aaron's voice rang out – with that familiar sneer so often heard when speaking to someone he considered to be inferior.

"I dare, because you gave me your permission!" the reply came. This second voice was known to Harry, but he could not put a name nor a face to it. "You said I was welcome to go butchering!" A wild laugh ricocheted amongst the churchyard trees and the ancient ragstone walls of St Peter and St Paul.

Side-stepping to partly conceal himself against the nearest object, Harry pressed up against the oak post of the gallows. The effects of the alcohol which, seconds before, had left him feeling pleasantly befuddled, somehow fled. He was now alert to every sound and movement, while his heart slammed against his chest and a light sweat covered every inch of his skin.

"Butchering?" Aaron repeated, now with a definite hint of fear in his voice. "Unhand me and allow me to go about my business at New Hall."

13

"Butchering! And there's no one on Romney Marsh who deserves it more."

"You'll pay for this…"

"I'll pay for nothing!"

These were the last words exchanged between the men and witnessed by Harry as clearly as if they stood beside him. A furious yelp shot from one of them, followed by a long, low groan, then a thud. Harry faltered, unsure of what to do next. Aaron's temper was legendary. He was unlikely to suffer this interruption to his plans and barrage of senseless words for long. This man, both landowner and jurat, carried a slim knife at his waist and was likely to use it.

Footsteps once more hammered on the path, coupled with a wild thrashing as a figure crashed against overhanging branches. A man emerged from the gloom and into the weak light cast by the moon. "You said I was welcome to go butchering." The words rang out, then again, "You said I was welcome to go butchering," as he ran across the road, past the Ship and in the direction of the seawall.

"Aaron!" Harry murmured, springing from his position and towards the shelter of the church and surrounding trees. "I thought…" But it didn't matter what he thought. The second man had run off, clearly without injury, and the first may well be wounded or worse… The churchyard was modest in size, although crowded with graves, oaks and an ancient yew. Harry knew it well and it took no time to discover the figure of Aaron slumped against a tombstone, his hand held over the left-hand side of his chest. Between his fingers, a dark liquid oozed, highlighted by a shaft of moonlight entering through a gap in the leafy canopy.

"Farrers," Aaron growled, low and husky. "Get some help."

Retreating, Harry ran from the churchyard, and across the rough track to New Hall. The front of the building stretched out: square windows, irregular in size, set in a red brick façade under a tiled roof. No light gleamed behind shutters or sumptuous window hangings – it appeared as if the inhabitants had settled early for the night, and Harry had no choice but to rouse them. He lifted the door knocker and rapped loudly while calling out, "Come quickly – a man is injured."

Almost at once, movement could be heard within the house – the clunk of a door closing, footsteps, then the smooth passage of worn metal upon metal as a bolt slid free. Before the manservant, Brown, showed his face at the door, Harry was speaking. "It's Aaron Chapman. Stabbed in the churchyard."

For thirty-five years, Brown had worked for the Bannerman family. He was often the first person encountered when visitors called at New Hall and over the years he had faced many dramas. Whether he naturally felt no emotion, or had trained himself to remain impassive, was not known. No one remembered the lively young man who had entered the world of work at fourteen years of age. Standing in his breeches and shirt, he merely checked, "Is he still alive?" In the hallway a grandfather clock ticked – its steady beat reminding Harry of Brown's ponderous manner. He glanced at it. *Only nine o'clock.*

"Alive," Harry confirmed, "but with a wound to his chest."

Now George Bannerman, eldest son of Sir Rupert and Lady Charlotte, thundered down the stairs and raced to the door. "Father is ill. In bed," he announced.

"I know," Harry replied. "But I had to come. Aaron Chapman has been attacked in the churchyard. Stabbed in the chest. It's serious."

"Can he walk?" Brown asked.

15

"Perhaps with help," Harry responded. "Maybe George and I...?"

"I'll go for the apothecary," Brown decided.

With no need for further deliberation, Harry removed his jacket and passed it to George. "Wear this," he said, grateful for the presence of the young man who was known to be of stable character and not likely to make a fuss about whatever was going to develop over the next hour. A man's life was at risk – both Aaron and Harry needed men with a steady mind.

George nodded and, thinking nothing of the incongruous sight he made, he pulled on the jacket as he stepped out into the night air with his nightshirt flapping at his knees and slippers on his feet. Meanwhile, Brown was seated in the wide hallway buckling his shoes and had already covered his upper body in the coat he usually wore about the house, complete with brass buttons and braiding.

"And the vicar?" Brown called as the younger men set off across the forecourt of New Hall.

"Fetch him!" Harry called back.

There were no more than two dozen steps between the Bannermans' home and the churchyard. They entered through a gap in the stone wall and were immediately cocooned by low grassy banks and trees. "There he is," Harry said, pointing to a hunched figure. "Aaron, I'm back with George Bannerman." In the darkness he saw no movement or flicker of recognition and, as he dropped to his knees, Harry believed they were too late.

"Will we carry him, or do you think he can walk?" George asked.

Harry faltered, thinking it would be better to return to New Hall for a ladder to place the body on.

At that moment, still showing the impatience and contempt for others he was known for, Aaron found the energy to snarl, "I can walk. I will walk."

Taken aback, Harry replied to George, "We'll walk him. I'll take this side." Then to Aaron, "We are going to take you to New Hall."

"We need to be careful not to pull on the wound," George observed, ripping a portion of his nightgown and folding it before lifting Aaron's hand and packing the bloody area.

Impressed by the young man's ingenuity, Harry said to Aaron, "We need you to keep your hand over the wound while we help you stand." He positioned himself on the side of the injury, and crouched to take the weight, with George bending to take his share. Together they eased Aaron to his feet.

Those few steps from churchyard to New Hall, so familiar to these three men, became an arduous journey. Their pace was slow and uneven, their breaths laboured. Every crunch on the gravel brought them closer, and all concentration focussed on the task. Before they reached the front door, all three turned to hear footsteps and a figure emerged from the street corner.

"The vicar," George announced.

At this, Aaron lifted his head, and his lips curled as if some spiteful tirade was about to pour forth. Yet nothing came and it appeared that he weakened, for the weight upon the young men supporting him became all the greater.

"He's not lifting his feet," Harry groaned. Together he and George dragged Aaron for the last few steps, while the vicar sprang forward to open the door fully, stepped inside the hallway and pulled a heavy oak chair forward.

Once lowered into the chair, Aaron merely lolled. "Some light..." the vicar ordered, glancing towards an oil lamp with a low flame still burning. His slim fingers shone pale as he pulled at the stiff stock clasped around Aaron's neck and then at the laces fastening his shirt.

George held the lamp, while Harry lifted a small side table, and they positioned them to cast the best light upon the injured man. The wadding, freshly torn from George's nightshirt, fell to the floor and the cut into flesh below the collarbone was fully revealed for the first time. It still oozed, and, to their horror, the three men could see the extent of the blood lost – both the jacket and shirt were soaked on the left-hand side.

Harry placed his hand on Aaron's forehead. It felt clammy. He turned to look at his companions.

"I fear there is nothing the good apothecary will be able to do," the vicar murmured.

No reaction came from the figure in the chair as the vicar held his hand and began to whisper, "For if we live, we live to the Lord; and if we die, we die to the Lord. Therefore, whether we live or die, we are the Lord's..." His words droned on while approaching footsteps sounded outside.

"Did you see it happen?" George asked Harry, his voice hushed. "Did you see who did this?"

"I heard an altercation," Harry whispered. "It was the butcher – Anthony Bushy. I'm certain of it. It was the words..."

"The words?"

"'You said I was welcome to go butchering'. Your father told him he could continue to butcher the animals but banned him from serving in the shop. I was in court on Friday, you see."

"But what does this have to do with Aaron. He wasn't there – in court?"

The apothecary and Brown entered, and the conversation between Harry and George ceased. The apothecary immediately dropped to his knees, taking Aaron's free hand in his own, turning it over and pressing a finger over the underside of the wrist. He said nothing at first, merely nodding his head slowly. Then, on releasing the wrist, he ordered, "Some warm water and cloths. At least we can clean him up a little."

"As you say, sir." Brown left for the kitchen.

"Shall we lift him to a bed? Or some place where you can see what is to be done?" George asked.

"His time on this earth is almost over," the apothecary replied without drama. "If he were distressed, I would offer valerian root powder or camomile, but he barely knows he is here."

"We must do something!" George insisted. "You'll be wanting to stem the bleeding. To close the wound. If the blood were to stop..." But George Bannerman was a sensible young man and he paused, realising that he was clutching at straws.

"Perhaps some whisky then? And some for you and Mr Farrers who must need it?"

Standing against the panelled wall, Harry considered this before responding, "Not for me, George. I need to keep a steady mind. The wine flowed freely in the Ship this evening."

George gave no reply but turned and walked away in the direction of his father's study.

While the doctor placed a fresh wad of material between the wound and layers of torn shirt and vest, the vicar's words of prayer continued in a low monotone. The scene became almost peaceful.

I would not expect it to be like this, Harry reflected. *I would expect him to fight to the last moment. Does he have no insults to fire at us? No demands that his assailant be hauled into the gaol and shackled to the*

19

walls? I would expect him to hate it that I am here to witness his life slipping away, or at least to muster some words to leave me dwelling upon the meaning.

Did Harry feel regret for the imminent passing of a man who was no older than himself – a mere twenty-six years of age? He kept himself a short distance away, leaving the vicar and apothecary to tend the dying man. *He is no more than a bully to those who work for him, the local villagers and, I fear, to his wife. I should be regretting this moment. I should be hoping that Aaron can live and prove himself to be a better man. Yet I cannot think it. I cannot be generous with my feelings.*

Sounds of movement came from the rear of the house bringing George, with a small tray and two glasses each with an inch of whisky, and Brown with a jug of warm water, a cloth over his arm, and a large bowl. They paused, still a few feet away, uncertain of how best to offer the whisky to the dying man or begin to clean the wound.

The administrations of these two good men were futile. Slumped on a graceful carver chair, Aaron Chapman of Burmarsh took his last shallow breaths, as the apothecary could do no more than hold a thick rag to the wound. The vicar, his eyes part-closed, murmured words of redemption and hope.

Time passed – each second marked by the soothing tick of the hall clock, while the vicar continued to pray. The other men stood at a respectful distance with their heads bowed. No doubt, like Harry, they contemplated the hours and days ahead when the repercussions of the murder would have to be dealt with.

The apothecary coughed, and the vicar uttered his final 'Amen'.

"My wife will lay out the body," the apothecary told them. "But where? Should we take him to Burmarsh by cart at night? It hardly seems right."

They looked at the vicar for answers, but he was a young man and, although used to death amongst the commoners, he was hesitant to decide what to do with the body of a jurat and landowner.

"I would be reluctant to suggest we place him on our dining table, but the clerk's desk is solid and over five feet in length," George Bannerman suggested.

Instinctively, the other men all looked to the back of the hallway and the staircase leading to the courtroom above with the sturdy desk.

"He could remain in the chair, and four of us could carry it up," Harry added. "It seems like a fair idea. George, should we wake your father? He should know about this."

"No – the last I heard he was vomiting and running a fever. He will be told as soon as he rouses himself in the morning." George turned to Brown and continued, "If you could fetch this good apothecary's wife, then we four will move the body in readiness for her."

Brown, although still stately in posture, was a man of nearly fifty years and none of them expected him to negotiate the stairs while taking the weight of a young man and the awkwardness of the chair. He hurried away, no doubt glad to be relieved of the task. The four remaining men manoeuvred into position.

Harry and George looked at each other, each wondering which of them should take the lead. Harry was a jurat and the elder by six years, but twenty-year-old George was the son of Sir Rupert Bannerman, and they were in his family home.

"Shall we lift on the count of three?" Harry asked. He saw the others nod or murmur their assent as they crouched and prepared to take the weight. "One. Two. Three!"

Aaron Chapman was not a large man and was lifted with relative ease. The men began an odd shuffle across the hallway and then step-by-step they negotiated the wide stairway, with the body of the dead man leaning upon the shoulder of the unfortunate vicar.

Chapter Three
Lydia

Lydia Chapman stood at her bedroom window, her hand resting on the slight swell of her stomach. She was tired, despite having slept soundly, and roused herself from bed at nine o'clock that morning. If her cousin had not been visiting, then she might not have bothered to dress at all that day. A maid or someone... anyone... could have looked after her daughter. The little girl was no trouble.

Glancing back at the breakfast tray, Lydia sighed, knowing she should try to nibble more than one triangle of toast. Her nausea would ease if she could force herself to eat, and when the maid came to tidy the room, her young face would smile to see the plate empty. *I could hide it.* She glanced towards a handkerchief and pictured the toast concealed within its folds. *No! I must eat it. I must or how will I have the strength to enjoy Gerald's visit.* Lydia snatched at the food, determined to relish the day ahead.

Favourite cousin and playmate from Lydia's childhood, Gerald Masters, had come to stay for a whole week at Rothschild Manor before travelling on to see his sister in Sussex. Today they planned to take a picnic and walk to Aldington Knoll with three-year-old Rebecca. Once on the knoll, the views across Romney Marsh to the coast would be outstanding and all the better if the day were not too bright. Her husband,

Aaron, did not like Gerald. Lydia smiled to herself – Aaron did not care for any young man who was taller and broader than himself.

The moment of satisfaction was short-lived, as Lydia glanced at the additional layer of lace adorning her sleeves. Hastily sewn on just two days beforehand, it made the dress appear unnecessarily fussy and the sleeve a little long for current fashions. She wiped the crumbs from her fingers and pulled it up – the bruise on her arm was beginning to yellow at the edges but would show for at least another week. Lydia had become an expert on knowing how long a mark such as this would last on her pale skin. *Perhaps if this child is a boy… Perhaps then I will please him.* She reached for another piece of toast, letting her sleeve fall into place.

With a cup of tea to hand, the breakfast was palatable and, encouraged by thoughts of a day away from Burmarsh with her beloved cousin and sweet daughter, Lydia ate three more triangles with gusto. Sounds outside drew her back to the window and she smiled to see Gerald and Rebecca hand-in-hand by the narrow dyke separating the patch of land in front of their house from the farmland. The little girl was laughing and chattering as she threw crumbs in the direction of a pair of ducks.

Gerald turned to look up at the house. He smiled, and Lydia beamed in return, then waved. Opening the sash window, she leaned out to call, "I'm just going to the kitchen to see what we can take for our picnic."

"Excellent!" Gerald replied, his voice merry. With Rebecca, he moved away towards the stables and was soon out of view.

As she lowered the window, movement beyond the driveway caught Lydia's attention. She frowned, not quite sure if her eyes deceived her. Yes – she was right – there was no doubting it! Young Master George

Bannerman and Mrs Phoebe Farrers were walking along the lane together, approaching Rothschild Manor. She watched for a moment, expecting them to stroll by. *I cannot imagine what brings them to Burmarsh at this hour. And why does Mrs Farrers accompany him when he has three sisters?*

Lydia watched Phoebe for a moment, allowing a pang of loneliness to take hold. Here was a local woman of the same age, liked in the community, known to be mild-mannered and kind-hearted. *Look at how she retained that poor maid of hers when the girl became blind after suffering from smallpox!* Lydia and Phoebe met regularly throughout the year, yet only exchanged polite greetings, each of them knowing it was only right to keep a tacit boundary between them. *She may not have come from a family with breeding or land, but I would have liked her as a friend.* Lydia sighed – it was not to be. Aaron had a passion for this woman, and she knew it to be beyond any attraction or affection he had ever held for her, his wife. It was unrequited – of that Lydia was certain – and stemmed from a romance in their younger days. His fury over the fact that she had chosen Harry Farrers seemed to have abated in recent years, and she knew it to be ridiculous because Aaron would never have married Phoebe. *He wanted her as his plaything and for her to remain a single woman in love with him.* There was no friendship, and could be no friendship, between the Chapmans and the Farrers.

But what can they want with us? Lydia remained at the window, her pale blue eyes widening with surprise. Mrs Farrers and Master Bannerman – *I should think of him as Mister now as he must be almost twenty* – had turned off the lane and it was clear they were intent on calling at Rothschild Manor. She turned and hurried towards the doorway.

Her husband – jurat, landowner and bully – had not slept beside Lydia that night. This was not unusual, especially as she was with child again. He usually nodded off on a bed in his dressing room, having satisfied himself with a village wench. There were times when he was not at home at all overnight, and she believed him to be at his parents' home in Dymchurch. Those were the occasions when he and his brother worked under the cover of darkness transporting woolpacks to the coast and, in turn, taking untaxed goods from the beaches to one of many hides within the lonely Marsh countryside. Lydia shook herself: *Do not even think of it. Do not even think what you have become a part of by marrying into this family.*

By the time Lydia was on the stairs, the sound of the iron knocker upon its plate was resounding through the house, and a maid appeared with a duster in hand. "I'll answer it," the lady of the house directed. The hallway was tiny – no more than a square at the foot of the stairs. *You can put a modern façade on the house and change its name from Farm to Manor,* Lydia thought, and not for the first time, *but this cramped space and the low ceilings tell a different story.*

"Good morning," she said, fixing a smile on her face and trying not to show any curiosity in her tone or expression. "Do come in."

The visitors murmured their greetings and followed Lydia into the front parlour. Before they had time to close the door, Gerald and Rebecca bounded in and suddenly the room became crowded.

"Let's sit down," Lydia gestured to the chairs, "and I must introduce my cousin, Gerald Masters, from Canterbury. Mr George Bannerman from New Hall in Dymchurch, and Mrs Phoebe Farrers also from Dymchurch." This was followed by polite greetings before Lydia continued with, "Shall I call for morning coffee?"

"Thank you," Phoebe responded. She glanced at Rebecca, appearing uneasy with the child's presence. "You must be wondering... I am sorry to call unannounced. Is it possible that your daughter... that we could talk in private?"

For the first time, Lydia felt a chill run through her body. She glanced at Gerald, who immediately responded, "Let's see if there is someone in the kitchen who can entertain my young cousin. Come along Rebecca – your mother will be busy for a moment, and we will ask if a pot of coffee can be made for her guests."

"Come back, won't you, Gerald?" Lydia called as they left. She began to twist one of her ash blonde ringlets that had escaped the neatly coiled and pinned hair at the nape of her neck. Then, without making eye contact, she spoke to the uninvited visitors, "You have come with news for me? Something has happened... in the village?"

"Something has happened," Phoebe responded, and Lydia noticed how gentle her voice was. "There has been a terrible accident. I am..." she glanced at George Bannerman, "we are so sorry."

"Is he? Is he badly injured?" Lydia felt the blanket of depression lift as she raised her face and looked directly at Phoebe.

"It is worse, and the only comfort I can give you is that he wasn't suffering at the end. My husband, Harry, and George were with him."

Gerald had returned – Lydia wasn't sure when – but he seated himself beside her and took her thin hand in his. "How did this happen? An accident?" She leaned into Gerald a little.

27

Thank you, Lord, that my cousin is with me. He will give me the strength to cope with the coming days and will stand beside me as the arrangements are made and while the people flock with their condolences. Not that they will be sorry. Those who work on our land will worry for their future. But the others… no one will be sorry except his family. Lydia's thoughts wandered as they were prone to, and she forced herself to await further news.

"It was in the churchyard," George told them. "Mr Chapman… Aaron… left the Ship Inn with some papers he wished to deliver to my father. It seems that he was accosted by a man and after a brief ruckus this person stabbed your husband. Harry Farrers was walking home and was disturbed by some shouting, then saw the man run off. He alerted us at New Hall, and Aaron was able to walk to the house. We tried but could not stem the flow of blood."

"Did he say anything?" Lydia asked. "Did Aaron say why this happened. Was there a message for his family? Anything?"

"There were no words," George replied. "I am sorry I cannot tell you different."

"The vicar came," Phoebe added. "He was with him at the end. And the apothecary, but there was nothing to be done."

"It's a terrible shock," Lydia said. She felt nothing, but they seemed like the best words to say. The housemaid had brought the coffee and some biscuits. "Would you pour?" she asked Phoebe. "We must do something. Keep busy."

Phoebe seemed to understand. "I am afraid there will be a lot to do. But give yourself time to rest. Perhaps you'll find peace in the church."

"I can help with whatever is needed," Gerald declared. He stood, coffee cup in hand, his head only

28

inches away from the heavily beamed ceiling. "I assume his parents and brother have been told. And the body? Where is he? He will have to be brought here."

"Harry Farrers and the vicar left to tell Mr and Mrs Chapman when we headed for Burmarsh," George informed them. "And the body... it is in the courtroom."

"In the courtroom?" Gerald repeated, his astonishment clear.

"Sir, the courtroom is in our own home – New Hall," George told him. "It was merely a case of carrying him upstairs, and the apothecary's wife came to make him decent. We could not be carting him here through the night."

"I understand. Forgive my surprise."

Once more Lydia could not help but admire her cousin for his confident manner and the respect he showed for the visitors. She extracted a handkerchief from her reticule and dabbed at her eyes. Not that she had shed any tears.

"Why would anyone want to kill him?" Gerald asked.

This was followed by silence. None of the others could protest that the victim was a man well-liked in the community.

"It is possible..." George began, "that Aaron was not the one meant to die. That it was a case of mistaken identity."

"Mistaken identity?" The words burst from Lydia, shrill and without restraint.

"We can hardly say at the moment, but Harry heard the killer shout some odd words: 'You said I was welcome to go butchering'. Only three days ago, it was my father who had Anthony Bushy standing before him in the courtroom, and it was my father who told him that he could not sell the meat in his shop, but he could still butcher the animals as he saw fit."

"And this Anthony Bushy is a local butcher, I presume? A Dymchurch man?" Gerald checked. "Are you saying you think your father was the intended object of this man's prey?"

"It seems likely." George slumped a little. He was young to be the bearer of such monumental news. "By now Mr Bushy will be imprisoned in the gaol – you can be assured of that."

"And the gaol is where?" Gerald asked. His knowledge of the Marsh was sketchy.

"In our home," George replied.

"You have a courtroom and a gaol within your family home?" Gerald asked, despite it being clear enough.

"New Hall is the seat of law and order within the Corporation of Romney Marsh," Lydia told him. She stood and placed a hand on his arm. "We are not in Canterbury now, cousin. Romney Marsh is an uncivilised place, and it makes its own rules. There are goings-on which you could not imagine. I wonder..." She stopped abruptly, knowing she had said too much and having a liking for young George Bannerman who was by all accounts an honourable character. "How my thoughts run away with themselves. No doubt my cousin will see New Hall for himself as there will be an inquest and a trial within the week."

"Mrs Chapman, I am sure there will be news within a day or so," Phoebe responded. "But Sir Rupert Bannerman is unwell and not able to deal with the repercussions of this tragic event. May I ask, although it is not my place to do so, if the body should be returned to Burmarsh? Or perhaps to his parents' home?"

"He would want to be here," Lydia replied without hesitation. She pictured a coffin placed atop a couple of sturdy trestles. *It will have to be here! Right here in the*

30

parlour. I would put him in an outhouse, but it has to be done properly. "Can you arrange... Would you mind arranging for Aaron's body to come back here? I should ask Gerald to go, but I can't bear to be parted from him. Not just yet."

Phoebe finished her coffee and stood. "You need not worry about asking. No one expects you to journey to Dymchurch and meet with the coffin maker. This news is so unexpected...and, well, you must look after yourself. Someone will..." She looked towards her companion and addressed him, "George, we should return to Dymchurch." Then back to Lydia and continued, "Someone will deal with it for you. There is enough for you to do here."

Once more Lydia regretted that the only time Phoebe Farrers had been welcomed into Rothschild Manor was when she came with news of Aaron's death. Bereft of companionship for days at a time, Lydia would have been grateful for the other woman's company, but the past love affair between Aaron and Phoebe, had robbed the women of being any more than polite acquaintances. *She is pretty, but without great beauty, caring and generous. Her friendship would have brightened my days here.* Perhaps, already, Lydia saw herself returning to Canterbury as not once did she consider that on this day a new bond could be formed. Once more her thoughts drifted until Gerald's words cut through them.

"We appreciate your coming here," he said. "This is a dreadful business, and nothing will induce me to leave my cousin before the killer is brought to justice." He walked into the hallway and opened the front door, stepping outside and once more thanking George and Phoebe.

Watching from the window, Lydia saw the unexpected visitors walk away. Movement in the nearby dyke – the same one at which Gerald and Rebecca had been feeding the ducks only a short time ago – caught her attention. The head and shoulders of a young man could be seen along with a rake and a clump of dead reeds.

"Hey! Yes, you lad!" Gerald shouted. "Do your clearing elsewhere. Keep away from Rothschild Manor for the next few days. Do you understand?"

If Toke Spicer responded, then Lydia could not hear him. She saw him doff his cap and haul himself out of the ditch before sauntering away. He was one of many boys and men who worked on the land, and she felt ashamed that she knew nothing about him, or any of the others.

"He's gone," Gerald said, as he walked back into the house.

His tone indicated that he referred to the loss of her husband, not the labourer. "He has," she replied, lifting the lace trim on her sleeve to reveal the purple bruise.

"We should go to church and thank the Lord." Gerald placed an arm around her shoulders and drew Lydia close to him.

Chapter Four
Harry

"We must face the inevitable: our children may not survive infancy, our fishermen may perish at sea, and the pox is ever present," the vicar began as he and Harry strolled away from the home of Mr and Mrs Chapman and along St Mary's Road. "But a young man such as their son... It comes as a shock."

"It does. The matter of the body and funeral will be dealt with by the family and vicar of Burmarsh," Harry suggested. "Although you will, of course, be needed to offer prayer and comfort. As for the jurats and Sir Rupert, we must now hasten to order the arrest of Anthony Bushy. But Sir Rupert is ill, so I will speak with the constable myself."

They paused at the bridge over the Clobsden Sewer, watching the sluggish movement of water towards the sea. A moorhen scooted about the withered reeds, and a boat rounded the bend from the direction of the coast. It was piled high with what appeared to be cut straw. October was the season for clearing the waterways, and bundles of reeds were commonly used as thatch throughout Romney Marsh and the surrounding area.

"I'll come with you," the vicar replied. "I heard nothing of what was said before the murder but at least I was with the poor man as he passed to a better place."

"Yes, of course and thank you." Harry started to stroll on. They passed the windmill and then the village school, where he couldn't help but look towards the windows and ponder upon what learning the boys were engaged in.

The annual voluntary role of constable was held by John Waller, who had gained the respect of villagers through his tireless work heading a team who laboured upon the seawall. Fortunately, the tide was subsiding from its full height, and so they were likely to find him at his home – one of a terrace named Mackett's Cottages, opposite the school. The houses, with long front gardens, were set sideways to the road. Harry and Reverend Green were not disappointed, immediately spotting John tending the last of his tomato plants, for these lengthy plots were put to good use.

"What's happened?" John asked before any greetings were exchanged.

"There's been a murder," Harry replied. "Aaron Chapman!"

"Lord save us! How?"

"Stabbed in the churchyard," Reverend Green responded without drama.

"Any idea why?" John asked as he led them towards the cottage. "I mean, I can't pretend the man was liked, God rest his soul. But murdered? Was there an altercation during the meal at the Ship or afterwards?" They walked straight into the front room, filling the modest space and drawing Mrs Waller from the kitchen beyond. "Constable business," John told her. "Can you tell Tom I may still be busy when he leaves for the Wall in an hour."

"I'll go now," she replied, leaving through the back door. Their son lived in the adjoining cottage.

"You asked for what reason," Harry said. "I believe it was mistaken identity and the intended victim was Sir Rupert."

"Sir Rupert?" the name burst from John. "Why? The man could not be better liked."

"Because on Friday last, I was in court when Sir Rupert forbade Anthony Bushy from trading in his own shop. The man took to the drink and was shouting about what had been said in court, or at least words very similar: He said, 'I could still do slaughtering'. Yesterday evening, I left the Ship minutes after Aaron and heard raised voices in the churchyard and a man shouted, 'You said I was welcome to go butchering!'"

"Then Anthony Bushy must be arrested immediately," John replied. At that moment, his wife returned, and he called through to the kitchen, "Ann, can you ask Tom to come here?" Turning back to Harry and the vicar, he continued, "The men will manage well enough without us on the seawall, and this will soon be dealt with. I won't go to arrest a man with his temper on my own."

"I'll come with you," Harry offered. Then to the vicar, he asked, "Could you go back to New Hall and let them know to expect their guest shortly? The gaol is empty, so Mr Bushy will have a room to himself."

Tom Waller, a man in his early twenties, entered through the back of the house. The vicar left, and Harry gave a brief account as to why the butcher was to be arrested. While they spoke, John took a pair of handcuffs from a hook by the front door.

There was no talk of the growing apprehension they felt as the three men walked the short distance from Mackett's Cottages to the High Street. Most likely, the butcher would be preparing the carcasses for sale that morning and have an array of knives to hand. He had proved himself to suffer from rage and could well lash

35

out without warning. They used an alleyway that ran beside his shop, stepping with caution into a yard where slaughtered animals were prepared in an outbuilding. Here they discovered Anthony Bushy, not with a knife in hand but a pail of water.

A look of surprise flashed across his face, immediately replaced with a scowl. "What brings you three gentlemen here? If I'm not mistaken, you're constable for a year, John Waller. I've not been serving in the shop. Been out here doing the butchering, like him at New Hall ordered."

"You have indeed been butchering," John retorted. "And you've taken it too far." As he spoke, Tom moved to stand behind Anthony Bushy, "I'm arresting you for the murder of Aaron Chapman in the churchyard yesterday evening."

While the enormity of these words sank into the sluggish mind of the butcher, Tom Waller clamped his large hands onto the forearms of the accused. At that moment, Anthony began to struggle, twisting from side to side and spitting his fury at the three men. "Murder? Is that what brings you three fools to my yard? Why would I go out murdering? So, Aaron Chapman is dead, is he? I can't say I liked the man, but it had nothing to do with me."

The commotion brought his wife from the kitchen at the back of their home. "What's all this about?" she screeched. "Get yer hands off him."

"Mrs Bushy, we are taking your husband to New Hall," John said, struggling to close the handcuffs over the butcher's wrists. "Anthony Bushy, you are under arrest for the murder of Aaron Chapman and will remain in gaol until your trial."

"My husband is no murderer."

"I've already told them that, you foolish woman. I told them I've not been out killing no one, not even you and I've a mind to sometimes," her husband snarled.

Unperturbed, Mrs Bushy continued, "Enough of that. Just tell Mr Waller again that you didn't do it." Mrs Bushy's wails brought their sons from the house and shop. "They're taking your pa to the gaol," she told them.

The longer they lingered in the butcher's yard, the more trouble they were likely to encounter. "Let's get moving," Harry said to John. To the Bushy family, he stated, "Aaron Chapman is dead, and the evidence against this man is strong. We have no choice."

"What evidence?" one of the sons asked. "When did he do it?"

His words were ignored as John and Tom began to push the cuffed man towards the alleyway. "If you don't walk, we'll drag you," Tom barked, his voice uncharacteristically vicious.

The Bushy sons stepped forward as if to block the way through to the High Street. Harry was quick to caution them, "We have four cells, as you well know. Any trouble here and I'll send men back for the pair of you. Then who will keep the business running for your parents?"

They stepped back, one of them taking the opportunity to brush against Harry. "It will be over by supper time," he retorted. "Fools you are! All of you. You need to find out who really done it."

"What's he gone and done?" Mrs Bushy wailed, as her husband and his gaolers funnelled into the alley. "God save me if there's any truth in it."

"Get on with swilling the yard," were the last words to be heard from one of the sons. "Pa won't be best pleased if he comes home and there's no work done."

Anthony Bushy, disgraced butcher and assumed killer, walked along Dymchurch High Street with his head bowed. He passed the women who regularly patronised his shop, anything from a whole chicken to a scrag end of mutton. He passed the other tradespeople – tobacconists and cobblers, bakers and coffin makers. As he was spotted, the villagers paused in their daily business, whether it was a purchase or exchanging recent gossip, and fell silent. Then the whispers began. Already the news of Aaron Chapman was spreading and now a man had been arrested. Even the humblest cottager of lowly intelligence could link the two events and reach the obvious conclusion: "They have found who murdered that Chapman fellow – it was the butcher. You know the one – Anthony Bushy."

At the fork in the High Street, they took the seawall road, passing the fishmongers' shacks and the City of London tavern. The butcher looked at neither. However, when an unchecked view of the bay was spread before them, he faltered in his step.

"We'll pause for a moment," John murmured, allowing Anthony Bushy this moment to appreciate the murky sea rolling towards and rebounding from the seawall. Despite the day being overcast, they could scan the coastline from the cliffs at Folkestone to the shingle peninsular at Dungeness, albeit in various shades of grey.

The track upon the Wall was empty, apart from a girl lugging a cumbersome basket and an old man drawing tobacco smoke from his pipe as he ambled along. Neither of them glanced at the handcuffed man or his wardens. No more words passed. No more needed to be said – they were all acutely aware that it was merely a step from gaol to courtroom to gallows. It was unlikely the accused man would ever see the coast again.

Raised voices and the slamming of a door from the tavern brought the men back to the moment and they moved on. Soon the cottages and shacks on the landward side of the Wall became sparse, with animal pens and allotments filling the space. The track forked and now they turned away from the sea, heading towards a triangle of substantial buildings important to both Dymchurch and the wider area – St Peter and St Paul Church, New Hall and Ship Inn. Which of these happened to be the most significant to village life was a matter for the individual to decide.

In the centre of this cluster stood the empty gallows, the noose swaying in the breeze. None of the men could even glance at it, but it was noticeable that the slump to Anthony Bushy's shoulders and the drop of his head became more pronounced.

The front of New Hall faced the church rather than the road. Approaching steadily, the men passed by the main part of the red-brick building, with Harry glancing up at the courtroom window. Then Tom nudged at Anthony Bushy, and they all veered towards a side entrance leading to the gaol.

Balking at the sight of the iron studded door, Harry relived the time he was imprisoned within the depths of New Hall. "I'm not needed here," he said, turning away. "I'm interested to find out how Mrs Lydia Chapman took the news, so hopefully Phoebe has returned home. Then my day's work beckons. He began to move away, offering a "Good morning, sir," to the keeper who had emerged from his home adjoining both New Hall and gaol.

Within minutes, Harry entered his home, Walker House. It came as no surprise to see Bess helping the twins down the stairs. As the person who had taken an injured Harry into her home when he first arrived in Dymchurch, the older woman had naturally slipped into the role of grandmother to Harry and Phoebe's young brood. Arriving at the house every morning to assist amongst the chaos that reigned over the kitchen table at breakfast time, she then wiped the porridge from rosy faces and chubby hands before removing the apron swathing each child. Next, alongside Phoebe, Bess changed the twins' soiled clouts and dressed the little ones. Owen and Bess had never been blessed with children of their own, and she knew herself to be fortunate to be both needed and welcomed into the Farrers' home.

"She's back from Burmarsh," Bess said, without preamble and barely glancing at Harry, for the stairs were steep and the children eager to descend them at speed. "Mary is upstairs with Esther."

Harry knew the household routine – although there had clearly been a substantial delay that morning. Phoebe and Bess would soon be going to the High Street to buy groceries to be delivered by a boy later that day. They always took the twins and Esther with them, usually walking atop the seawall, but staying within the shelter of its vast bank on the days when the breeze blew briskly. The walk there and back could take an hour or more, especially now young James was toddling, and all the children given some freedom to escape the adults' hands and explore.

In his mind's eye, Harry saw another scene – next summer when the little ones would be able to chase and kick a ball on the beach. He knew that to ferry them to the shops and home again was a challenge to Phoebe and Bess, but it would get easier. On their return, Mary would help settle the children – after replacing more soiled clouts. The women would then be able to relax for an hour or more while the toddlers slept deeply in their shared nursery.

Phoebe appeared from the kitchen, an empty pail hanging at her side. Harry smiled. *Caring for the children is almost relentless. By lunchtime it will be half-full of wet linen.* "Thank you for everything you have done already this morning," he said to Bess. Then to Phoebe, "Did you see her? How was she?"

"We saw her and the gentleman who is staying there. She was calm." Phoebe frowned a little, reflecting. "It seems an odd word to use – calm – but that's how she appeared. I don't know that she realised Aaron was missing, despite him being gone all night."

"That man would live by his own rules, and I doubt it included sharing his plans with his wife," Harry observed.

"She will be in shock," Bess suggested, allowing the twins to wriggle free from her grip. They raced through the open doorway towards wooden blocks awaiting them on the rug in the front parlour.

"She will," Phoebe agreed. "She is… Lydia is with child. I didn't realise before."

"We see little of her in the village," Bess pointed out, "and a full skirt hides pregnancy for several months."

"We can talk more of this later," Harry said, eyeing the hallway clock – it was about to chime half-past ten. "The children's day is all out of sorts, and I must hasten to the forge."

"We are merely taking them to the seawall and back, then I will shop while they nap," Phoebe told him. "It will be enough."

"It will be a day when nothing falls into place as it should," Harry commented. Reaching forward, he took Phoebe's hand for a moment. "I know it's been a difficult morning."

"The disruption to our time is nothing compared to that of the Chapmans." She squeezed his hand. "I shall pray that Mrs Lydia Chapman has the strength to

41

endure the coming weeks. But we'll speak of this later…"

Harry moved at a fair pace through the village, offering no more than a brief greeting while passing friends and acquaintances. "Yes, it is true. You will hear more of it in the coming days," he said to anyone who attempted to stop him in his tracks.

His forge was the last property on the road to New Romney before it continued to the town, flanked by the seawall on one side and a deep drainage ditch to the other. Double doors were wide open, and a ribbon of smoke from the charcoal fire wafted out. Opposite, the Ocean Inn slumbered, with the front door open and a broom propped against the outside wall.

"I'm sorry – late again," Harry said, walking in and immediately reaching for an apron. "You've heard, I presume?"

Matthew Alder pulled a piece of iron from the fire and replied. "We heard that Mr Chapman is dead, and the butcher has been arrested."

"And that you were with him when he died," Jack Jones added. He was a steady young man of seventeen years who had served his apprenticeship with Harry and was proving himself to be a reliable and skilled metalworker.

"That's right. But we have work to do, and I am determined to complete these wheel rims before I meet with Joshua Smith later today. If my plans run smoothly, then you, Matthew, will be running this place while I look at getting the new forge as we like it."

The men settled to their tasks. Despite the front doors being open, there was little activity to distract them that morning. Perhaps the village was quieter than usual. Perhaps the landlord of the Ocean noticed a lack of patrons when he later opened for business. The people of Dymchurch were a curious lot and they lingered near the church or the Ship – both places which afforded a fine view of New Hall. When the body of Aaron Chapman was placed within an oak coffin and settled upon a cart bound for Burmarsh, the villagers would be there, looking on wide-eyed and silent.

Chapter Five
Lydia

The dress Lydia selected was modest in style, lacking the lacy layers with which she tended to adorn her outfits. Yet the linen chemise resting on the swell of her stomach and the wool kissing her calves and upper arms were soft and of a fine weave. In a moment of defiance, she had decided not to cover the bruise, now a mottled greenish-yellow. *If they see it and choose to consider it may have come from the hand of their son and brother, then it will do no harm for them to recognise my husband for the bully he was.* Dove-grey skirts brushed against papered walls as Lydia descended the staircase and turned into the parlour without a glance towards the coffin in the dining room.

"I shall be glad when he is gone from this house," were her first words to Gerald. "I am ashamed that you, dear cousin, must eat in the kitchen while *he* has commandeered the dining table."

"These are the last moments when he will intrude on your life." Gerald stepped forward and placed a hand on her arm.

"And yours... to think that you had to sit up through the night with *him,* when there is a bed for you in the room above."

Gerald gave a small smile and glanced towards the back of the house where the cook was busy preparing breakfast. He lowered his voice, although it was unnecessary, "No sooner than the girl had crept up the stairs to the attic, and I was bidding your husband a good night! I slept in my own bed, Lydia, just taking care to wake in time to resume my duties!"

"I am pleased to hear it!" she exclaimed. "Very pleased indeed." She stepped towards the window and tweaked the curtain. "It is too dark in here – did Minnie not think to light a lamp?"

"Just allow that shaft of sunlight in and it will serve us better than any lamp," Gerald suggested. "By midday, all the curtains shall be opened, he will be gone, and the house will be yours to do with as you please."

"What would please me is to leave this place and return to Canterbury." Lydia turned from the window and looked directly at Gerald. *What would please me would be for you to take me as your wife – what a fool I was to succumb to Aaron's attentions when I had admired you for as long as I can remember. There is no harm in cousins marrying.*

Gerald's attention was on the length of silk tied loosely at his neck and his reply came without understanding the true meaning of her words: "I am sure your family would welcome you. If the baby is a boy, the Chapmans will expect him to grow up here, but no doubt you could spend the winter months in Canterbury."

Lydia shrugged. "There is nothing to be done until he or she arrives." She scowled at her stomach. "I used to pray for a boy so *he* would be satisfied that I had done my duty. Now I pray for a girl and pray twice as hard."

Movement on the stairs caused them both to turn and all talk of Lydia's wishes ceased. Rebecca, dressed in the same dove-grey as her mother, came into the parlour hand-in-hand with the maid. "She's eaten her

45

breakfast and, if it pleases you ma'am, I'll take Rebecca to see the lambs when... when they – his family – arrive. Or...?"

Lydia considered this for a moment. "Thank you, Minnie. I don't think they will expect to see her until afterwards, but don't dally as cook will be needing help. I'll take care of her until the family arrive."

The girl bobbed her head in respect and moved through to the kitchen. Here she could chatter freely, where the light poured in through the open back door and windows had no drapes to shut out the sun.

Time passed while Lydia went through the motions of helping Rebecca dress her two cloth dolls, then they flicked through a book of watercolour paintings of animals. The little girl fretted over the room being so dark, and her mother tugged at the curtains once more, allowing light to spread into the room. Gerald paced about, his strides too long and his figure too tall for the room. He made some excuse about tending his horse and sidled out.

The clock on the mantelpiece ticked and Lydia glanced at it frequently, certain that its rhythm had slowed. "What is wrong with the clock?" she almost snapped at Gerald when he returned. "Now I shall have to find someone to repair it. I cannot abide its ponderous tick... tick... tick."

"There is nothing wrong with the clock," he told her.

Lydia didn't reply. For the first time since she had been told about her husband's death – *Was it only four days ago? How could that be?* – tears began to well. Embarrassed, she stood abruptly, surprising Rebecca, who was mid-flow in her chatter about a painting of a frog, and walked through to the kitchen.

"I'm going to make tea," the lady of the house said to the startled cook.

"The kettle is on the boil," came the response. "I'll bring a pot through for you and Mr Masters."

"I should like to do it myself," Lydia countered. "If you could just show me where the caddy is? Best to keep busy."

For ten long minutes – according to the cook when the event was reported first to her sister, and then to other women in the village – Lydia Chapman measured tea, set out a tray and fussed over the smallest of details before carrying it through to the parlour.

"I made the tea!" she announced to Gerald.

"How frustrating for cook!" he replied with a grin, while turning the page of Rebecca's book. His arm circled the girl and when he spoke again, it was on a different subject. "Tomorrow we shall picnic on Aldington Knoll – just the three of us. It has been delayed long enough."

"That would be wonderful!" Lydia exclaimed, unable to keep the pleasure from her voice. "To leave this house behind us, if only for a few hours, will be so refreshing for us all." She pictured Rebecca between them as they clambered up the knoll, stopping frequently to both admire the view and to catch their breath. "The thought of it will carry me through the day."

The crunch of wheels on the driveway brought them back to the present. "They are here," Lydia said. "The Chapmans. I will answer the door." She had already sensed that her cousin's presence at this time was an affront to Aaron's family, but one she largely chose to ignore. With every hour that passed, the young widow felt an increasing boldness, and now, finally, her late husband would be both dead and buried within the hour.

The Chapmans – Aaron's parents, his brother, and sisters with their husbands – spilled into Rothschild Manor, parting in the modest square of a hallway. The sisters had not yet seen their brother lying in his coffin, and Lydia winced to hear their protesting that a man of such good character should be snatched from this earth.

"God takes the best first," Mrs Chapman senior proclaimed.

Then he made a grave mistake, Lydia thought.

"He has gone to a better place. A better life," the vicar of Burmarsh stated, his voice smooth and without drama.

When did he arrive? Lydia wondered. *This farmhouse – this manor – is too small for the crowds descending on it. And the coffin maker too...*

"Lydia, we are saying our final goodbye," Mr Chapman said.

Standing at the doorway, she watched Aaron's father place a square of the finest linen upon the face of the dead man, then he drew the woollen shroud across. From the corner of the room, the vicar offered prayers of faith and redemption.

While Lydia turned away, she heard the lid closing and the tap of a hammer on nails. *I have seen the last of my husband!*

The unborn baby moved and pressed outwards, providing Lydia with the excuse she needed. "The baby is restless," she said to Mrs Chapman, "I'll just step outside... fresh air..."

Without waiting for a reply, Lydia slipped through the hallway and crossed the driveway to stand under the shade of a willow tree. She gazed across the flat pastureland towards the coast, seeing but barely noticing the lush grass with stocky Romney Marsh sheep grazing, and the trails of withered reeds lining the wandering waterways. It had rained overnight, and she breathed deeply, absorbing the scents of damp earth.

48

From this spot, Lydia watched the six men – Mr Chapman; his remaining son, Daniel; the sisters' husbands; George Bannerman and Gerald – carry the coffin on a bier. Their hats were bound with long black ribbons, and they focused on the path ahead. The women kept a respectful distance, and Lydia stepped from the protection of the willow to join them. It was unthinkable that a female would walk with or seek the comfort of a man at this moment when any weeping or weakness was frowned upon. After all, the deceased had gone to a better place, and this was a matter for rejoicing.

The following day – five after Aaron's death – the horse and trap were led to the front of Rothschild Manor, a picnic basket pushed under the bench seat and a thick rug folded to cushion Lydia and Rebecca against the oak plank.

"I would have been happy to walk all the way to the knoll," Lydia protested, "and would have matched you stride for stride." Her manner with Gerald was easy, lacking the formal politeness which was the norm. As cousins, they had met frequently during childhood – at a time when they were free to ramble about the countryside surrounding Canterbury and to chatter without the restrictions that came later in their lives. In company, she was the Lydia Chapman known by her neighbours and family on Romney Marsh – reserved, uninterested and unfocussed. Beside Gerald, she became the person she wanted to be, the person she used to be before her marriage. She had opinions and an interest in the world around her.

"We must show some decorum," he replied. "Moreover, you must be weary after all that has happened… and…" He gazed at the gentle swell of her stomach, visible where her skirt billowed out at the waist.

Aware that she could no longer tie the ribbons of her bodice as tightly as just a week before, and that the baby had been fidgeting since the early hours of the morning, Lydia conceded. "It is a long way for Rebecca to walk or for us to carry her. Thank you, cousin, for the care you show us."

"Let me help her up," Gerald suggested. "Come, Rebecca, Cousin Gerald will lift you up high. Now don't wriggle!"

To the little girl's delight, he reached down and scooped her up, lifting her higher than necessary then dropping her into the trap.

"A step for my lady cousin," he announced, taking a wooden box from the porch. "Now let me support you."

Lydia laid one pale hand on the side of the trap and the other on Gerald's forearm, using him to help her remain stable while she swung her leg over the low side of the trap, taking care not to catch her skirt on the wooden rail. No sooner had she placed her arm around Rebecca than Gerald was at the horse's head encouraging it to walk on.

They passed through the village of Burmarsh, with Lydia giving all her attention to Rebecca. She didn't want to know if the people would judge her for going on an outing the day after the funeral. She didn't want to see them turn from their work or their gossiping and watch her trundle by. Only once did she glance up to see the mound of fresh earth in the churchyard and gave a slight nod to acknowledge her husband's grave.

Gerald led the horse past the small collection of cottages, the tiny church and the alehouse. Within moments Burmarsh was behind them, and Lydia could straighten her back, breathe in the slightly damp, earthy air and shake off the feeling of hopelessness that had so often cloaked her during the past couple of years.

The lane turned one way then the other, as those on Romney Marsh so often did. The fields were mostly pasture, irregular in size and surrounded by drainage ditches. "I suppose it's an interesting sort of place," Lydia conceded. "He told me, in the early days when we were still speaking a little, that these waterways follow the paths of the ancient sea creeks, and that Burmarsh is the oldest settlement on Romney Marsh, or at least one of the oldest."

"He would say that!" Gerald let out a brief laugh. "It made him feel more important when, in truth, it is nothing much at all, despite having a manor house."

"Rothschild Manor!" Lydia scoffed. "It is a mere farmhouse, with ceilings so low I can touch them with ease. I have a mind to return it to its rightful name."

"Take care with the changes you make," Gerald cautioned. "His family are grieving, and you may cause affront."

Lydia ignored this and her conversation returned to the countryside. "You know about the thorn trees, I assume?"

Large trees grew sparsely, with a regal oak or chestnut being an occasional feature in the landscape, but blackthorn grew in abundance, frequently hedging the roadside. Gnarled and armoured with spikes, the dark leaves were beginning to wither and fall amongst ragged grass and weeds on the verge.

"I know I would have my ear cut off if I took a branch!" Gerald responded, referring to the fact that the wood was impervious to seawater and used to strengthen the seawall. It was a crime to take it for any other reason. "That is, if anyone saw me do it!"

"Oh! They would see you," Lydia replied, her tone dark. "This place looks deserted, but you can be sure there is someone sneaking about, watching and listening. These people... these Marshmen... they appear to be tending the sheep or clearing the ditches or catching eels, but all the time they are plotting and planning. I swear that if you were to cut a blackthorn, even out here where it seems so remote, then Sir Rupert would have heard about it by nightfall."

"You have been here too long." Gerald tightened the rein and quickened his pace. "It plays tricks with your mind."

"I *have* been here too long," Lydia agreed. "But my mind is clear, and I should hate to be a riding officer, sent by the King to deal with this unruly lot."

The hedging dwindled away, and they took a turn to the right, heading directly for the escarpment marking the edge of Romney Marsh. Lydia and Rebecca clambered down from the cart and walked along the narrow lane, seeking out the last of the fluttering butterflies, and hovering dragonflies whose slim bodies flashed turquoise or red. The landscape was now completely open and flat, with very little rising above the dry and colourless lines of reeds. Every so often they stood on a plank bridge and from here they could look directly into the water, searching for fish, frogs or, if they were lucky, a snake.

"These waters look idyllic while the water flows thanks to the recent rains," Lydia remarked. "But you would not want to venture here during the heat of the summer. Just six weeks ago, it lay stagnant, and mosquitos gathered to breed. How they love sweet human flesh to feast on."

"Oh! Everyone knows the Marsh is rife with disease!" Gerald said. "But you fare well enough in Burmarsh, for it lies a little higher than the surrounding land. Not that I noticed, but your late husband told me, and I will give him credit for knowing."

"And we are not far from the sea," Lydia admitted.

"Well, let us not dwell on disease and these Marshmen lurking about the place." Gerald took Rebecca's hand. "Let us continue along this lane before we climb the hillside and explore the knoll."

Despite her resolve to enjoy the day, Lydia's thoughts kept returning to melancholy matters, and she moved away from the water. "You are right, cousin. I was so looking forward to this outing before... before everything changed. Now, I shall say no more unless it is good. Do you see how the reeds sway and whisper? It is the thing I love the best. Climbing the hillside will be a challenge, but I promise you that the view is outstanding."

With that, the little group walked on and after a while, Lydia and Rebecca rode once more in the cart. The countryside they travelled through was almost devoid of cottages and farm buildings, but there was a beauty in its being desolate, and with every pace the escarpment loomed larger before them, its outline a dramatic contrast compared to the flat marshland.

A red-brick house sat at the base of the hill, and here Gerald sought someone to leave the pony and cart with. He then carried Rebecca, and Lydia took the picnic basket as they began their slow ascent, first walking on a stony track and then a footpath.

When the knoll emerged before them, Gerald voiced his confusion, "I thought it just to be a hill – a promontory on this hillside – but this is a mound upon the natural landscape. I am certain man has shaped it."

Rebecca now scrambled up the chalky bank, delighting in the freedom, grabbing at grassy tussocks to keep her steady. Her mother smiled, allowing her daughter to enjoy this moment of adventure. "I think you are right," she agreed, "but I am unsure of the reason why it is like this." Her head spun a little – perhaps due to the exertion, or perhaps due to the fear of seeming foolish before Gerald. "It's the Romans!" she clutched at a vague memory of Mrs Chapman, Aaron's mother, telling her some tale of the place. "The Romans came here."

"Ah! The Romans," Gerald's answered. "Let us find the easiest way up." He took the picnic basket and offered his arm.

They set off, all the time assessing the steepness of the knoll, rounding a point and coming to the landward side. By now Rebecca had reached the top and was waving madly, encouraging them to join her. Taking a route that wound around badgers' sets and areas of almost vertical cliff, Lydia and Gerald finally reached the summit.

The details, previously eluding her, now surfaced. "It was a burial ground! For the Romans," Lydia proclaimed.

They pointed out landmarks: the seawall at Dymchurch, the church tower at Newchurch, the distant hills of France, and marvelled at the flatness of the Marsh which faded away as it crossed the Kent Ditch into Sussex, wrapping itself against the sea cliffs at Rye. Then the three of them flopped upon a rug and emptied the contents of their picnic basket, relishing the freedom of this time away from Burmarsh.

They discussed the oddity of the mound – its irregular shape with three spears pointing outwards from the centre – and wondered if the long-gone Romans were lying there beneath them. Inevitably, their thoughts could not remain free of recent events forever and it was Gerald who mentioned the court hearing due to take place in four days' time. "There seems no doubt that the man who..." He glanced towards Rebecca. "... The butcher... He is to stand before Sir Rupert, but the outcome seems certain."

"It does," Lydia agreed, "but it makes me uneasy, nonetheless."

"I have to travel to Sussex," Gerald told her. "I have sent a note to my sister to tell her I am delayed, but she will be expecting me soon. My plan is to stay for the court case, go to see her, and then call in here on my return trip to Canterbury."

"I knew it," Lydia replied. A feeling of heaviness descended upon her, and where the sun had warmed her body, her arms and legs now felt chilled. "I knew you had to leave, although we have not spoken of it. Perhaps my mother will stay when the time nears for the baby to come into this world. She will bring me comfort, as none of *his* family could."

"But I will visit again, and soon," Gerald declared. "You have months of waiting before you, and in that time there will be things to deal with. You will be pressured by your late husband's family and need a trusted friend to guide you."

"I have no such friend here," Lydia admitted. "I have no friends at all, despite my living here for six whole years."

"Then we will pray for this child to be a daughter, and for the Chapmans to agree to you returning to your family in Canterbury. They will have no desire to keep a granddaughter close to them."

"They won't!" Lydia agreed. "They won't!" A sense of exhilaration soared through her body. "I will pray daily – no, hourly! The good Lord in Heaven is sure to hear my wishes. My dear cousin, when you leave, I shall console myself with thinking of your return and awaiting that time when I am recovered enough for my daughters and myself to leave this wretched place behind us."

Chapter Six
Harry

"It's a shambles!" Sir Rupert blurted out before any pleasantries were exchanged.

"I am so glad to see you recovered," Harry replied, determined not to encourage Sir Rupert's tendency to be overly dramatic.

"If I had not been forced to take to my bed, then the wrong man would not have been arrested for murder," Sir Rupert declared as he dismounted his horse and stood beside the bay gelding. He appeared dishevelled, with his cravat badly tied and unruly waves of greying hair unleashed when the tricorn hat was swept off his head. "A whole week has passed, and only now I learn of this…"

Harry wore a leather apron and held a rod of unheated iron in his hand. The summons to attend the Leveller of the Marsh Scotts in the yard had taken him aback. He recalled the summer of 1762 when the Whitsun Gallop cup had been stolen, and how Sir Rupert had often demanded that Harry call upon him at New Hall. Never had he arrived at the forge.

"I don't understand," Harry responded.

"Neither do I, but the schoolmaster has been to see me, having just learned the full details of the events, and he swears he was with Mr Bushy at the time of the murder."

Sir Rupert's horse stamped his foot, causing a metallic ringing sound to echo in the confined space. Harry's sturdy chestnut whinnied a response.

"Why would the schoolmaster be with the butcher?" Harry asked. "I can't see them as drinking companions."

"He is helping him learn to read," Sir Rupert told him. "Mr Bushy's family knew nothing of it. They could only assume that he was at one tavern or the other and later in the churchyard."

"'You said I could still go butchering' – that's what he said. It's what I heard the murderer say, and the day you convicted Anthony Bushy, he came over here saying the same thing, or near enough."

"I did say that in court, or so the clerk tells me. I said he couldn't serve customers but could still butcher the animals. It was a fair punishment, but it appeared that our butcher took offence."

"I believed, having heard those words, that it was you who was meant to be killed in the churchyard that night," Harry said. "I discussed it with George, and it seemed likely – more than likely – that had you been at the Ship that evening, then you would have been the victim."

At these words, Sir Rupert lost some of his usual buoyant manner and turned to stroke his horse's neck. "It is a terrible thing to believe," he told Harry. "To think that someone meant to murder me, and because I was bedridden another man died. This business of the butcher being at his lessons turns it all on its head. He will have to go to trial, but who knows what the outcome will be."

"His knife was found," Harry stated. "In the churchyard."

"Exactly! There is everything to say he is the man we seek and just one piece of evidence to say otherwise. The trial must go ahead. The schoolmaster is mistaken – he must be. I am wrong to take his word so seriously."

"It will make an interesting hearing," Harry reflected. "I cannot see how the man can be innocent, yet it appears our schoolmaster will give a compelling testimony. When is it to be? I assume the Chapmans will accept no delay."

"On Thursday – the tenth day of October," Sir Rupert replied. "My clerk has drawn up the indictment and the jury will receive letters within the hour. You cannot be on the jury, of course."

"No, I have evidence to give. I assume Mr Chapman will also be exempt, given that he can hardly be impartial."

"Damned awkward." Sir Rupert gathered the gelding's reins and looked for the mounting block. "Two jurats unable to take a place on the jury and another dead. George suggested that I ask some men of property within the village, and it seemed like a good idea."

"You have your men then?" Harry asked. "And you want me there as witness on the tenth – in two days' time." He gestured to the mounting block and reached for the bridle while murmuring soothing words to the horse.

"I believe that is what I said." Sir Rupert swung into the saddle. "Take care, Harry. Take care to think about what you saw and heard that night. I can't say I like Anthony Bushy, but neither do I like to think of looking from my windows to see him swinging from the gallows if he is innocent of murder."

As the bands of orange and pink intensified in the sky to the east, Harry eased himself out of bed.

"Are they awake?" Phoebe murmured from the depths of their blankets.

"Sorry, I didn't want to disturb you," Harry whispered. "No. At least I've not heard them. I need to go to work…"

"Work?"

Harry reached over to kiss her. "I have to be in court at ten."

"Of course!" Phoebe leaned forward, responding to his embrace.

There was no need for him to explain that the court hearing would take hours – hours when Matthew would be left to run the forge with Jack to assist. "It's not fair to leave them again," was all Harry said while pulling off his nightshirt, then feeling his way through a pile of work clothes. It would be another half an hour before the sun offered any useful light in the room. By then he would be stoking the fire in the forge.

As Harry secured his breeches, there came a familiar patter of small feet, and the bedroom door was pushed open. "Papa?" Esther enquired, seeing his shadowy figure.

"Good morning, my sweet." Harry scooped her up and kissed a soft, warm cheek. He breathed deeply, inhaling and appreciating the infant's scent. "Are the twins sleeping?"

"Yes. And Mama?"

"Mama is awake. I woke her," Harry confessed.

The little girl clamoured to be released from his arms, and he placed her on the bed beside her mother.

"Stay here. Papa must go to work now," Phoebe whispered. "Let's not wake the babies."

Harry left his wife and eldest daughter and crept down the stairs. In the kitchen he exchanged a few words with Janey while pulling on his work boots, then left by the back door.

The streets of Dymchurch were empty and he passed no other soul. In their homes, the villagers began to prepare for the day ahead. Harry pictured them fumbling about in the half-light, bemoaning the fact that winter was fast approaching. The bang of a door, the clatter of a bucket lowered into a well, the squabbling fuss from impatient chickens – Harry heard them all clearly in this short time before the place was fully awake and each sound mingled with the next. His thoughts drifted from the domestic scene at home to the work he planned to achieve within the next few days.

"It's for the best, Ma. Leave it be."

The words surprised Harry. They seemed to blurt from nowhere – harsh, and shocking Harry from his reverie. He slowed his pace, now alert to the slightest sound. A reply came – it was indistinct. If the first person gave a response, then it went unheard. Perhaps he had moved away from the open window. Harry looked at the name above the shop he was passing: 'A. Bushy & Sons – Butchers'.

Mid-morning saw Harry striding through the open front door and into the familiar hallway of the New Hall. Here he joined a gathering of locals, some intent on enjoying the sport of a murder trial, and others for whom either outcome promised an impact on their lives. They filed along the flagstone floor, barely glancing at Brown who stood at the doorway to Sir Rupert's study, ensuring that no one could slip into any of the private rooms. The air buzzed with murmured words – the odd comment or greeting passed about. Pushing against one another, the villagers moved upstairs before spilling into the lofty courtroom. Now some of them faltered, deciding on the best place to stand, for most were not there by invitation and the seating was limited to judge and jury.

In a decisive move, Harry stepped to the right, placing himself by the window overlooking New Hall's garden. He nodded to members of the jury and to Sir

Rupert Bannerman, who sported a wig of curling silver locks and a bottle-green jacket with the froth of a cravat at the open neck. Reaching to the linen at his own neck, Harry adjusted the folds of his scarf, and marvelled on his swift transformation from scruffy blacksmith to tailored gentleman in a jacket and breeches made from the best Romney Marsh wool. He caught William Payne's eye and remembered a comment thrown in his direction when they had passed in the street less than an hour beforehand: 'Look at you, Farrers! You'll never get cleaned up in time for court.' Harry grinned. Like all the jury, William also had a day's work to complete as well as his duties to the Corporation. The friends exchanged a smile. *If he is lucky, he'll be back working on his land by early afternoon.*

The menfolk of the Chapman family assembled, not on the rows of narrow jurors' benches nor beside Sir Rupert on the dais – both positions where they often took their places – but near Harry on some hastily gathered chairs. With them, although not seeming to be on amicable terms, was a tall, pleasant looking man. *Ah! He must be the cousin Phoebe spoke of.* The vicar and the apothecary appeared at the top of the stairs, they scanned the room and moved across to stand with Harry. The men murmured a greeting.

From his raised platform running the length of the room, Sir Rupert stood and leaned forward on the balustrade of oak panelling. Unheard by those in the room, he spoke to the clerk and then straightened himself to stand tall. This was the cue for those in the courtroom to fall silent.

"Gentlemen, we shall begin." He turned to the bailiff seated beside him and asked, "Can you escort Mr Bushy to the dock?"

The bailiff, Jeremy Parris, responded with a nod, and those in the crowd swivelled to watch his progress across the room. He weaved his way around heavy oak furniture and curious villagers before reaching the top of the stairs. Here they heard a few words exchanged as Mr Parris met with the gaoler and the shackled man. His head lowered and encumbered by the iron rings at his wrists, the butcher made his entrance into the courtroom. At once the whispers began as comments and opinions flew about from those pressed against hessian-draped walls, oak railings and panelling, to the twelve men of property seated on the two rows of narrow benches.

"I hope he's not brought his knife!" one villager dared to call out.

This was followed by nervous laughter.

"He left it lying about in the churchyard, the damned fool!" another answered.

"Silence! Silence!" Sir Rupert bellowed. "Any more disrespect in my court and those responsible will leave immediately. I have three free cells and will not hesitate to use them all."

The onlookers quietened, partly because they knew the Leveller of the Marsh Scotts would be true to his word, and more importantly because they wanted to hear what was to follow. Family and friends who were not a witness to the butcher's fate would need to hear all the details – these may be embellished over the coming days but must be based on the truth of what happened in court. With bated breath, everyone watched and waited as Sir Rupert took a deep breath and exhaled slowly, while all the time keeping a steadfast gaze fixed upon the butcher.

"Anthony Bushy, you are accused of the murder of Aaron Chapman. How do you plead?"

"Not guilty," the butcher replied without hesitation. "I didn't do it."

The Leveller of the Marsh Scotts gave an audible sigh. *I can't help admiring Sir Rupert's optimism,* Harry reflected from his position at the side of the room. *There is a trustworthy witness in the schoolmaster, yet he still hopes this case will be over within the hour.*

"Not guilty," Sir Rupert repeated. "Very well. Let us return to Friday 27th September. On that day you appeared in this court accused of cheating your customers by using flawed weights and measures. Is that true?"

"It's true I was here."

"And on that day, I forbade you from serving in your shop or on any other premises within the Corporation of Romney Marsh. Is that correct?"

"It's right enough," Anthony Bushy replied, his tone implying that he was already weary of the process.

"But you, Mr Bushy, are a butcher. If you could not serve, please tell those gathered here what you are allowed to do."

"Allowed to do?"

"Allowed to do," Sir Rupert repeated. "Mr Payne – you were in court that morning. Please remind Mr Bushy."

William Payne, stood from his seat on the jurors' bench and looked about the room, cleared his throat and began, "Your Worship, Mr Bushy was allowed to butcher the animals. He could prepare the meat for sale, but not sell it."

"Aha! Those are the words I was expecting to hear – 'butcher the animals'. Do you know why the word 'butcher' is so important, Mr Bushy?"

The accused shrugged his shoulders in response.

"Thank you, Mr Payne. I would now like Mr Farrers to step forward."

For a moment, another time in this same courtroom flashed before Harry: A newcomer in the village, his head pounding from an injury, he had stood to face Sir Rupert Bannerman. He shook himself back to the present and turned to look out of the window taking in the view of New Hall's Garden. A young man was raking fallen leaves and, further away by the brick wall, Miss Eleanor Bannerman selected a late bloom to add to her trug of cut roses. Harry stepped away from the window and faced Sir Rupert once more.

"Mr Farrers, you were also in court on 27th September. Afterwards you returned to your forge. Did you see the accused again that day?"

"I did," Harry said. "By the time I reached the forge, there had already been some sort of altercation in the street outside the Ocean. My employee told me that Mr Bushy had been upset about something. Then he came across the street – drunk, he was – and he started complaining about being mistreated. He was saying that I should watch out, that before long you, Sir Rupert, would be at the forge or in Giles Woods' shop and looking to make trouble. They were the words of an inebriated man." Harry paused, seeing the scene and reflecting on what happened next. "He left and his parting words were something about how he could still do the butchering – or slaughtering… Yes, I think it was slaughtering."

"I can still do butchering… I can still do slaughtering… They mean one and the same to me," Sir Rupert asserted. "If any man can say different then I am happy to be corrected. There was silence in the room, other than the inevitable shuffling of feet and the brushing of fabric upon benches and chairs. Someone coughed and muttered an apology. Outside the window, a gull screamed.

Jeremy Parris coughed and stood, "Sir, if I may?"

Sir Rupert nodded and replied, "Of course."

"Slaughtering means to kill the animal, whereas butchering is to cut and prepare the meat, or so I believe."

"Thank you. The clerk can make a note of this, but in this case either word could be used for Mr Bushy does and can both slaughter and butcher."

"I agree." Mr Parris seated himself.

"Did you hear those words again?" Sir Rupert asked Harry.

"I did, sir." Harry paused, remembering the heated exchange in the churchyard. "I was just across the road from here – between the Ship and the church – when I heard raised voices. It was the evening of the Michaelmas Meeting – the 30th September, due to Michaelmas being on a Sunday this year. Aaron Chapman had already left the Ship, having said that he had some papers to deliver to you. I followed just minutes later. As I walked home, I heard Aaron shouting for someone to take their hands off him."

"Did he say the person's name?" Sir Rupert asked.

"He did not," Harry replied. "But then I heard those words: 'You said I was welcome to go butchering'. Aaron sounded surprised by this – the words meant nothing to him. Then it was said again – and something about no one deserving it more. And that was it. I thought he would have it all under control, but the next minute someone was running out of the churchyard and towards the seawall, and that's when I found Aaron injured."

"What time was this?" Sir Rupert asked.

"It was before nine o'clock, sir. I know that because when I was in the hallway here at New Hall waiting for George and Brown, the clock chimed nine. I also know that you take a pride in keeping your clocks running to the correct time."

"I do!" Sir Rupert agreed. "Before nine o'clock it was then." Pointing at Anthony Bushy, he demanded to know, "Was this the man you saw running off?"

"I can't say either way," Harry admitted. "I wish I could."

Sir Rupert then spoke to his son, the vicar and the apothecary. A picture of Aaron's last moments was painted for the jury. Not one of them could place the butcher as the killer, for no condemning words were uttered from the dying man, and no one had been witness to the attack.

Finally, the accused man was told to step forward once more. He did so with a confidence rarely seen in the courtroom, even going as far as to glance along the line of Chapman men seated to one side and allowing himself the pleasure of a slight smirk.

"Did you see that?" Daniel Chapman yelled, stepping towards the butcher. "Do you see how he killed my brother and now he laughs about it?"

Harry froze. The men of the Chapman family were known to have a temper which flared suddenly, and they reacted without thought. The bailiff was standing nearby and stepped forward, placing a restraining hand on Daniel's chest. In tandem Sir Rupert prepared to bellow an order, but before any words passed his lips, the butcher hollered, "I wouldn't mind him being dead, but I didn't do it. Bravo to the man who did!"

These words silenced the courtroom in a way Sir Rupert could never have managed. The villagers... the jury... the witnesses and the Chapman family stared at Anthony Bushy, then turned to each other. Now the room was on the brink of uproar.

"Return him to the cell," Sir Rupert thundered in an unprecedented move.

The gaoler leapt from where he loitered at the head of the staircase, while immediately the bailiff was at the butcher's side.

"We meet again in half an hour," Sir Rupert stated. "You, Mr Chapman, will be allowed in court, but any trouble and I will have you removed. Other than the jury and the family of the deceased man, I only want to see the witnesses. The session will not be open to the commonality."

From the doorway of New Hall, Harry glanced across to the Ship Inn. *They will gain a good trade today,* he mused. *Those words from Anthony Bushy will be repeated over and over, and those excluded will make their own judgements. No, I shan't go there. I don't care to be caught up in it all.* Instead, he wandered towards the small forge he was in the process of buying and there he chatted to the owner, Joshua Smith. The heat of the fire, coupled with the sweet smell of iron mingling with the comforting aroma of charcoal smoke, offered Harry a respite from the rigors of the trial. He looked at the tools and materials offered with the sale of the business and left having thanked Joshua for his time.

In the courtroom, the jury filed through a doorway and silently seated themselves as Harry took his former place by the window facing the garden. No one spoke, merely acknowledging each other with nods and a twitch of the lips. Bounding up the stairs, Sir Rupert paused at the top and turned to call his stoical manservant, "Brown! Ask for the accused to be brought up."

"He's on his way, sir," Brown called, forever respectful.

This was followed by ponderous footsteps on the stairs and the clank of iron chains. Everyone swivelled

67

to see Anthony Bushy appear in the courtroom. There came an audible sigh from Daniel Chapman, but nothing more was said.

No sooner than the accused was standing in the dock, than Sir Rupert addressed the clerk, "If you could repeat the last words spoken by Mr Bushy…"

The clerk stood to do as instructed, his face expressionless and tone flat: "'I wouldn't mind him being dead, but I didn't do it. Bravo to the man who did!'"

Murmured words flowed about the room, none of them clear enough to reach Sir Rupert's ears. He coughed and began: "Brave words from our man in shackles, but I am going to ignore his opinions and concentrate on his words declaring he did not murder Aaron Chapman. It is for the jury to decide today if there is any truth in his plea of innocence. Mr Bushy, tell me – what were you doing at quarter to nine on the evening on Monday 30th September?"

"I was doing my learning with the schoolmaster!" Anthony Bushy replied with relish.

"You were with Mr Dickens. Can you explain why those words you were known to have said previously were repeated when Mr Chapman was savagely killed? Or why your knife was found at the scene?"

"I can't explain any of it, sir. Someone wants me to hang for this – a scapegoat, that's what they want. But they didn't know about me doing my learning."

Harry allowed his attention to wander to the view of the garden. A gust of wind blew, shaking leaves off the chestnut, causing conkers to fall. *Sir Rupert knows of this. Why does he speak as if it comes as a surprise? Does he hope that Mr Bushy will admit to a crime it appears he didn't commit?* He turned back to focus on Sir Rupert's next words:

"It is a mystery to me, Mr Bushy. I would like to call Mr Dickens as a witness."

Harry's concentration drifted once more while Sir Rupert repeated what was known of the events before and when the murder took place. *A needless exercise. The schoolmaster has waited patiently until we reached this point and does not need to hear this. And the jury are well-versed with proceedings so far. Oh… I missed a bit.*

"That's right, Your Worship. He's been learning to read and write for the past month and is making good progress," Mr Dickens explained. "Mr Bushy came to me at eight o'clock and left at nine. Those are his usual times and I keep a sharp eye on the clock." The schoolmaster was a man known to be precise with his habits.

Further unnecessary questions followed, and Harry's thoughts roamed to his dinner. *Janey will be dishing it up now, and Phoebe will be wondering if I'll be home. But she knows Sir Rupert well enough to appreciate that he too will be thinking of his stomach.*

"That's enough for now," Sir Rupert said as the clock struck one. "The court will adjourn to give the jury time to discuss the matter. We meet again in one hour."

"You're not letting me go?" the butcher asked as the gaoler stepped forward to take his arm."

"I have not heard the verdict yet," Sir Rupert barked as he left the court.

Chapter Seven
Phoebe

Three days had passed since the court hearing. October was upon Dymchurch and had arrived with a definite nip in the air. Phoebe held her shawl snug about her shoulders when she left her home for the shops or to go visiting, and the fire in the front parlour was lit by mid-afternoon. She welcomed every day when the twins' freshly washed clouts could be pegged on the washing line, recalling the previous winter when the drying rack was lowered to be filled with damp wool and linen, then raised so the kitchen ceiling became festooned.

Sitting at the kitchen table, Phoebe gazed up at the empty rack, then in a seemingly unconnected comment she said, "There has been so little rain lately, I think I'll take the field tracks and enjoy the walk."

Using a crust of bread, Harry wiped the last of the gravy from his plate. "Where are you going?"

"Esther and I are going to call on Mrs Lydia Chapman," Phoebe told him. She smiled, noting his surprise. "That woman has not one friend on Romney Marsh and through no fault of her own. Her husband is dead, and we are none the closer to finding out who killed him. I cannot imagine how she must be feeling."

"It won't be easy," Harry pointed out, unnecessarily.

"She's a cold one." Janey offered her opinion while wiping Clara's mouth.

"Is she unfriendly, or is she lonely and aware of her late husband being unpopular hereabouts? Marianne Payne and I have spoken about it, and she is going to ride from St Mary in the Marsh tomorrow afternoon, although I am to send a note to her if I think it unwise." Phoebe stood to start clearing the table. "Look at how lucky I am, surrounded by my friends and family, while poor Lydia spends her days in that remote hamlet, her only visitor being her mother-in-law. Janey and Mary will look after the twins, and we will leave immediately." Phoebe turned to her elder daughter to ask, "Esther, will you fetch your cloak. We're going on a countryside walk."

The village of Burmarsh was no distance away, and the church tower served as a constant guide while Phoebe negotiated dry mud tracks and plank bridges. The countryside awaited its winter slumber, but amongst the bleached greens and dull golds the hawthorn berries shone a glorious, rich red. In contrast, thistle heads and reeds were faded, their stems ragged and virility forgotten. Labourers were at work on the fields, and Phoebe spotted two teams of horses ploughing the wheat stubble back into the land, while here and there the dykes were being cleared to keep the water flowing towards the outlets in the seawall.

Esther chattered, watching the men at work from her elevated position on Phoebe's hip, or plucking at flowers or long grass heads as she rambled along the track. They paused frequently to inspect a delicate web or busy beetle. On the bridges they stamped, enjoying the thud of their steps.

After a while, mother and daughter joined the country lane and Rothschild Manor loomed before them. Glancing down at Esther, Phoebe was glad of her daughter's company. If Lydia was at home to receive a

71

visitor, then to speak of their daughters would ease the flow of conversation. They walked up the gravel driveway and stood under the shelter of a wooden porch before rapping on the front door.

It was Lydia herself who answered, and Phoebe was relieved to see a look of pleasure on the widow's face, swiftly replacing the initial surprise.

"Mrs Farrers! How good of you to call. Come in... Do you come with news or just to... And you have brought your daughter – how lovely."

"I hope I'm not intruding," Phoebe replied as she followed Lydia into the parlour. "I come with no news, but wondered if you might care for some company?"

"I would!" The lift to Lydia's voice and the smile that followed reassured Phoebe that her decision to call unannounced was the right one. "Do sit down." She gestured to the couch, while walking towards a doorway leading to the kitchen. "Rebecca! Come here please. We have visitors – a little girl has come to see you." Then to the cook, "Mrs Farrers is here. Could we have a pot of tea, please." Turning back, now with her daughter at her skirts, Lydia continued, "This is Rebecca, and I'm sorry... I should know... but I don't know her name."

"Esther," Phoebe responded. "This is Esther. Hello Rebecca, how lovely to see you."

The children eyed each other, Esther from the safety of her mother's lap. Phoebe noted that Rebecca had the same blonde hair and pale skin as her mother. Her features were delicate, and she was no bigger than Esther, despite being four or five months older. Their mothers waited for a moment before Lydia suggested, "Rebecca, do you think Esther might like to see your dolls?"

Although she said nothing in reply, Rebecca's face showed her eagerness and she scampered free from

72

her mother's skirts to haul a wooden cradle from its tucked away place between the couch and a well-worn chair. Esther looked at Phoebe for approval before sliding off her lap. For the next few minutes all the attention was on the children, encouraging them to each take a doll, and gradually they began to chatter between themselves without further persuasion from the adults.

Tea was brought on a tray, and Lydia busied herself with pouring it, then offering shortbread biscuits. The bustle of the arrival of unexpected visitors passed, and Phoebe found herself wondering how to fill the time while the tea cooled. "Is your cousin still here?" she asked, immediately feeling that her enquiry appeared gossipy, for he was undoubtedly a handsome man.

"Gerald – yes, yes he is." Lydia appeared a little flustered. "He went to Sussex as arranged – quite a dash it was – then returned for the trial, and now he insists on staying until the... the person responsible is found."

"You are fortunate to have a family member with you at this time." Phoebe recalled the times when, as a younger woman, she had visited Mrs Chapman, Aaron's mother, on Saturday afternoons. "His mother... your husband's mother is a good support, I'm sure. But..."

"But she is inconsolable," Lydia interrupted. "I hardly know what to say to her."

"It must be difficult. Besides, she is some distance away." Phoebe took a tentative sip of tea. It was still too hot. She changed the subject, "This house is charming. Sometimes people say that the beams in old houses have come from ships, and I can well believe it. They must have had a life before becoming part of all this."

"Rebecca, sit still with the shortbread," Lydia reproached her daughter before considering Phoebe's words. She looked at the ceiling: heavily beamed, with cuts and marks telling a story of an earlier construction. "I can reach and touch it," she said. "I should prefer a loftier space, but my husband was doing his best to modernise the property. It used to be two cottages, you know."

"I remember it when Aaron's grandmother lived here," Phoebe replied. "It was one house then but looked very different without the recent façade. It's changed a lot since you married and came here."

"My father paid for it as our wedding gift – the modernisation, I mean." Lydia gazed into the distance, beyond the huge brick fireplace, as if looking back to a time when she arrived in Burmarsh young and hopeful of a happy marriage.

They spoke more of the changes to the house and of Lydia's particular interest – her rose garden. "They are past their best now, but maybe you would like to…?"

"I'd love to see them," Phoebe said. "I often think that I should take more interest in my own plot, perhaps you will inspire me."

"I hope so. We'll go shortly; it seems a shame to interrupt the girls when they are playing so nicely."

A second cup of tea was sipped while they talked about the children, although Lydia said nothing of her pregnancy and Phoebe took care not to refer to it. Then Esther and Rebecca placed the dolls in the cradle and followed their mothers through the kitchen and into the garden. Here the girls skipped about, and Lydia revealed her special spot where the roses still bloomed. The suggestion that Marianne Payne might visit the following afternoon was agreed to. "I have never had a visitor that was not his family before… before now."

"I thought that might be how it was," Phoebe responded. "We'd better walk back now, and if you would care to bring Rebecca to Walker House, I know

Esther will be pleased to see her. She finds the twins rather tiresome!"

On leaving Rothschild Manor, Phoebe felt a sense of having made her peace with Aaron's wife. The unease experienced by both women since Lydia came to the area as a new bride could finally be left in the past. At the roadside, she hauled Esther onto her hip and resolved to set off at a fair pace to Dymchurch.

After ten minutes or so, a young labourer approached pulling a small cart laden with cut reeds. His clothes were caked in dry mud and a knife with a curved blade hung from his belt. The lad doffed his cap as he neared Phoebe and Esther, and she responded with a smile, fully expecting him to walk by.

Just as they were on the verge of passing, he spoke: "It's Mrs Farrers, isn't it?"

There was something familiar about his russet curls and freckled face, but Phoebe couldn't place him. "Yes," she replied with caution.

"You won't know me, but it was me who told about the blacksmith taking the prize cup."

"Of course it was. What do you want?" Phoebe answered, now very much on her guard. It was clear that this young man, Toke Spicer – she recalled his name now – had something to reveal. She lingered, aware of Esther's weight on her hip.

"I'd like to come and speak with your husband," Toke continued. "He's a good man – that's what they say and it's what I see of him. There's things that need telling about that day."

For a moment, Phoebe was back at the racecourse in New Romney at that time when the gilt cup was stolen. She remembered the look of satisfaction on Aaron's face when he produced Toke – his witness to the theft of the prize cup. Looking at Toke, now fully grown into a man, she saw the boy he had once been, and recalled the glee in his eyes. To receive attention from Sir Rupert had given the lad a sense of pride. A shilling or two in his pocket, courtesy of Aaron Chapman, had added to his feeling of importance. There was never any proof of Toke being paid to bear false witness, but both Phoebe and Harry were certain of it.

"My husband is fair," Phoebe said, her voice uncharacteristically firm. "But he is also a man who lost a good employee that day and wasted a great deal of time trying to prove Jesse Alder's innocence."

"I've done wrong by your husband and his apprentice," Toke admitted. "Now Mr Chapman is gone – and I can't say 'God rest his soul' even if I should – I need to start putting things right."

"Come to my home, Walker House, at five o'clock today," Phoebe said, determined not to be drawn further into this conversation. "Mr Farrers will see you then."

"That's most kind." Toke doffed his cap once more. "Take care on these roads, Mrs Farrers. They are mighty muddy in places. Dry mud, but mud nonetheless."

Phoebe nodded, her expression haughty but belying her true feelings. *I won't let him see it, but I can't help liking Toke Spicer!*

The trek home became arduous with Esther begging to walk, but soon tiring, and then falling asleep in her mother's arms. Phoebe took the field tracks once more, passing through pastureland and ploughed fields, across plank bridges over waterways and dry ditches. Burmarsh church became distant while the features of Dymchurch's church materialised. Esther woke as Phoebe trudged up the path to Walker House, her mind still buzzing from her encounter with Toke Spicer.

Once home, Phoebe was plunged into family life. From their highchairs at the kitchen table, James and Clara squealed for their mother's attention, while Esther clambered onto her seat, and Mary fastened an apron around the little girl. Janey spooned a thick broth into bowls while saying, "It's not too hot. I've let it cool."

Phoebe settled herself between the twins, Mary helped Esther, and Janey prepared a cup of tea. The talk was of how Rebecca Chapman had enjoyed the company of another three-year-old girl, with enquiries about Mrs Lydia Chapman being put aside until the women could speak without interruption. Phoebe said nothing of her meeting with the lad in the lane, conscious that Harry would be home shortly and Toke due not long after.

No sooner had Harry stepped through the back door than Phoebe was ushering him to the parlour.

"My clothes!" Harry gestured to the soiled breaches and tunic. But Phoebe would allow no delay to her telling of the chance meeting on the lane. She gave a brief account, aware Toke was due and sensing that he would be punctual. They avoided the urge to discuss the matter further. Instead, Harry raced upstairs to scrub the worst of the day's dirt from his hands and forearms. Then he was returning downstairs as Mary shepherded the children into the parlour, and Phoebe was at the back door facing Toke Spicer once more.

"Harry will see you in the dining room," she said, leading the way through the house to the room so rarely used. Harry and Phoebe chose to live as one family with their housekeeper and maid, and this included eating together in the kitchen.

In the centre of the room there stood a mahogany table – polished and pristine, large enough to accommodate eight. The iron grate was both unlaid and unlit, emphasising how infrequently the room was occupied. It was a pleasant, well-proportioned space – a twin to the front parlour – but almost devoid of life. Almost, because to one side of the fireplace, positioned to benefit from the morning sun, there sat a desk, its surface laden with ledgers, loose papers, quills, nibs and ink. It was here Harry attended to his paperwork connected with the running of his forge and the purchase of his second business in the village. Phoebe found him seated at the desk as Toke was led into the room.

"Toke Spicer, I understand you want to see me," Harry said, without the usual warmth to his voice. Looking towards Phoebe, he continued, "I'd like you to stay and hear what this is all about."

Phoebe had rarely seen her husband looking so stern. *Whatever Toke has to say, Harry is determined not to make it easy for him.* Weary from the walk to Burmarsh, she pulled out a chair and sat down, while aware that Toke would not be offered the courtesy of being made comfortable in their home.

"Well, Mr Farrers... Mrs Farrers, you're not going to be pleased with me, and perhaps I'll end up in that courtroom either here or at New Romney, and perhaps I'll end up the most hated man here on Romney Marsh Proper." Toke paused and rubbed at the wisps of hair growth on his chin. He chewed on his lip and let his gaze roam about the room, then he blurted out the words they had been waiting for: "It was Mr Chapman who stole the cup. Mr Aaron Chapman – him who's dead now."

Chapter Eight
Toke Spicer
1762 – Three years earlier

"What are you up to, boy? Dressed like a toff you are when there's clay to be carted up to the Wall."

Toke tugged at the fancy piece of material he had cut from a dress in his mother's rag bag and hemmed when none of the family were looking. "It's my cravat, Ma. I'm off to see that race what they call The Whitsun Gallop and I'll be back moving the clay tomorrow."

"A cravat?" The mother of five cackled, giving her youngest a playful cuff about the ear. "Going to be sitting on the stand with the gentry, are you?"

"Of course not, but there's no harm in looking my best. I've got plans, Ma. One day people will look at me and say, 'There goes Toke Spicer – he's done well for himself', and I'll be proud to hear it."

"And what are you going to be doing to have people say that?" Ma Spicer asked.

"I've got to go now," Toke replied as he sidled into the room he shared with the two siblings remaining in the family home. The truth was that Toke didn't know what he wanted to do. His world was limited to the lanes and dykes around Burmarsh that led to the great seawall and Dymchurch. He was in awe of the huge barrier between sea and low-lying land and the men who worked upon it. Even to be one of the boys who led the donkey with its clay cart, and to know those clods of clay-earth were to be packed into the Wall, made him feel as if he were a part of it. *Please God, please keep the Wall good and strong, and protect them men who work on it.* Toke folded his socks to hide the ragged top then remembered to offer a hasty *Amen.* Minutes later, with a piece of bread and dripping in his hand, and one precious penny in his pocket, he left for a day at the racecourse.

Nearly two hours passed, and having reached the end of the seawall track, Toke joined a trail of people walking on the roadside. Astounded by the volume and variety of traffic upon the road, the boy kept his eyes open and his mind alert. Elegant horses passed, some with riders seated upon them and others pulling lightweight traps. Sturdy beasts hauled equally sturdy carts, and within these traps and carts all eyes were focussed on the dunes in an area known as The Warren, where a racecourse had been carved out between the sand hills.

Constantly having to move aside for the faster traffic, those on foot were often brushing up against each other. Toke glimpsed tempting leather purses hanging from wrists and belts, and his fingers tightened on the bone handle of the knife hanging at his hip. There were rich pickings here for someone who was deft enough to choose their prey with care. However, eager to see the horse race, the boy had no plans to scupper the chance of such unique entertainment. He had never suffered the misfortune of spending a night in the Dymchurch gaol and was not going to end his outing in one of the damp, dark cells.

Nearing the pest house, Toke avoided even a cursory glance. *I've heard of that place and if I don't look then I won't end up one of them poor folk who have to go there.* Before he could dwell on those who suffered from the pox, dysentery or tuberculosis, Toke noted a wide path leading to the racecourse. He moved with the mass, his shoes touching against ridges of sandy soil topped with tough grasses and ragged weeds. Every so often he would kick at ribbons of shingle and shells. *This is a place where the sea came not so long ago. It's a different sort of area to Burmarsh. This is new land, and my place is ancient.* Deep thoughts for a boy who knew little of life beyond his village, but he worked on the land, and it was something he understood.

Racegoers now spilled in all directions – some choosing their spot at the trackside and others heading towards staging erected for the well-to-do. They lingered in groups, sharing the news and gossip, or meandered towards carts offering food and drink. Beyond the areas where the gentry would sit, behind some makeshift fencing, the racehorses and their grooms awaited the first heat. *I'll keep my eye on them – no need to go by the track until I see them moving to the start.* Toke stood on his own and allowed his eyes to scan the whole area, waiting for that moment when something would catch his interest.

What's that? He narrowed his eyes and began to walk towards the staging. *Gold and shining.*

It took a few minutes for Toke to negotiate his way past people wandering aimlessly, while being wary of the numerous rabbit burrows in the sandy landscape, and all the time keeping his gaze fixed upon this glorious gold object. Placed upon a navy-blue velvet cloth draped over a small table, the graceful shape of a lidded cup with large, slim, yet curvaceous handles came into focus.

The prize cup – the cup that one of them gents will be taking home with them! Still keeping his distance –

for it was not for the likes of him to go too close – Toke stood and allowed a sense of awe to wash over him.

"Hurry up – the seats are filling." A bewigged gentleman strode past. His wife, with a baby in her arms, struggled to keep up. Her straw hat tumbled from her head, and she paused, looking almost helpless with the bundle of infant and vast shawl, as well as a basket at her elbow.

"Here Mrs, I'll fetch it," Toke leapt to help, recognising his near neighbours Mr and Mrs Aaron Chapman from Rothschild Farm. The couple paused, and the baby passed to her father while the hat was accepted and returned to Mrs Lydia Chapman's ash-blonde hair. "I hope you have a spendid day, Mr Chapman… Mrs Chapman…" Toke dared to say.

Perhaps surprised that the boy knew his name, or that he dared to speak to him, the gentleman enquired, "Do I know you from hereabouts?"

"You do, sir. You do!" Toke chirped. "My pa and my brothers and me, we all work down the lanes and in the waterways around Burmarsh. And my pa does a bit of lookering for your sheep in the springtime."

The gentleman gave no immediate reply, but his eyes narrowed and he stared intently at Toke as if all sorts of plans and schemes were churning about in his mind. Then he passed the baby back to his wife, reached into his purse, withdrew tuppence, and tossed it towards the boy, causing him to scrabble about in the sand for it. "Get yourself a muffin or a pie." Then, just as Toke thought their dealings were over, Mr Chapman stepped forward and said, "Meet me by the ale stand and don't mention this to anyone."

There was no chance for the boy to give a grovelling response, for the gentleman turned and continued on his way to the stands.

82

Well, that was a lucky thing when his lady wife let her hat go flying. I've got tuppence in my hand and now he knows me and wants to talk business. He's an important man, Mr Chapman is, and he's asked to meet Toke Spicer!

The food and drink stalls were closer to the road, so Toke turned his back on the golden cup and the track where the horses would soon be racing, and took a meandering path to a trestle table where trays of warm pies tempted him. Gravy oozed from their lids, and his mouth began to water. "A mutton pie, please," he said, handing over his penny and keeping the tuppence safely tucked away. The savoury treat came on folds of newspaper, and Toke instantly began picking at the pastry, then nibbling at the meaty filling. As he did so, the boy wandered towards a stall where ale was being served, eyeing the crowds for the gentleman he had agreed to meet.

He lingered for so long that it all seemed to be a waste of time and Toke began to fret that the race would begin while he was far from the trackside. *And then what will I do because he gave me tuppence, but I came to see them horses, not be waiting about just in case…*

As these thoughts batted about in Toke's mind, he spotted Mr Chapman, sporting a wig of dark waves on his head and a scowl on his face. The coat tails of his burgundy velvet jacket took on a life of their own as they bounced along, and his silver buckled shoes almost danced amongst the hillocks and tufts of long grass heads. Toke watched the progress of this individual whom he privately saw as a 'bit of a toff' and doffed his cap as he drew closer.

"What's your name?" Mr Chapman asked, his words short and sharp.

"Toke. Toke Spicer." The boy beamed with the pleasure of the honour bestowed on him in being singled out for attention. The gentleman had land, money and a wife from 'off the Marsh'. He was still a young man too, with so many opportunities ahead of him, and if Toke could ingratiate himself with this fine person then he too could have prospects beyond the clay carts and the dykes.

"Can you be trusted?"

"I can, Mr Chapman, I can."

"And you're a Burmarsh boy?"

"I am, Mr Chapman. And my father before me and his father too. We go to the church on Sunday and work the land on the other days."

"Would you like to earn a shilling? And another if I'm pleased with you?" The rim of a silver coin showed between the slender fingers of the gentleman.

Toke nodded.

"I want to have a bit of sport today, and if you help me then the shillings will keep coming. Do you understand? You'll need to do as I say and not go talking to anyone else about it. I'm looking for a bright lad who I can trust. Are you that person?"

"I am, Mr Chapman. I won't tell a soul."

Aaron Chapman looked towards the prize cup and then to the cart where Harry Farrers, blacksmith and jurat, was setting up his mobile forge with the help of his assistant. His thin lips curled, and he gave a slight nod, then Mr Chapman continued, "When the race begins, it will be all eyes on the horses. Most of these people you see here will be at the trackside or up in the stands, and they will all be facing over there." He gestured towards the track. "But not you – you will wait around the back of the stands, and when I pass you the prize cup, you'll wrap it up in sacking. Have a look behind some upright posts and you'll spot a piece I left there for this very purpose. Stuff it down your shirt for now so no one sees you with it. Then, when you have the cup, wait until the fuss starts and people are here and there and everywhere. That's when I want you to hide the cup at the blacksmith's cart."

"At the blacksmith's cart?"

"Oh yes! Harry Farrers took my wife away from me."

Toke looked towards the stands where Mrs Chapman and the baby sat.

Aaron Chapman let out a short burst of laughter. "Not that wife – the wife I was meant to have. The woman I planned to marry."

This was beyond Toke's understanding, so he nodded furiously as if to show that he knew the ways of men and women. "I take the cup and leave it at the cart. Hidden."

"Then later, when the cup has been found and everyone thinks Mr Farrers' apprentice is a thief and it's caused a lot of trouble for our jurat-blacksmith, people will be asking if anyone saw him take the prize cup."

"They will!" Toke could imagine the scene – the chaos and disruption for the Corporation of New Romney who had planned this glorious day.

"That's when I'll find you at the trackside, as if you've been there all the time, and you'll tell me that you saw the apprentice – Jesse Alder – running from the stands with a bundle of sacking. It will be as if he took the cup, and you will be witness to it. When I find you, that's when I'll give you the second shilling."

"The second shilling," Toke echoed.

"There will be lots of questions from important people, so you'll have to stick to what I tell you. Please me and there will be more shillings – a tidy pile in the end!"

"I can answer questions," Toke assured him.

"Good! Now go to the back of the staging and pick up that sacking I told you about. Then walk over as if you're about to watch the race, and when it starts you move away and wait for me." Aaron Chapman didn't wait for a response, instead he called to the wench at the ale stall and made his demands for a drink.

Toke faltered for a moment, taking it all in, then he set off for the great wooden edifice which supported rows of benches from where the race could be viewed. There was no one lurking to the rear, but the wooden planks and beams groaned under the weight of the gentry. Toke held his breath and looked up, expecting at any moment for the whole thing to come crashing down and crush him, then he dashed under, retrieved some sacking and stuffed it up his shirt. He scurried off to the trackside, wanting to see King's Sovereign and Dandy Dancer approach the start line for the first of three heats.

It didn't feel right – leaving his position amongst the jostling crowds to sneak around the back of the staging. Toke felt uneasy. Surely later, when the great fuss began, someone would remember that they saw him on that patch of open ground between those gathered at the trackside and the gentry sitting high on their benches. However, it proved easy to slip back as all around him pushed forward, intent on watching the dash. He could feel the ground vibrating under the horses' hooves, and for the first time he doubted if pleasing Aaron Chapman was worth missing the race for. Then he thought of the silver shillings and how they would lie snug with the coppers he had collected over the past year and stashed under a plank in his shared bedroom.

Although Toke saw it as a vast plain, the open ground between racecourse and staging was no more than a few yards. With the horses still on the first straight, all eyes were on these athletic beasts and, while his heart pounded with a mixture of excitement and anxiety, the distance was soon covered. Soon he stood snug within the shadows of the wooden planks and posts with the well-to-do seated above.

The structure swayed, taking on a life of its own – leaning with the eager spectators in the direction of Dymchurch and then the coast. It thundered as feet were stamped, and dropped particles of mud, splinters of wood, then – to Toke's delight – a New Romney token. He waited, part curious, part nervous as to what would happen next. If he lay on his belly, then the edge of the velvet draping the small display table could be seen, and he knew that the prize cup still sat upon it.

He was in this position when Mr Chapman dropped down from the side of the staging. Without a word to Toke, he discarded his jacket, tore off his wig, and he too lay flat on the ground, then proceeded to worm his way towards the front. In a movement so swift that Toke could not help but be impressed, this gentleman slithered out, snatched at the cup and retreated. He gestured for the boy to move forward and almost flung the cup in his direction. "Take it," he barked.

Toke did as ordered, wrapping the cup in the hessian sack while Mr Chapman replaced his wig and jacket. "Wait!" came the instruction. "Wait until there are people all over the place. Then do as I said." With this he tossed the first of the promised silver coins in Toke's direction and the boy almost swelled with pride for being singled out to help Aaron Chapman in this important task.

Chapter Nine
Harry
1765

Of all the scenarios which had played out in Harry's mind over the past three years, none had included Aaron taking the cup. It seemed most likely that he had paid – and paid handsomely – some young villain to snatch the cup while all eyes were on the race. Perhaps the sea had been an unwitting accomplice – as the sun shone upon the waters, they sparkled, dazzling those who gazed in that direction. It had been obvious that Toke, and later another Burmarsh lad, had been paid to lie during the aftermath of the theft and later in court, but never had he considered…

Shaking himself, Harry pulled his thoughts back to the present. Looking at Phoebe, seated on one of the dining chairs, he saw the confusion in her face as she too tried to picture the scene. Her brown eyes were solemn and her brow creased with a slight frown. "How could he dare?" she asked, her voice little more than a whisper.

"Excuse me for answering, Mrs Farrers," Toke piped up, "but he was a man who would have come up with an excuse if he were caught, and he was a nasty sort so easier for people to believe him than cross him."

"You've grown wise in the past three years," Harry reflected. "You understood about the Marsh, but now you understand about people too."

"You're good to say that, Mr Farrers, and I'll tell you that the Marsh is easier to understand than people. She has her moods, but they make sense to me, and I know how to handle her. Now people… they confuse me more."

During this tale which had taken them all back to Whitsun in the year 1762, Harry had moved from his desk and was standing at the window. Toke remained upright, never having been invited to sit. "I suspect the person who you have learned most about is Aaron Chapman."

"I soon learned to keep away from him," Toke acknowledged. "He was vicious with his whip. That man wasn't my friend for long."

Phoebe reached out, placing her hand on the lad's arm. "Sit down and I'll ask Janey if we can have a plate of her spiced apple cake. Would you like some ale?"

Toke considered this for a moment, then responded, "If you don't mind, Mrs Farrers, I'm partial to a cup of tea, if you happen to have any."

Harry grinned. Toke Spicer had a lively mind – he knew as well as the next man that tea was no luxury on Romney Marsh if you had a friend who traded by night with the French. He watched as the lad seated himself, adjusted his breeches and looked down at his well-scrubbed hands in his lap. "A good man was at risk of being deported," Harry stated, his voice stern. "He had everything to look forward to – marriage to a lovely woman, a decent job, a cottage of his own. That was taken away from him by Aaron's scheming and your lies."

"You're right. I feel bad about it and won't deny it."

"However, if it hadn't been you, it would have been some other young lad eager for coins and attention from an important man. Jesse Alder would have lost his

89

future here in Dymchurch with or without your influence."

"I'm glad he got away." Toke smirked. Without doubt, stories of Jesse's release from New Romney gaol would have circulated to the hamlet of Burmarsh. "Mr Chapman was angry. That's when I got a beating." He paused for a moment and gazed out of the window into the greying sky. "My first one."

"I'm sorry that happened. You did as Aaron Chapman asked, and he must have been pleased with you. It's not right that you suffered when his plans went wrong."

Phoebe entered the room with a lamp and pulled the shutters, fastening them and closing out the impending nightfall. She left and returned with a tray of tea and the cake. Placing a chunk of the sweet treat in front of Toke, she said. "This will fill you up before you walk home. I hope your ma saves some supper for you."

"Oh, she will." Toke beamed as if seeing a full dinner plate in front of him. He stuffed a piece of cake in his mouth, then said, "I've wanted to come and tell you or Sir Rupert Bannerman. I've thought about it over and over. But once you had let me go... if you let me go... I'd have had to leave the Marsh because he'd kill me. That's what stopped me – knowing I'd have to go."

'Because he'd kill me.' Those words reverberated in Harry's mind, reminding him of something else... or someone else. His brow furrowed, and unsure of how to express himself, he asked, "Toke, do you remember... on that day... do you remember seeing a young man standing within the circuit of the racetrack? Someone standing on a sand hill?"

"Yes!" Toke replied, brightening up. "I saw someone there and I said to Mr Chapman that I hoped he hadn't seen him take the cup. Everyone was looking at the racecourse then out to sea, you understand. But that man, he was looking towards the racecourse and inland."

Harry kept his voice calm, "That's right. It seemed strange to me." *I won't say another word. This lad was only a boy when he played a part in ruining Jesse's plans for the future, yet those words – they led to the rabbit keeper being murdered. I'm certain of it, but there's no need for Toke to suffer for it. Perhaps some things are best left unsaid?*

Toke marvelled at his tea being served in a matching cup and saucer, and they all ate cake, despite Janey keeping supper warm for Harry and Phoebe. Their talk drifted to life in Burmarsh. "There's always work to be done," Toke told them. "This time of year, I'm clearing the dykes. But the best jobs are them that help us keep safe behind that old wall. There's nothing more important than the Dymchurch Wall hereabouts, is there? Carting the clay is a mucky job, and cutting the thorn gives me more holes in my hands than I care to think of, but I know I'm part of the Marsh when I'm doing them."

"What do you want for the future? Is the money steady enough for you to have your own cottage and to be able to support a wife one day?" Harry asked.

"It's not steady, Mr Farrers, and that's the truth of it. Mr Chapman, he said I had to stay in Burmarsh and do jobs for him. He liked to keep me nearby. But now... I don't want to go far but I'd like to look for a steady job."

"What would you like to do?" Phoebe asked. "You're still young enough to learn a trade."

A broad grin spread across the lad's face. "Mrs Farrers, I'd like to work on the seawall! Wouldn't that be a fine thing?"

"I did it myself," Harry told him. "When I came here as a young man." He said no more, but over the next few days he would ponder over what could be done to help Toke achieve his dreams.

The sun had set by the time Toke left Walker House. The last of its light would see him on his way out of the village, then the moon would guide him, along with Toke's longstanding knowledge of the road to Burmarsh. His revelations filled Harry and Phoebe's thoughts and conversation for the rest of the evening as they agonised over the best path to take if they were to restore Jesse's good name within the Romney Marsh community.

On Monday morning, the new week began with Harry saddling his horse and setting off on the road to New Romney. The air was crisp, the day bright and, to his left, he caught glimpses of sparkling turquoise sea. On the seawall, there were small groups of workers, some who turned upon noticing the horse and rider. They raised their arms in a greeting then continued their labours. It was the type of day that made Harry feel glad to be astride the chestnut and moving at a fair pace. He journeyed with good news to report and a smile on his face while passing trundling carts and the occasional individual travelling along the coast road. No conversation stalled him, and he paused once to allow the chestnut to rest. Soon they were passing the racecourse and Warren House, then approaching New Romney. Once there he would seek Sir Julian Craythorne who had been instrumental in the arrest and conviction of Jesse over three years earlier.

On the outskirts Harry faltered, unsure of which direction to take – would Sir Julian be at home or in the town on some business? He decided on a road leading inland, then turned down a track, finally dismounting outside a modest manor house. Spotting someone raking fallen leaves, he asked, "Is there somewhere you could tie my horse for a moment and keep an eye on him?" With the chestnut secured, and the lad given a penny, Harry approached the front door.

A woman of mature years answered and, unsmiling, she brusquely asked his business. Giving no indication as to whether her master was at home, she gestured for Harry to wait in the hallway.

"Mr Farrers – Harry!" Sir Julian appeared, with his arm outstretched. As they shook hands, Harry could not help but notice the older man was becoming frail. Without a wig, there was little to be done to improve his thinning hair, and the lines across his face had deepened over the last few years. "How can I help you?"

"Good morning, sir. Might you be able to spare me some time? Something strange happened on Saturday evening: Three years after all that trouble at the Whitsun Gallop in '62, I've had a new witness come forward, or rather an old one has changed his story."

"I'm curious, but fear the outcome of this," Sir Julian responded, reaching for his walking stick resting against the panelled wall. "It bothers me to go back over old ground. Come to my study and we'll have coffee while you enlighten me." With the stick tapping on the stone floor, he led the way into a snug sitting room.

With the fire smouldering, a cup of good coffee and the comfort of an old leather chair, Harry found it easy to relay Toke's revelations to the elderly gentleman. Sir Julian reacted with none of the drama that Sir Rupert Bannerman of New Hall was renowned for.

"It happened on New Romney land, so I rode here to tell you first," Harry concluded as the tale came to an end. "But the men involved are all from Dymchurch and Burmarsh, so I'll tell Sir Rupert as soon as I can, but I do have work to attend to."

"Do you believe this lad?" Sir Julian asked.

"I do," Harry replied. "He has nothing to gain. However, if I could find David Williams who also stood as a witness in court, then his words could confirm it all."

"If he dare tell the truth," Sir Julian pointed out. "These young men will have serious concerns about the repercussions they may face, although I am not minded to punish them for their part in it. As I said, I do not wish to go back over old ground and have no doubt they were desperate for the money offered at the time. Then there is the matter of Jesse Alder... Wherever he might be, he could now return to Dymchurch but the matter must go before the court for an acquittal. He need not be there for his name to be cleared – the evidence offered by these two should be enough to satisfy me, and it can be a private hearing."

"And into all this, we must bring the Chapman family who are grieving for a man who is to be revealed as a thief and a bully. They will not want these revelations to be made public knowledge."

"It's a shambles," Sir Julian said, using one of Sir Rupert's expressions. "There are so many strands to be unravelled and followed that I hardly know where to turn first." However, the older man's mind was undeniably sharp and as they spoke, a plan was formulating. "I think the priority is to question this other lad," he said. "Make it clear that whatever the truth of it is, he will not be punished." He paused, "The worst of it, as you mentioned, will be to face the Chapmans and the widow with this allegation. I see no need for them to attend court unless they wish to. First, we must speak to Sir Rupert. By the way, has he recovered from his illness?"

"He's in fine form," Harry responded. "I suggest that I return to work now, and tomorrow I'll go to Burmarsh, then see Sir Rupert. Hopefully I can find David and he will be willing to confirm his part in the lies told three years ago."

"I appreciate you coming to see me." Sir Julian drained his coffee cup and reached for a biscuit. "The news is troublesome, but it pleases me to think of a man's name being cleared. I recall feeling uneasy about his conviction back in '62."

"Thank you for your time, sir." Harry appreciated the older man's honesty and his willingness to deal with the matter. "I'll look forward to seeing you tomorrow and hope this matter is easily resolved, although I doubt it will be straightforward."

Sir Julian raised himself from the chair, taking time to straighten himself. "Could you leave a message at New Hall? Tell Sir Rupert that you and I will call tomorrow at two o'clock in the afternoon. If it doesn't suit him, then please ask that a note is sent advising me of a suitable time. Ideally, I would like this settled immediately, so, if possible, we will meet with Toke and David at the New Romney courtroom on Thursday – that gives us two days to invite a few others, such as the town constable from that time and members of the jury."

Returning with the wind on his back, Harry steered the chestnut towards the seawall track, joining it at Wall End. As always, he felt a sense of exhilaration on seeing the vast sweep of the bay. The moods of the Channel changed daily, taking her colours from the sky, shoals of fish or the sediment on her bed. She slapped gently or pounded rhythmically upon the great clay-clad bank, depending upon the strength of the wind. She rolled in barely breaking or spat with fury at those who ventured on the Wall at high tide. Sometimes you could taste the salt in the air or, on days such as this, the tide shimmered in the distance beyond the golden sands and the darker mudflats. Whatever the season or weather, the view changed by the hour and never failed to impress Harry.

Harry came across John Waller, who separated himself from his team of workers and raised an arm in a greeting. He sprang up a wooden ladder with the agility of a man ten or twenty years younger and stood upon the summit of the Wall.

"You're lucky to be released from jury duty," were his first words to Harry. He referred to the fact that as a witness to Aaron's murder Harry could not investigate alongside the jurats.

"I don't get away scott-free," Harry confided as he dismounted. "The case of the Whitsun Gallop cup is to be reopened, and both the murder and this case have one person in common."

"Our dead jurat?" John asked. "What's happened?"

"You weren't involved at the time," Harry began, "but do you recall there being some witnesses? Nothing more than a couple of boys."

"Burmarsh lads?" John asked.

"That's right." Harry gave a brief account of recent events to his friend and current village constable. "But let's not say a word to Jesse's family. I've not told Sir Rupert yet."

"So now we speak ill of the dead," John surmised. "While the jury seek out his killer, it is about to be revealed that Aaron stole the cup and made sure that Jesse was convicted of the crime."

"Exactly."

John looked across the sea towards France. "At least Jesse was not transported to America as planned. What chance would there be of getting word to him if he were there?"

"I know." Harry pictured the small fishing village of Wissant, home to Phoebe's family, and now Jesse. "At least he will have a choice of whether to remain where he is or to come home. It's been three years and he has made a good life for himself there." Bringing his thoughts back to the recent crime, he asked, "Now our butcher is a free man, what news is there of finding the killer?"

"Wait a minute." John dropped down from the Wall and onto the sands. After speaking with a couple of the workers, he returned to Harry. "I'm heading back to the village. We can walk together." Returning to Harry's query, John continued, "It's obvious that whoever murdered Aaron knew how angry the butcher was and they had heard his words, most likely more than once. Our killer ran off repeating a phrase which Anthony Bushy was known to have used, and they repeated it enough times that it was likely to be heard. On top of that, they left the butcher's knife at the scene of the crime. It looked as if it had been tossed without care, as if the man was in such a temper that he gave no thought to it being spotted. Most likely it was thrown by the killer, knowing full well that it would be found and place Mr Bushy at the crime scene."

"So, who heard those words 'You said I could go butchering'?" Harry wondered. The chestnut strained towards a clump of grass but was encouraged to walk on at his master's side.

"You, for a start!" John reminded him.

"I did!" Harry agreed, knowing that he was both liked and respected in the village and that while his name was clearly on the list of suspects, it would not be taken seriously. "I heard Sir Rupert Bannerman say it in court, but it was afterwards that Anthony Bushy was repeating it."

"Yes, he was outside the Ocean shouting about the injustice of the court hearing that morning. He walked across the road to your forge, still saying those words."

97

"To have heard Sir Rupert state that Mr Bushy could still slaughter or butcher animals is not enough for our killer," Harry mused. "For example, William Payne was in court with me. He heard the judgement, but presumably returned home to St Mary in the Marsh and knew nothing of those words being shouted about the village. Our killer needs to know that 'You said I could go butchering' was said over and over, and people would connect it with the butcher."

"We have created a list of those who we know will have been familiar with what was said, but there is something else..." John paused as they passed a couple of fishermen, and then a woman clutching a capacious wicker basket. They were still some distance from Dymchurch, and this part of the Wall was usually free of villagers. "Who was meant to die?" John asked when they could again speak privately. As head of a team of wall-workers, he was a practical man, and these words were uttered without drama. "It would help if we could be certain who the intended victim was."

"Yes! We said it at the time... on the evening when it happened... that Sir Rupert was the man meant to die. After all, it was he who stopped the butcher from selling meat. But you also must consider that Aaron was the man our killer was after."

"Which of the two is, or was, the most disliked"? John said, without needing or expecting an answer, for Aaron Chapman was loathed throughout the area and Sir Rupert Bannerman was well-liked. "If we knew who was meant to die, then it would help immensely."

Chapter Ten
Harry

"Excuse me," Harry approached the first villager he came across on nearing Burmarsh. "I'm looking for a young man named David Williams. He works on the land, or so I believe."

"Oh, yes?" the elderly man replied with caution. His gnarled fingers rested on the handles of a small pushcart laden with cabbages and, while he paused in his labours, his breath whistled and chest heaved.

"I'm not looking for trouble," Harry continued. "Just hoping he can help me." As he spoke, a lone cabbage rolled from the cart and settled on the tatty grass at the roadside. Harry retrieved it and placed it with the others.

"Help you?"

"That's right. Or Toke Spicer – would you know where I can find him?"

The man studied Harry's face, then answered, "You're that smithy from Dymchurch, I believe."

"That's right."

"They say you're a good-un. David Williams is at Abbotts working on some fencing. As for Toke, I've not seen him this morning."

Harry gazed across the fields towards Abbotts Court Farm. *I'll be there in ten minutes and hopefully on my way back within another ten. It all depends on how quickly he can be found.* "Thank you. I appreciate your help." He gave the man tuppence and, to his surprise, received a cabbage in return.

"Give that to your lady wife," the old man said, offering a toothless grin.

Harry was in luck that morning – he came across a familiar young man on the track to the farm. *I'm certain that's him. Thank you, Lord! I could have been searching for an hour or more.*

"Toke said you might come looking for me," David said before Harry uttered a word. "I'm busy."

This didn't bode well for Harry who responded carefully, "I can understand you don't want any trouble over what happened. It was a long time ago now."

David merely shrugged and turned back to survey the rotting fence.

"I can't say I was a friend of Mr Chapman," Harry told him. "I wouldn't want him dead, but he was a bully, wasn't he? A bully to me, and I would guess that he was a bully to you and other young men around here. Decent young men who needed to earn an honest living."

He was well aware that the term 'honest living' was largely inappropriate, but just as David shrugged his shoulders, Harry shrugged away the knowledge that many Marshmen were involved with the smuggling trade.

"He was a bully," David admitted. "Far too free with his whip. I'm not sorry he's gone. Dead."

"I've spoken to Sir Julian Craythorne," Harry told him. "He doesn't want this to go to trial again. Not when the man who caused all the trouble is dead. All he wants to know is if it is true that Aaron Chapman paid you to lie in court."

David kicked at a broken branch on the ground. "He did."

"Did you see my apprentice take the Whitsun Gallop cup?"

"No. I was watching the race. He told me to say it. Said there would be trouble if I didn't – said he'd stop me and my pa and my uncle getting work."

Harry sighed. "I can see why you lied. Thank you for telling me."

"It's good that he will have his name cleared," David responded. "That apprentice of yours."

"It is," Harry agreed. "But I do need you and Toke to come along to New Romney on Thursday. Sir Julian and a few others who were in court back in '62 will have a talk with you – they need to hear it for themselves that you were forced to lie. You won't be in trouble."

At this David perked up. "Then they'll know he was rotten. He can't pay for it, but those important people will know Mr Chapman was a bully through and through."

"You'll come then?"

"I won't be on trial?"

"Not at all."

"All right. I'll be there."

"You'll be losing your wages, and we'll see that's covered," Harry told him. He had stayed long enough and knew that, unlike Toke, David wasn't inclined to chat. As he turned to walk away, he said, "I'm going to meet Sir Julian at New Hall today. He and I can tell Sir Rupert that it's all true – Jesse didn't take the cup. Thank you. But one last thing: Will you see Toke? Can you tell him? I'll meet you both by Slodden Farm at ten in the morning, then we'll go by cart to the town."

"I'll tell him," David confirmed.

"What a time to come forward with this turn of events." Sir Rupert stood at the window of his study. Restless while listening to Harry's account of his meeting with

101

Toke, he now turned and almost threw himself back in his chair, his mood one of a petulant child. "And this other lad, David – he says the same?"

"He was reluctant," Harry admitted. "But Sir Julian said yesterday, and.." he glanced at Sir Julian Craythorne, "I hope he's not changed his mind. Sir Julian said that neither Toke nor David will be punished for their lies in court, and I was able to tell him that. There seems no doubt that what Toke told me is true, and David says the same."

"But he didn't see Aaron take the cup?" Sir Rupert queried, despite this being made perfectly clear when Harry first told him about meeting David that morning.

Inwardly Harry sighed. *How can every conversation with Sir Rupert turn this way and that with the same details explored from all angles?* "He didn't see the cup being stolen. He saw nothing at all. David was approached by Aaron the next day and paid to lie in court."

"It came as a surprise on the day," Sir Julian recalled from his chair beside the fire. "I hadn't expected a second witness to be brought in. I'd say that was the worst thing that could have happened to justify sentencing Jesse Alder. The jury had no choice but to convict him."

"Blazes! Those boys should stand up in this court and answer to their lies." Sir Rupert gestured towards the courtroom upstairs, catching his coffee cup with his hand. It toppled, slipping onto its side in the saucer and slopping the dregs onto the leather top of his desk. Sir Rupert tutted and mopped up the puddle with his handkerchief.

"A man is dead," Sir Julian stated, his voice calm. He made a reassuring figure, thinning hair now topped with a grey wig and an outfit of muted browns cladding his tall, slender figure. His legs were outstretched,

102

soaking up the warmth from smouldering logs. "He cannot stand trial for theft or for his persuading others to lie in court. Is it right that these boys – for they are still no more than boys – should suffer for what they did when the true perpetrator cannot be punished?"

"They took a few shillings, and in doing so they became beholden to a man of standing in this area who was also a bully. They have both suffered at Aaron's hand, or his whip to be more accurate, and both regret their choice to lie for him," Harry told him. "I have no wish to see Mrs Lydia Chapman and, in time, her children suffer any further by having his name tarnished. I cannot bring myself to say 'his good name' for that would not lie easily on my tongue."

"Very well." Sir Rupert appeared to relax a little. As Leveller of the Marsh Scotts, he held the most senior position within the area, but he was not one to press his beliefs or wishes on others. "I will not create a fuss if it can be avoided, or cause distress to a family who grieve for their son, brother, husband and father. Mr Chapman senior is a jurat and will need to be informed of this, otherwise I propose that we let the matter lie."

"We cannot keep the issue wholly to ourselves. The local people must know something of this," Sir Julian asserted.

"Why the devil not?" Sir Rupert, his thoughts leaping about from one extreme to the other, began to loosen his necktie, needing to keep his hands busy. "It was all done and dusted years ago and his apprentice…" he looked at Harry, "…his apprentice escaped from gaol. No need to ask where he is. He does not take me for so much of a fool that I would see no connection between Jesse being released on the very evening Phoebe Farrers sailed to Wissant. And there he was eating dinner at my table to give himself an alibi!"

103

Sir Julian gave a knowing smile. No doubt he had heard whisper of this before. "I maintain," he said, "that this cannot be kept amongst the three of us because Jesse Alder was convicted, and it is only right that he can live as a free man. I've thought about this since I saw Harry yesterday and have arranged for us to meet in New Romney courtroom on Thursday with some of the jury who were there at the time and the constable from '62. Then it can be announced that Mr Alder is to be a free man. Posters can be pasted about New Romney and Dymchurch declaring his innocence."

Full of enthusiasm for this plan, Harry suggested, "Then if it happens that anyone can get word to Jesse, he can choose whether or not he should return to Dymchurch."

"Splendid!" Sir Rupert stood. "There will be some difficulty ahead when the truth of the matter is revealed to the Chapman family, but they will – in fact, they must – be appeased by this matter not going before a full court hearing."

"It is more than a touch complicated," Sir Julian surmised. "We find Dymchurch to be at the centre of two great scandals and both involving one man – he is a thief and murder victim and all in the course of a couple of weeks!"

"Pah!" Sir Rupert moved to the door, ready to bid goodbye to his guests. "This business of the stolen cup will soon be forgotten, and the killer swinging from the gallows in no time."

"Are your men ready to make an arrest?" Sir Julian asked.

"They are collecting evidence and I am certain news of one will reach New Romney within days," Sir Rupert replied.

Harry smiled to see the competition between the two men. He walked with Sir Julian through to the stable yard where they bid their farewells before returning home.

The next afternoon Harry, Phoebe and their children took the track from the Ship Inn to the seawall. Holding the hands of the little ones, they encouraged them up the steep incline to the top of the Wall, then lifted them down the wooden steps until they all stood on the golden sands. Now Esther and the twins could at last run free, but with firm reminders to keep away from the puddles. They explored ridges created by the tide, strands of seaweed, shells and pebbles of various shades of brown and grey. All the time the young family investigated, they were moving along, negotiating the upright stakes and rocks which created the knockes stretching down the beach. Taking their time, and keeping snug within thick cloaks, they eventually clambered back on top of the seawall, joining the road running parallel with it.

Here they passed shacks selling fish before reaching the main road. Then, almost immediately, they turned to an area of rough land, and the children ran the best they could towards their grandparents' cottage constructed of planks with a neat hat of reed thatch.

Owen answered the door, and the children bundled in. Although not strictly Harry's parents, he and Bess had filled the role for the past six years. Unlike Harry and Phoebe who had adopted babies, the childless couple had taken Harry into their home when he was already a man of twenty-one years. Owen still kept busy with the woodwork which had provided a living all his life, but it had taken its toll. His hands were becoming gnarled, while an arthritic hip and swollen knees restricted his movements. Colder weather would only cause him more aches, but he made sure there was plenty of seasoned wood stacked by the fire and fixed a smile on his face whatever the discomfort. The arrival of the children gave him immense pleasure and his greeting showed this.

"Come on in! Go on Esther, pull out the box of animals so the twins can have a look." Owen smiled at Harry and Phoebe, and continued, "Kettle's on the boil, and you've come with news, I believe. I've heard you and Sir Julian were at New Hall this morning."

"News travels fast," Harry responded. "It's private, you understand."

"I do, but an old man can't help wondering…" There was little that Harry didn't share with Owen and Bess. To sit in their cosy home with the low ceiling and comforting smell of woodsmoke and to have them listen to his concerns or help him sort his thoughts into a logical order was a blessing. Over the years, their quiet intervention had prevented him from making foolish mistakes, despite him usually being a steady character.

"Papa!" Esther was at Harry's breeches, pressing a wooden animal on his leg. "Look!"

"Have you been making more?" Harry asked Owen with a grin, taking the sheep and examining its curling carved coat.

"Just a family of sheep."

"Big ones and little ones," Esther supplied more information.

"How lovely!" Phoebe exclaimed, kneeling on the thick rug and taking a couple of lambs from the box. "You're so clever, Owen."

"It gives him a lot of pleasure," Bess said as she entered from the bedroom. "We've got quite a farm now, and more to come, no doubt." She busied herself making a pot of tea while instructing Phoebe to place biscuits on a plate.

They settled at the central table, leaving the children playing on the rug. This room may lack the luxuries of some of the homes Harry and Phoebe visited, but it remained a firm favourite in their hearts. With the one main room and two bedrooms, it was the place they lived in for the first year of married life. Built by Owen, the cottage had been improved over the years and was always kept in good condition, with strong shutters to keep out the savage sea winds. Thick rugs covered an earth floor and in the depths of winter the bed was hauled from the adjoining room so the couple could benefit from the main fire which burned boldly behind an ornamental guard crafted by Harry.

While the wooden animals were cantered off the rug and across the floor, with the sheep showing the agility of a horse, Owen asked, "Any news on what happened to that Chapman fellow? There's him buried for over a week now, and whoever did it to him is walking free about the place."

"There's no news that I know of," Harry replied. "If there had been an arrest then word would have spread through the village and beyond. No, there's something else though and it's about Aaron Chapman. You wouldn't believe what trouble a dead man could cause."

Harry relayed Toke's account of what really happened on the day of the Whitsun Gallop, with Phoebe adding extra details. Owen and Bess listened, occasionally commenting or asking a question. "Yesterday I went to Burmarsh and tracked down David," Harry added as he came to the end of the story. "He agreed to come to Dymchurch tomorrow morning, and I'll take him and Toke to New Romney."

"Best you do take them," Bess responded. "The last time those lads were in the courtroom, they were clearly telling terrible lies and they will be nervous about

107

admitting to it. It will calm them to have you drop them off."

"I hope so."

"And Sir Julian Craythorne says there will be posters put up about the place announcing that Jesse is an innocent man," Owen interjected as he gazed across the room and through the small window to the village centre. "Now that will excite the locals. Imagine them seeing those words and most of them unable to read them, but they'll find out soon enough and it will be the talk of the inns and alehouses."

"There's nothing like the magic of unknown words to get their imaginations going!" Phoebe said. "No sooner than the last poster is pinned up and the whole village will know Jesse is a free man."

"But is he free to return?" Bess wondered. "You took on his cousin as an apprentice, and then he married Jesse's young woman."

Harry gave a shrug and reached across the table for a spiced biscuit. "I did employ Matthew – I needed to replace Jesse, and the Alder men are good workers. Would I have employed him if I'd known that within weeks he would have taken the job and Lucy too? I can't say I felt comfortable when I learned about his intentions towards Lucy, but he made a fine apprentice and I'm pleased to leave him in charge when I have other business to attend to."

"But now, three years have passed," Phoebe reflected, "and I wonder how Jesse would feel about returning? There's Matthew and Lucy in their own cottage, a little boy and another baby on the way. This is the life Jesse saw for himself, but circumstances changed all that. Bess is right – is he free to return or would it cause too much upset?"

"That will be for him to decide," Owen, ever practical, said. "He's a grown man and can weigh it up

108

in his own mind. Three years is long enough for him to become used to being parted from Lucy, and no one could have expected her to wait for this moment we never thought would come."

Having visited Wissant every spring, Harry and Phoebe knew better than anyone how well Jesse had settled into life in the French village across the Channel. But to their knowledge he had no new romance. "It would have been wonderful to see Jesse with a local woman, a Frenchwoman," Phoebe said. "Every year I hope to see him married."

They spoke a little of Jesse's life across the sea, and their last visit, but the children's attention was wandering from the toy animals, and they were wanting new entertainment. It was time to walk home and soon they were being wrapped up in their woollen cloaks, then leaving Owen and Bess with promises they could visit again soon.

The next day, Thursday, Harry took David and Toke to New Romney and paid for them to be taken back to Burmarsh by a man who ran goods or passengers about in his cart. He then returned to work alongside Matthew and Jack in the forge. Meanwhile, the jury who had convicted Jesse Alder met in the town's courtroom. The meeting was not public knowledge.

That same morning, rain hammered down upon Romney Marsh. It rode on the coastal wind, forcing Harry to keep the front doors of the forge closed. With a fire blazing and soaking wet cloaks hanging about the place, the windows misted, cocooning the men in their workplace. Occasionally one of them would take a rag and wipe the glass, letting in some light, and giving a brief view of the empty street. The back door was left open intermittently, but rain fell from the roof and bounced into the forge, creating a puddle on the earth floor, which in turn added to the damp atmosphere.

Harry said nothing about the meeting but worked alongside his employees, guiding young Jack with his metalwork. Not long after midday, they donned their now dry cloaks, wrapped them tight around themselves and raced home for dinner, darting around the puddles and rivulets on the High Street. On their return, the rain had lost much of its fury and settled into a steady drizzle. The wind eased, making it possible to open the double doors fully and have both a view onto the street and a better light to work by.

Being the first property reached when travelling from New Romney, news of Jesse's innocence reached the forge first. Although later, those who assembled in the Ocean Inn may have claimed that privilege.

"Oyez, Oyez." The words of the town crier were accompanied by his bell.

"What's this?" Matthew asked, darting to the doorway.

"News of some sort," Jack replied, standing beside him.

"By order of Sir Julian Craythorne, Jesse Alder of Dymchurch is proved innocent of theft!" The bell rang again. "Jesse Alder of Dymchurch is now a free man. God save the King!" With these words a poster was extracted from the crier's shoulder bag and nailed to the doorpost of the Ocean Inn. Before he had stepped back to inspect his work, the crier was being crowded upon. Not to be thwarted nor drawn into any talk, he turned on his heel and set about walking the length of the High Street as far as the Ship Inn. "Oyez, Oyez! By order of Sir Julian Craythorne..."

"Did you hear that?" Matthew almost demanded of Harry. "Did you hear...?"

By now Jack had darted across the street to gaze at the words on the poster. He could barely read them, something he had in common with the others gathered. Yet having heard the crier's words they picked out those they did know and guessed the others. Turning to meet Harry and Matthew midway across the road, Jack said, "Jesse is innocent. He didn't do it. Didn't take the cup! That's what it says."

"I never doubted it," Harry exclaimed. "The same as everyone who knew him." Then to Matthew, "Your cousin is free now. The family will be pleased." As he said these words, he knew that the good news would be mixed with confusion, perhaps uncertainty, in the home of Matthew and Lucy.

At the door of the Ocean, Harry read the words: "'By order of Sir Julian Craythorne, let it be known that Jesse Alder of Dymchurch has been proven innocent of the theft of the Whitsun Gallop Cup' and it has today's date on it."

"Did you know?" Matthew asked.

"I knew a witness had changed his story," Harry admitted. "I couldn't be certain the jury would accept it."

"Well, that *is* good news," Matthew stated. "Better get back to work. It won't finish itself." He returned to the forge, leaving Harry wondering if while the Alder family celebrated, this news would cast a shadow over two of its members.

Chapter Eleven
Mireille

The stem gave way, and Mireille felt the weight of an apple in her palm. She wrapped her fingers around it, detecting a rough blemish, and lowered her arm. Turning away from the tree, she kicked at the crisp leaves, frowning as they scattered. The apple joined others in a wooden crate, and Mireille stomped back to the tree.

The day before, a letter had come. At first the family feared the worst when the fishermen from Dymchurch were seen walking up the beach and along the sandy track to the Bernard family home – 'the worst' being something awful had befallen Phoebe, Harry or one of their adorable little children. News of their coming had reached the marketplace, causing Oncle Jacques and Mireille's father, Marc, to race to the home where her mother, Marie, was preparing supper. At the time, Mireille had been in the upstairs bedroom straightening freshly washed and aired blankets on her bed. She had spotted the fishermen from the window and almost plunged down the steps to the living room.

Thankfully, 'the worst' was not the reason for Joshua and Walter's unexpected arrival in Wissant. They had brought a letter for Jesse and would not reveal its contents but could only say that the news was good. Oncle Jacques had taken it to Jesse at his lodging house and returned with him not long after.

112

Mireille had been looking out for them, assuming everthing would be divulged by the expression on the Englishman's face. However, he looked pleased and confused all at once, and she had to wait until he told the whole family his news. Minutes later, when the wine was opened and laughter filled the house, the young woman had left unnoticed and raced to the dunes where she buried her feet in the white sand and stared unseeingly out to sea.

The next apple had a blackened hole where an insect had burrowed deep into the crisp, juicy flesh. Mireille scowled at it and placed it in the second crate. She continued with this task – good apples and bad apples – and after a while the second crate was carried to the back kitchen and slammed down on the wooden counter.

Mireille wore a scarf around her long brown hair which swung as she plodded back to the apple trees. Her eyes were dark, and more so due to the fury smouldering within her. At the garden table she picked up the first crate, balancing it on the slight curve of her hip and proceeded at a slower place to a wooden storeroom. The doorway was low, and she stooped a little – at seventeen years of age, Mireille was now a touch taller than her mother, her figure slender, yet maturing. To manoeuvre the crate up the steps was awkward and, although she would not admit it, the physical challenge of first hoisting it into place and then stretching to put each apple onto the slats helped release some of her temper.

Leaving the crate propped against the store, Mireille returned to the end of the garden where branches reached out to each other and an old wooden table, the place for summer gatherings, stood solid. In her mind, she saw Grand-mère seated in a low chair with her shawl of Romney Marsh wool across pointed knees and

113

another around her bent shoulders. Mireille felt the weight of her loss sweep over her – next spring when the leaves unfurled on the trees and the sun warmed this patch of the garden, Grand-mère would not return to her chair.

You would understand. Mireille slumped on the end of a bench, resting her elbows on the table. *If you were here, Grand-mère, then you would know he should not leave. He is happy here. I know he is. He dresses and speaks as a Frenchman now, and we see him as part of our family.* She smiled to think of the time they spent together – from the moment Jesse had arrived in Wissant it was she, Mireille, who encouraged him to learn not just the language, but the words and phrases unique to the region. 'Teach me something that the others would not think of', he would say, and so she did. In turn, Jesse taught her English, and they spoke about the Romney Marsh with its low-lying land and the vast seawall.

"But he sees me as a sister, or a favourite cousin," Mireille wailed out loud. "Can he not recognise I am grown up now?"

After the outburst, Mireille sat quietly and listened hard for Grand-mère's response: *'My child, he will see it. Already he seeks your company and appreciates your interest in his homeland. I hear your shared laughter as he perfects his French, and you learn to speak English with ease. If he does not know it yet, then soon he will see you as the beautiful woman you have become.'*

"And if he doesn't?"

'Then seek Phoebe's help when she comes next spring. By then you will be eighteen and he can no longer deny that you are ready for marriage.'

But Phoebe would not return to Wissant until late spring, and if the talk around the supper table was to be believed, Jesse might leave for Dymchurch before the winter set in. During their last visit, there had been much talk of Mireille visiting and it had been agreed she would return with Harry and Phoebe the following year. Her fascination with the village had grown over time, and she longed to see the place where her English family lived. Her thoughts flitted from the planned visit to Jesse's likely departure.

If he returns to Dymchurch, by next summer he will have changed. His years in Wissant will be forgotten and he will have found an Englishwoman to share his life with. I will arrive and find him different. I cannot blame him for wanting to return to his family, but I don't know how I shall bear it.

Staring towards Grand-mère's vacant chair, thoughts of unrequited love and lost opportunities churned over in Mireille's mind. She did not consider that Jesse might have noticed the rosy bloom on her cheeks, her dainty waist, or her soft, yet playful, voice. She believed that her growing into a woman had passed unnoticed.

If Phoebe had been in Wissant, then she would have suggested that the Englishman had come to France as a man needing to hide and, without the acceptance of the Bernard family, he would have struggled to find work and lodgings in the village. Perhaps he feared that to take the daughter of the house as his wife would be to violate his welcome. But these conversations between the cousins had not taken place the previous spring, so Mireille was left to her own imagination.

"Mireille!" Marie called from the back door. "*Les pommes...*"

Of course – Maman is waiting for me to prepare them. She says we must make tarte aux pommes for supper – Jesse's favourite. Mireille stood and ran back to the house.

"Grand-mère would not want you to sit under the trees feeling sad," Marie said, misunderstanding her daughter's melancholy. "She had a happy life and lived to a good age with her loving family around her. Now let us prepare this fruit, and we will all enjoy supper when the men are back. We have much to celebrate, and a great deal still to learn – who would have thought that a letter would come telling of Jesse's freedom."

"I don't want him to go," Mireille countered. "Isn't he happy here?"

"I'm sure he is, and perhaps he will choose to stay, but now he has that choice."

Mireille considered these words while she began to peel the apples. *He cannot be with that other woman – that Lucy who married his cousin – but he could return and choose another Englishwoman. Now Jesse has the choice, and if he were to choose me then it would be all the better.*

"If he leaves, it will be soon," Mireille stated. The Dymchurch fishermen were staying in Wissant for three days. They would then return, either with Jesse or with a letter from him.

"If he leaves, then he may come back," Marie suggested. "Jesse may visit his family and choose to return to his life here."

"He might," Mireille conceded as she tipped the apple peel into the bucket at her feet on the back kitchen floor. "I'll make the pastry," she suggested, wanting to change the subject. *There will be enough talk about Jesse and Dymchurch later.*

A couple of hours later, when dusk shrouded Wissant and the oil lamps had been lit, the men crowded into the Bernard family home. They scraped wooden chair legs

116

across the stone floor, poured red wine into tumblers, broke chunks from loaves of bread, then began to spoon *bouillabaisse* into their mouths. Amongst them, Jesse appeared as if he were one of the family. In fact, after three years, they had almost forgotten that he was not one of them. He spoke French with ease, his voice low and gravelly. At his neck he wore a knotted scarf, and on his head a beret flopped to one side. His hands were rough, not from handling the nets in all weathers, but from working at one of the forges to be found in a street leading from the marketplace. The Bernard men could not support another crewman on their fishing boat, meaning that once Jesse had been accepted within the small village, he had been driven to find his own employment. Six months after leaving Dymchurch, he had returned to the trade he was fast becoming skilled at before being forced to flee Romney Marsh. Alongside the job, there came an offer of a room in a cottage, and Jesse began to make his own way.

With his thick blond hair and clear blue eyes, Jesse attracted the attention of the young women of Wissant, but he remained a man seemingly content with the company of his new family and those he worked with. Now, as he wiped the plate with a *quignon de pain,* he raised the subject of returning to Dymchurch.

"I've decided to go to see my family – just for a week." Silence fell upon the table. Although the men kept their fingers busy packing tobacco into pipes, and the women began to tidy the table, all attention was on Jesse. "Walter and Joshua say they'll bring me back, as long as the weather is fair. So, it may be a little longer if the sea turns rough, but I plan to return. I've spoken to Monsieur Laurent, and he is allowing me the time off work."

"He's a good man," Jacques murmured.

"He is," Jesse agreed.

"You leave tomorrow then," Vincent stated, for they all knew when the Dymchurch fishermen planned to leave Wissant. Mireille rolled her eyes, recognising her older brother's friendship with Jesse and resentful of the time they spent together in the local tavern.

"That's right," Jesse agreed. He took a sip of wine, and they waited, knowing he had something more to say. "I reckon this is my home now, and I don't forget how you took me in."

The Bernard men murmured their appreciation of his words. They were enough, and it was the women who would have more to say about this over the coming days.

As plumes of tobacco smoke began to roll above the table, Marie and Mireille finished clearing away the plates and serving platters. Mireille turned towards the vast fireplace and braced herself against the heat before lifting the great kettle of scalding hot water. "Let me," Jesse spoke to her in English.

"Thank you," she replied, also in English. A glow of satisfaction flowed through her young body. *He speaks to no one else in English. I am the only one who wanted to learn.* Stepping aside, she followed him into the narrow corridor of the back kitchen. "I hope you have a… a good… a pleasant… time with your family. They will be pleased to see you."

"I didn't expect to go back, not even for a visit."

"I know."

Having emptied hot water into the great basin where the crockery and pans would be washed, Jesse backed away. If he were to linger, then he would soon be in Marie's way and face a lashing from her sharp tongue. "I'll come and see you tomorrow – late morning – before I leave." He flashed a smile at Mireille.

She said nothing in return. Before her thoughts had formed into English words, Jesse was seated once more at the table with the men.

"What did he say?" Marie asked.

"Only that he will see me before he leaves here tomorrow." Mireille returned to her own language.

"You'll be at work!" Marie's voice rose a little.

Mireille shrugged. She was no longer a girl who needed reminding where she would be or what she would be doing. "I know. I think he meant that he would wave as he passed by," she replied, hugging at the pleasure she felt in knowing that Jesse intended to seek her out before leaving Wissant the next morning.

Mireille had long admired Phoebe, relishing the time they spent together every year. Determined to emulate her cousin's manner, the young Frenchwoman was mastering a way of being serene rather than fiery. The letter from Dymchurch had caused a darkness to fall upon her while silently she screamed at Jesse to notice her becoming a woman, yet outwardly she remained calm. If her family members had noticed any difference in her mood, then perhaps they would have said she was a little quieter than usual. They saw none of the confusion raging as Mireille faced losing the man she idolised to an unknown woman who he would meet – she was certain he would meet a new love – across the water in the English village of Dymchurch. Other than that magical summer of 1758, when Phoebe had arrived and stayed with the Bernard family for months, her influence on Mireille was limited to about two weeks a year. It was enough to help Mireille consider the woman she wanted to become.

The second placid female character in her life had been Grand-mère, who had lived to a ripe old age as matriarch of the family, and no doubt the hours spent in her company had moulded Mireille, but this is not something the seventeen-year-old had considered.

A fascination with Phoebe's life before marriage had led to Mireille working in the village store every morning. She hankered after meeting her cousin's aunt and uncle – Peggy and Giles – and to see the shop which was part of a terrace fronting Dymchurch High Street. That longed-for visit would happen, and most likely the following June. In the meantime, she weighed oats and dried beans, reached up to release spiced sausage from hooks, or twisted small paper parcels of dried herbs.

The morning of the departure the weather was mild and the slatted tables on the street outside the shop were loaded with turnips, cabbage, beetroot and leeks, enticing potential customers into the shop. In contrast, baskets of clogs sat on the pavement. With the door wide open, Mireille bustled about, all the time able to keep an eye on the marketplace, the area around which, along with the church, life in Wissant revolved.

Any fury or resentment felt about Jesse's impending trip had vanished; in its place there was a pent-up excitement, coupled with an intense fear of his rejection. In the darkest hours of the night, Mireille had conjured up a plan – a scheme not yet revealed to her family as she set about preparing for it to come to fruition. The first part had been to pack a small bag with some essential clothes and to place it under her bed with her thickest cloak. The second part had been finalised once she arrived at work.

"It will be for a week, or as soon as the weather allows," Mireille had explained, having asked for permission to leave work if the men agreed to take her to Dymchurch.

"You'll be back?" Madame Blanchett had asked, her suspicion clear.

"I'll be back," Mireille had confirmed, eyes bright and images of her arriving in Dymchurch blossoming in her mind.

Madame Blanchett had made it clear that no pay would be given for hours unworked, and Mireille had happily nodded and agreed to everything, knowing that her plan was taking shape.

Despite Jesse having told her that he would say goodbye before leaving, Mireille was on edge. *If he were to forget, then I may miss his going. And how could I blame him when his mind will be full of Dymchurch.* Yet Jesse was known to be reliable: if he said he would help Marie move logs, repair the chickens' pen, or brush the cobwebs from the shutters, then that is what he would do. A game of dominos... a tankard of beer... they would not delay him lending a hand as agreed. *But today may be different. Today he will be thinking of his family across the sea.*

Mireille kept a keen eye on any fishermen she spotted in the marketplace. Once they began to disperse, it was a sign that they were preparing to go to sea, and then Jesse's departure would be imminent. She was helping a busy mother load her basket when he came into sight – there was a freshly scrubbed look about him, as if he had taken time to scour away any signs of long days working in the forge. Knotted at his neck, Jesse's scarf looked newly washed, as did his tunic. He gave a wave and flashed a broad smile. "I'll see you soon, Mireille."

"Wait!" With an apology to the customer, she found her way past the counter, open crates and barrels, and ran out into the street.

"I'll see you next week," Jesse said, reaching out to give her a quick brotherly hug.

"No!" She freed herself. "I've packed a bag, and Phoebe has said I can come."

121

"How?"

She laughed at his confusion and babbled, "She always says I am welcome. We thought of next summer, but as you are to return in a week, Madame Blanchett says I may go."

They glanced towards the shopkeeper who smiled and nodded her encouragement. "Mireille can go but bring her back next week! I cannot manage for long without her." Jesse might not yet recognise his future, but the older woman liked the Englishman and saw him as a good match for the lovely young woman who had worked with her for the past three years.

"It's a terrible journey," Jesse stalled.

"I know." Mireille began to walk away from the shop, turning back to call her thanks to Madame Blanchett.

"Your parents?" he asked, already aware of her response.

"I'll tell them now. When I fetch my bag… and my cloak − I have the thickest one ready." Her pace was quick as they left the marketplace for the Bernard home, and Mireille spoke in a mixture of French and English about the joy she felt in knowing that soon she would be with her dear cousin and seeing Dymchurch for the first time. She barely allowed herself to think that her parents could stop her from going, but as her excitement mounted with every step, so did the fear of being thwarted. Alongside the visions of being in Dymchurch, Mireille also pictured herself standing alone on the white sands of Wissant, waving goodbye to Jesse.

Chapter Twelve
Jesse

Standing at the prow, his shoulders hunched and eyes half-closed to the sea spray, Jesse felt torn between gazing towards the beach at Wall End, where he could see a dozen figures gathered, or looking down upon the hunched figure of Mireille who was missing this opportunity of seeing the Romney Marsh coastline for the first time.

Mireille had suffered seasickness to the same magnitude as her cousin, Phoebe, and the journey had been one of utter misery. Her hair, usually so beautifully glossy, lay limp, trailing from the hood of her cape. Her skin, usually so soft and fresh, became clammy and pale. The dark eyes, shining bright when they departed Wissant, were now dulled, as was the eagerness in Mireille's voice so recently heard when she chattered about the wonders of seeing Dymchurch and the joy of being with her cousin. All Jesse could do was offer ineffectual words of comfort and encourage her to sip on a flagon of cold camomile tea, provided by Marie as they left.

Unseen to the Dymchurch fishermen manning the boat, or the miserable young woman seated on a narrow plank bench, a huge force was building within Jesse. He struggled to contain it as he staggered about *Louisa-Ann*, gripping at her small cuddy cabin, or rounded gunwale. This man, returning to his homeland for the first time in over three years, was not filled with the anticipation of seeing his family, although he did have those feelings, but consumed with a need to protect Mireille.

"We are nearly there." Jesse spoke in French to ensure she understood. "Can you stand and look at the beach?"

"I must," she replied, raising her face towards his. She shuffled about a little. "It's so hard."

"Once you are standing, the breeze will be on your skin. It will be better." Jesse crouched and placed a hand under her elbow, encouraging her to stand.

Mireille raised herself and turned to lean on the smooth, curving edge of the gunwale. "*Merci.*" Her response was simple as she breathed deeply, and it seemed to Jesse that already some warmth returned to her face.

Glancing to the beach, Jesse saw one of the figures, then another, wave. Beside him, a strand of Mireille's long hair whipped about, and he caught it between his fingers, tucking it into the hood of her cloak without thought to the intimacy of the gesture.

"That's my father over there." The figures were now distinguishable. "And my mother beside him, and my brothers, Joe and Philip. They work on the Wall, you know."

"Your mother?"

"No, not my mother!" Jesse smiled, recognising the easy banter which usually flowed between them, lost for the past hours at sea.

"And Lucy?"

He frowned. *How odd that I have thought nothing of her since… since Mireille became sick. I imagined that she would be on my mind the whole way.* "She won't be here," he said. "I will see her, of course. But she married my cousin."

124

"I know," her voice was thoughtful. Then it rose and words streamed out, "Look! There's Harry. Over there. Can you see him?"

Racing along the top of the seawall, Harry neared Jesse's family who were following the progress of *Louisa-Ann* as she sailed into the shallows.

"That's good of him – coming to meet me. He'll have quite a surprise when he spots you." Jesse looked towards the sails, then back to Mireille. "I should help them. You'll be all right now."

Without waiting for her response, Jesse, well-practised in handling a boat, helped with the sheets of canvas, while Joshua poised ready to jump into the breakers with the end of a rope clutched tightly in his hands. Sand gave way to shingle at the top of the beach, and the waiting men stumbled over the stones towards them, eager to play their part in hauling the small boat home, and to welcome their returning son, brother and friend.

Before the sails had been furled and fastened, Albie Alder, having waded through the shallows, had clambered on the deck. "You're home!" he greeted his son with those simple words and a slap on the back. "We never thought we'd see the day."

"I've been lucky, Pa," Jesse told him. "They treated me well in Wissant."

Glancing towards Mireille, he noted that Harry was encouraging her to climb down, and conversation in English and French was passing between them. Jesse caught the odd word or phrase, but mostly he heard the excitement in her voice and briefly wondered at how she had recovered so swiftly from such debilitating seasickness. She glanced towards him and smiled, then turned her attention back to her long skirts and full cloak, as she tried to keep them free from snagging.

125

"Who is the girl?" Albie asked, as the last of the sail was secured.

"She's Phoebe's cousin – come to stay with them," Jesse replied. *She will be safe now and Harry can answer all those questions about Dymchurch while he takes her home. I'd have liked to show her myself, but it can't be done.* He turned his attention back to his father. "Mireille. Her name is Mireille."

"Sounds French," Albie responded. "Come on, lad. There's your Ma and the rest of them – some you've never met. Your brother's had two youngsters since you left, and your sister is at home nursing hers."

Jesse barely noticed Mireille leave. He had heard Harry call his thanks for looking after her, and had waved his acknowledgement, but now he too was jumping down from *Louisa-Ann,* scrambling about on the steep bank of stones and wrapping his arms around his mother while others crowded in on them.

"Sir Rupert will want to see you."

"And no doubt, John Waller – he's constable, you know."

"They'll want to tell you that it's official – they know you didn't take that cup."

"There's a nice bit of mutton roasting."

"Harry's bought himself a new forge."

The talk batted about from one topic to the next, with Jesse barely answering before another question or announcement was fired at him. Wall-workers left their tasks to run up with words of congratulations before returning to their tools. All the time, amongst the chat and the greetings, the Alder family walked the stretch of seawall towards the centre of Dymchurch. If Jesse would have liked more time to gaze across the familiar flatlands of Romney Marsh, to watch the tide as it neared full height, or to take in the details of the village as they approached, then this went unnoticed by his eager family.

They left the Wall, using a well-worn track that took them to the road by the Ocean Inn. With curiosity Jesse gazed at the forge opposite, his place of work until his sudden arrest at Whitsun three years before. The door was open, and a figure appeared.

"There's your cousin, Matthew," Albie said, his tone carefree as if he remembered nothing of the fact that his son had intended to marry the girl who became Matthew's wife.

He took my wife and my job. It's not going to be easy, but time to lay any bitterness to rest. Jesse raised his arm in a greeting and forced a smile. Matthew did the same but did not cross the road to welcome his cousin home. *It will be difficult for them too,* Jesse realised.

There was a sense of being in a dream, with everything feeling familiar but not quite as it should be, as the family filed into a cottage within a terrace known as Dormers. *It's so small.* Jesse immediately felt guilty to think such a thing about the family home. He accepted a mug of ale and pulled up a chair at the table. *And so dark.* The light was fading fast now, and his mother busied herself with the lamps.

For a moment, Jesse felt trapped within the babble of their voices... the closeness as they crowded upon him. His home in Wissant was a room under the eaves in a cottage he shared with an elderly fisherman, but his true home – the place he felt was home – was the Bernards' cottage. Although humble, it was built on land with plenty of space for vegetable plots, a chicken pen, fruit trees and various outbuildings. Here, Dormers Cottages were squashed, one against another, fronting the street. To the rear, outbuildings crammed up against them, restricting the light. There was a strip of land, reaching out from the back, but unlike the garden belonging to his French family, it was not used as a place to eat and linger when the weather allowed. In Dormers, family life took place within the old, beamed walls, and beneath low ceilings which creaked under the weight of anyone moving about in the two small rooms above.

"Philip! Take your brother's bag upstairs," their ma called from her position where she crouched by the fire, lifting a joint of mutton from the spit and placing it on a tray. "No need to share a bed now!" she continued, reminding Jesse of a time when the two younger boys slept head to toe.

"He's not got much," Philip commented as he picked up the cloth bag from where it lay against Jesse's feet.

"It's enough for a few days," Jesse replied. "The mutton looks great, Ma. They don't have that in Wissant."

Sarah didn't respond. The meat tray was lowered to the ground and there it rested on the hearth. The adults paused, some mid-sentence, and the only sounds came from the baby fretting over trapped wind, and the crackling and gentle hiss of damp wood burning in the grate. For that moment, the room and the silent people in there stifled Jesse as he resisted the urge to run to the seawall and relish the space it would offer him. *And from there, it would be no distance to Walker House where Mireille could tell me what she thinks about Dymchurch so far.*

"When you say it's enough for a few days," Albie began. "You meant before you sort out new clothes. Proper clothes."

"He does." Sarah clutched at her husband's words. "That's what he means. You're looking a bit different, son. A bit French perhaps?"

128

"It's been three years, Ma. Three and a half. I didn't have a lot of choice if I wanted to fit in."

"Do you speak it?" Philip's wife asked. "Do you speak like them?"

"Not like them, but I get by," Jesse told her.

"Fancy that!" she replied, looking at him as if he had journeyed from exotic lands.

"He'll soon forget it," Albie stated. "He'll get over it in no time at all."

The others nodded their agreement. Jesse took a long sip of ale. It didn't taste right – not what he was used to. Every one of them was staring at him, while the mutton remained on the floor and the bread on the side uncut. *They don't know me anymore,* he realised. *They don't know me, and I don't know them. They look at me as if I've emerged from the pest house after all these years. As if I need to adapt to life again. No, it's worse – it is as if I need to be cured still. Cured of the habits and language I learned in order to help me adapt.*

"That's right, isn't it, son?" Albie said. "You'll soon be putting all those French ways behind you."

They waited for Jesse to respond. All of them. Even the baby had fallen silent.

"I don't know about that, Pa," Jesse answered. "I've been a long time gone and I've made a new life for myself now – a home and a job. You know how it is. It's all there waiting for me after I've spent a week here with you."

"Mr Farrers, Harry, he's getting himself a new forge. That's your job," Albie persisted. "And up there…" he jerked his head towards the ceiling, "is a bed all aired nicely and your own trunk and row of pegs. Up there sharing with Joe."

The tears rolled down Sarah's face. "I'm sorry, Ma," Jesse said. "Let's not spoil our meal with bothering over where I'll be living. I'm here now and it's a moment we never thought would come."

Sarah wiped her face with her sleeve. "You're right. We just weren't expecting…"

"It's only been an hour or so." Jesse attempted to ease the tension. "It all feels a bit strange, being back. But I'm happy. Don't think I'm not happy to be here. I'll go to see Harry tomorrow – I'd like to see this new forge."

"That's right, son. It will all seem different when you see what's on offer here." Albie looked at his family, then moved to his wife's side and lifted the tray with the joint of mutton, placing it in the centre of the table. "We've got a feast here, so let's not spoil anything."

Stretched out on the freshly-filled mattress, for the first time Jesse had a bed to himself under the eaves of the low cottage. Nearby, Joe's breathing was deep, punctuated by the occasional snore, while behind the wall he heard his parents' bed creak, and his father mumbled in his sleep. Wind pressed through gaps in the window frame – *I'll plug some rag in there tomorrow,* he thought, while his mind drifted in that state between wakefulness and sleep. Not for the first time, he wondered how Mireille was settling into Walker House, and felt envious for knowing she was accepted as French, whereas his 'foreign ways' were clearly a source of shame for his parents. *I'll go there tomorrow. See how she is. They'll say I shouldn't go calling at the Farrers' house, but things have changed. They are like family to me now, and she… Mireille… she's like a cousin too.* But something had shifted during that long voyage from Wissant to Dymchurch. The pleasure he had always felt when he saw her had been replaced with a yearning to be with her. The long hours of darkness could not pass quickly enough. *I'm tired.*

That's what it is. I'm missing home and she's a part of it. Jesse finally drifted off to sleep without having come to terms with his conflicting feelings.

The next morning, Jesse walked with Albie and Joe towards the High Knocke area of the Dymchurch Wall where John Waller's team of workers assembled. The wind was brisk and the skies grey, and now he finally shook off that feeling of being stifled by Dormers Cottage and ... he loathed to even think it ... his family. The men spoke a little: the occasional comment as they pointed out a familiar figure, or changes to village properties were remarked upon. Once on the seawall, to his left the beach view altered with the weather and the tides, and to his right the land was, as he remembered, sheep pasture intersected by winding drainage ditches. Here the reeds remained resiliently upright, their stalks straight and seedheads withered. A line of short stems showed signs of recent harvesting of the reeds for thatch, and Jesse wondered if the labourers would be resuming their work that morning.

At High Knocke, where a sturdy construction of wood and stone stretched away from the Wall towards the sea, they joined the workers. Jesse was greeted with enthusiasm, and he happily answered questions about life in Wissant while parrying the assumption that he had returned to Dymchurch for good.

"I'll see you later," Albie said to Jesse, as John Waller prepared to talk his team through the day's work.

Jumping off the Wall and onto the firm golden sands, Jesse then ambled along the beach towards the village. For the first time since arriving, he was truly alone and appreciated the solitude. Walking at a steady pace, he soon found that he had passed the point where he should have climbed the wooden steps leading onto the seawall and the central area of shops.

He was now nearing Church Knocke, and so he climbed a ladder there, waved a greeting to a small group of workers and took the track on the landward side. Gazing at St Peter and St Paul, he faltered, thinking of the gravestones for family members, but decided to go to Walker House. It was still early and likely that Harry would not have left for work.

The beautiful modern house sat back from the road, its red brick walls unblemished by age, and sash windows elegant. For a moment Jesse faltered: In Wissant he lived as a member of Phoebe's family, whereas in Dymchurch he was a former apprentice at the forge. Taking a path to the side of the house, he rapped on the kitchen door.

It was opened almost immediately by Janey who smiled to see him. "I was hoping we might see you today. What good news – we could hardly believe you were coming back!" She ushered him through to the kitchen. "Mr Farrers is in the dining room – I'll call him – and Mrs Farrers is upstairs. She's with her cousin and the children. I can't quite get the hang of the girl's name, but you'll know it well enough."

"Mireille," Jesse said.

"That's it. My goodness! You sound all French when you say it!" As she spoke, Janey topped up a teapot and placed a mug on the table. "I'll give you a cup and saucer when you're in one of the front rooms," she said, then laughed.

"It's been a while," Jesse said. "I guess everyone will say I look a bit different or sound a bit foreign!" Somehow in the airy kitchen, with the housekeeper bustling about, he didn't feel as if sounding French was a concern – something he needed to be cured of.

"There's not one of us who hasn't aged," Janey commented. "Now, wasn't that a surprise when Mr Farrers went off to meet you and came back with a

132

French girl, and doesn't she speak English well! I hear you taught her."

"You're right. Mireille really helped me with my French and she wanted to learn English. She's been wanting to visit for so long."

"Lovely girl, she is. Or young woman, I should say." Janey moved towards the hallway. From his place at the kitchen table, Jesse saw her tap on the dining room door. "Mr Jesse is here to see you." Then she was back in the kitchen resuming the conversation. "And how are your parents?"

Jesse paused, only to be saved from having to skirt around the uncomfortable feeling hanging over the Alder home, as at that moment Harry appeared. "Ah! I was going to walk along the road to find you. We should go to see Sir Rupert – set this matter straight about the Whitsun Gallop cup. It's too early, of course, but I hoped to show you my new forge beforehand."

"I'd like to see it," Jesse acknowledged. "But did Mireille say... did she say I've made a home in Wissant now?"

Harry was prevented from answering as there came the sound of hurried steps on the stairs and they both turned to the doorway.

"*Bonjour!* Good day." Mireille beamed at them both.

She looks at home here, Jesse realised. *Yet in my parents' cottage, I feel like an outsider.* Then he recalled those hours on the boat shared with Mireille, and how he felt compelled to care for her. His heart swelled and for the first time Jesse found it difficult to speak to this person who was so familiar to him. "*Comment ça va?*" he asked.

"I am very happy to be here," Mireille replied. "Soon we will walk into the village, and I shall meet Aunt Peggy!"

"Harry and I are going to the forge," Jesse told her.

133

"It will be your work if you choose to stay," she stated.

Does that make her sad? he wondered. *No, she just thinks as they all do. She thinks I will want to stay.* "I'm going home to Wissant," Jesse insisted. "But I want to see the forge."

Jesse glanced at Harry. He was watching Mireille with a slight frown on his face. *Has he realised that she is part of the reason why I must stay in Wissant? I only just recognised it myself. She will marry a Frenchman, of course. Perhaps then it will be my time to return to Dymchurch, so I must see this forge and try to imagine a future back here.* He took a sip of his tea. It had turned cold.

Chapter Thirteen
Mireille

On Mireille's arrival in Dymchurch, she had felt exhausted from the journey and anxious about her unexpected appearance at Walker House. Jesse had been attentive during those long hours at sea when the nausea took over her whole being, and the care he showed had strengthened her love for him. The turmoil in her stomach had matched the thoughts churning about in her mind – those visions of Jesse regretting the loss of his first love and seeking a suitable Dymchurch woman to settle down with. Mireille had heard his assertion that he intended to return to Wissant, but she was a young woman suffering the pangs of first love and revelled in the trauma of it being unrequited. Thankful to see Harry on the beach, she had walked beside him, first on the seawall and then through the High Street until reaching his family home. The next morning she woke and having only taken in parts of the village she was eager to see it afresh.

Jesse's appearance in the kitchen had been unexpected and he had seemed uncomfortable. As she plodded back up the stairs, Mireille began to reflect on why this would be.

"Mireille! Here she is!" Esther shrieked.

"Here I am!" Mireille replied, all her attention returning to the moment and the chaos of three young children with their mother and family members caring for them. With Bess, she helped take them to the parlour, leaving Phoebe and Mary to tidy up.

As Mireille squatted on the rug, creating towers of wooden bricks, Bess gathered tiny shoes and woollen cloaks. "We always walk to the village, as long as the weather is fair," she explained. "I can't say if it's easier or not with the little ones walking now."

By the time the children were clad in their outside wear, Phoebe was downstairs. "I'm ready," she called. "We can walk along the beach today."

They headed up a path leading directly to a wide track running alongside the seawall. Here Mireille marvelled at a collection of substantial cottages all facing the Channel. The largest of them was not as grand as it appeared, Phoebe told her, looking towards the village workhouse. Gazing up at the rows of windows, Mireille wondered about the hopeless people who lived there and how they spent their days. But these thoughts were interrupted by Phoebe, pointing out Cluny Cottage, a place to which she used to deliver groceries when she worked for her aunt and uncle. Now she pondered upon her cousin's life as a young woman before marriage, then Clara wriggled in Mireille's arms and all attention was on the little girl and helping her down the steps to the beach.

The tide was low, and the sands flat and firm. For the first time, Mireille took in the full extent of Dymchurch beach. Used to the dunes at Wissant which were never engulfed by the sea and where each step led to her feet sinking a little in the sand, she marvelled at the ease of walking here.

"It's not so easy nearer the sea," Bess explained. "You need to take care there – see how wet it is? The sand can be very soft. It's so flat – never dries out."

"Our sand is white," Mireille told her, "and with... I don't know how to say it – hills with grass." She looked at Phoebe.

"Dunes," Phoebe supplied. "Your English really is superb, Mireille."

"Ah! It is the same word!" Mireille laughed. "And thank you!"

"He did well." It appeared for a moment that Phoebe was lost in thought as she gazed across the Channel towards Wissant. "We must talk later," she said, partly to herself. "When the children have their morning nap."

Wondering what was meant by these words, Mireille was now being led by the children to another set of steps, and soon they were clambering up them. Now back on top of the seawall, they took the track leading to the centre of the village. Although lacking the marketplace so integral to life in Wissant, the women with their baskets and boys with barrows for deliveries were a familiar sight. Mireille's eyes darted from one place to another, until she spotted the general store run by Phoebe's family.

"I heard you had a visitor!" Aunt Peggy lifted her ample bottom from the stool behind the shop counter. "Fancy that – you arriving unexpectedly, just like Phoebe did when she went on the boat to that Wee-sunt place all those years ago. It was very upsetting for her uncle and me, you know." She scowled at Phoebe and then turned her best smile back on for the newcomer.

"This is Mireille," Phoebe said. "My cousin."

Despite only following half of Aunt Peggy's opening words, Mireille's face lit up. "I have wanted to meet you for so long."

Swelling with the pleasure of hearing these words, Peggy addressed Phoebe, "She speaks very nicely, doesn't she?"

"I enjoy learning English with Jesse," Mireille told her, unable to resist mentioning his name.

"Nice young man, he was," Peggy replied. "Not like I mean to speak as if he's gone. But he hasn't been seen around here for a few years."

"No doubt you'll spot him soon enough," Phoebe said, keeping half an eye on the street and not liking to leave Bess with the three children for too long.

"I see a lot from the shop," Peggy agreed. "And what I see now is those children needing a firm hand. Did you want to buy anything?"

"Just some oats please, and a pound of cheddar," Phoebe edged towards the door. "I'll leave Mireille with you and wait outside."

There was little difference between this general store and its counterpart across the Channel. Mireille scrutinised the lengths of shelves, some needing a step-ladder for the produce to be reached. She looked into the barrels of flour and the tubs of seeds, and at the cheese and butter alongside a neat pile of paper squares on the counter.

"Your cheese is different," she commented.

With a wire, Peggy cut a triangle from the yellow block and passed it across the counter. "Try a piece," she offered.

Knowing this English aunt had a fearsome reputation, Mireille understood this gesture showed that she was both liked and welcomed. "Thank you." Holding the wedge with her fingertips she nibbled at the end. Her mouth was flooded with a taste both saltier and stronger than the cheese she was used to, but she liked it and said so as she licked her fingers. Next her eyes fell upon a jar of barley twists on the counter. There was a family story about these – something to do with Harry and Phoebe first meeting, and now Mireille was eager to find out all the details. "Can I have some of those please."

"Have you got English money?" Peggy asked suspiciously. Her generosity was limited.

"I have English money!" Mireille replied. Phoebe had given her some coins that morning, including tokens to be used instead of standard currency.

Looking at the coins which had been retrieved from Mireille's purse and now nestled in her palm, Peggy said, "I'll weigh out a token's worth." She tipped a dozen golden twists onto the scales and then into a paper bag. "The cheese and oats go on the tab."

"On the tab?" Mireille enquired.

"They pay later."

With polite assurances that she would see Aunt Peggy again soon, Mireille left. The family group moved on to the butcher and then the haberdashery shop before Bess returned to her cottage. "You don't need three of us to settle them for a nap," she pointed out. "I'll be glad of the rest today."

This was met with some concern from Phoebe – the older woman had appeared pale that morning and had complained of a headache. "With Mireille here to help, I'll come and see you on my own later," she offered.

The children's energy had not yet waned, and Esther led the way, while Phoebe and Mireille kept a firm grip on the twins' hands as they all raced back along the sands. The skies remained grey and the wind fresh, but to run with the children was exhilarating and by the time they returned to Walker House, Mireille was feeling thoroughly at home in Dymchurch.

With cups of tea on a tray, and these in turn on an elegant mahogany side table, Phoebe and Mireille sat in the parlour. Mireille loved this room: she admired the square proportions and high ceiling, and its position setting it apart from the kitchen and scullery. The sash windows with their thin glazing bars, she saw as an object of art, along with the decorative cast iron fireplace.

"I am so pleased you came, but does this mean you won't return with us in June next year?" Phoebe asked. "I know how awful it is crossing the Channel."

"Jesse looked after me," Mireille replied, unwittingly giving Phoebe the opportunity to probe further.

"I can't think of a nicer man," Phoebe said. "We liked him so much as Harry's apprentice and now he is part of my Wissant family."

"I wonder if he will see Lucy today." When she thought of Jesse, all Mireille could visualise was him seeing his love for the first time in years.

"He may," Phoebe responded, "And he will certainly see her husband, who is also his cousin. I hope it won't be too difficult for either of them."

Mireille shrugged. "It will be difficult. Perhaps this is why he says he must stay in Wissant."

"Perhaps Jesse has an attachment to someone in Wissant?"

"There is no one!" Mireille's response was immediate. "I would have seen. He spends his time with our family – with me! But he sees me as a cousin, or worse – a sister."

"You already have two brothers, there is no need for another."

At last Mireille had found someone who she trusted to discuss her love for Jesse and she allowed her thoughts and feelings to flow: "We eat together... our house is a home to him when he is not in his lodgings... he sits outside the tavern with Papa, Oncle Jacques and now Vincent. How can I be anything but a sister to him? He forgets I am a woman now. He forgets I am no longer fourteen."

"Listen to me, Mireille," Phoebe replied, her voice soft but the tone firm. "I saw you together last spring and am certain that something has changed between the two of you. Jesse does see you as a woman. But think how difficult it is for him. He arrived in Wissant as a man who had escaped from gaol, and our family welcomed him. With their support he gained the acceptance of the local people. Does he feel comfortable with the idea of asking to marry their daughter?"

"They would not mind! Papa and Maman know he is a good man – the best!"

"But I wonder how Jesse feels. Perhaps he thinks it would be taking advantage? He came to Wissant with nothing; does he deserve you?"

Forgetting her resolve to always remain calm – to model herself on her cousin and not her mother – Mireille blurted, "Jesse thinks nothing of me at all! Everyone would be pleased. No, Jesse thinks of coming back to Dymchurch and marrying an English woman. Perhaps this Lucy..." the name was almost spat out. "Perhaps this Lucy has a cousin or a sister as lovely as she is, and everything will be settled." She paused, waiting for Phoebe's response and feeling months of tension released from her young body. *Phoebe will help me make sense of it – she is young enough to understand my anguish and she knows how English men think and behave.*

"Mireille – this is nonsense rattling about in your head," Phoebe responded immediately. "It is quite clear to me that Jesse is fond of you and his feelings have grown since last summer. I have not seen you together, but Janey has and the first thing she said to me was, 'I see there is a romance between Jesse and our Mireille'. Perhaps Jesse doesn't know it yet, men can be slow to notice these things, but he will..."

141

Mireille fell silent as she pondered on these words for a moment. She had expected to be soothed – to be reassured that she would meet a suitable Frenchman in time. Instead, her love for Jesse, and – dare she believe it? – his affection for her had been justified. Her spirits soared. "Janey saw it? She noticed?" She wanted to hear it again and to revel in the giddy feelings the words evoked.

Rather than exploring the enthralling prospect of Jesse returning her feelings, the confidences ended with the arrival of the man himself. In Harry's wake, he entered the hallway and then the front parlour. Mireille beamed and felt herself redden. She glanced at Phoebe and saw her eyes dart between her and Jesse.

"We've seen Sir Rupert," Harry said. Then, "Sit yourself down, Jesse."

Mireille watched as Jesse sat on the edge of a chair. *He feels uncomfortable here.* She frowned a little. *At home he comes in and sits as if he is part of the family, but here in Dymchurch… Ah! It is not Dymchurch – it is this beautiful house that makes him out of sorts.*

"How was he?" Phoebe asked, referring to Sir Rupert.

"He was both pleased to see us and complaining about Jesse's escape to Wissant." Harry grinned. "It's all settled though – Jesse is free to be in Dymchurch and, as the man who framed him is dead, there will be no trial. It is just as he and Sir Julian Craythorne said before."

Mireille, not knowing the great man, was confused: "He is not pleased that Jesse escaped?" She wanted no ill feeling, and the need to defend Jesse was strong. She didn't understand why but knew the return to Dymchurch brought with it some unease.

"That night when we came to Wissant, Harry dined with Sir Rupert," Phoebe explained. "It meant that he could not have been at the gaol in New Romney and accused of being a part of the plan to release Jesse. Sir Rupert knew he had been tricked into giving Harry an alibi – *un alibi*."

"I understand – you did not want to be in trouble when Jesse was freed and put on the boat to Wissant." Mireille knew the story well, but now she saw it from the perspective of those who remained in Dymchurch.

"I didn't choose to escape," Jesse mentioned. "I was pleased, of course, but I didn't plan or expect it."

"Sir Rupert cannot blame you!" Mireille leapt to his defence. It seemed that their comfortable friendship had returned as she and Jesse exchanged smiles. His appearance in the kitchen earlier had confused her and she had sensed some awkwardness between them. "Others arranged it for you."

"Then gave themselves an alibi!" Phoebe grinned. "Harry didn't even tell me. What a wonderful surprise to discover you there on *Louisa-Ann* and leaving Romney Marsh to be with my family in Wissant."

"I've been very lucky," Jesse said. "Lucky to be introduced to people who gave me such a welcome."

"What plans do you have for the rest of the day?" Phoebe asked.

Mireille's eyes narrowed as she considered Jesse meeting the young women of Dymchurch. *He is so friendly, and everyone will be eager to hear about his time away. Not a stranger in this village, but a hero returning with a job offer and the friendship of my cousin and her husband.* She listened, not only for his response but for the words left unsaid.

"We are going to the other forge now." Jesse referred to the place where he had served his apprenticeship under Harry. "Then I'll spend time with Ma."

"She must be so happy to see you," Phoebe said. She had been parted from her father and understood the joy of a family reunion.

"Yes, but she knows there are difficult conversations to come." Jesse referred to his plans to return to Wissant.

While Jesse remained determined that his future lay across the Channel, the others knew there were six days before he sailed for France – his loyalties and attachments could change within that time. *Perhaps he will return with me. No, I am sure he will return with me, but will it be to stay or with thoughts of leaving again for Dymchurch?* Lost in her imagination once more, Mireille became quiet, allowing the others to continue with the talk of their arrangements for the day, and by the time the men left, James was stirring in his cot – family life moved on.

Chapter Fourteen
Harry

Trudging along the High Street, Harry kept his head bent towards the wind howling from the west, his hat pulled low and scarf high. In time, he became aware of a horse's hooves hammering upon the road and turned to see a grey gelding, clearly of good breeding, with a rider equally muffled as himself. The horse came to a snorting halt and the rider swung elegantly to the ground, showing himself to be a tall, agile young man.

"Mr Farrers? Harry?"

Not recognising the horse, nor rider at first, Harry frowned. The man was well-spoken – most likely a landowner or man of business and not hailing from Romney Marsh. Both his voice and attire indicated that he enjoyed some wealth. "Yes?" As the brief response came, Harry realised he knew the gentleman. "Mr Masters – I didn't recognise you. You're still in the area then. Do you suffer such dreadful winds in Canterbury?"

"I'd say they are worse by the coast," Gerald replied, his tone confirming Harry's first impressions of him being a sociable fellow and of good breeding. "Yes – I remain in Burmarsh for the foreseeable – and it's damned awkward, I can tell you."

With the reins tight, and the disciplined steed at his side, Gerald fell into step beside Harry who now realised that there was a purpose to this conversation and, most likely, their meeting was no coincidence. "Did you want to speak to me?" he asked.

"I had hoped to." Gerald loosened his scarf, uncovering his freshly shaved chin and full lips. He smiled, revealing a set of even teeth. "You seem like a sensible chap, so I decided to seek you out. What news is there of them finding the killer? I made a promise to Lydia that I would stay until this was resolved but have business in Canterbury and did not plan to be away so long."

"You expected the butcher to be found guilty and the case closed within days." Harry nodded towards the shop 'A. Bushy & Sons', and Gerald followed his gaze. "It seemed so obvious."

"The words overheard by your good self that night, echoed those spoken by Mr Bushy, and the knife – his bloodied knife – was found nearby. The jury should have made their decision within minutes." Gerald made a swift summary of events. "Yet it was not to be, and I had told Lydia that I would stay until the killer was convicted."

"When you thought the killer was known." It was clear that Lydia Chapman's cousin had made a pledge he could not keep over an indefinite period. Obviously a true gentleman, Harry realised that it would not come easy for Mr Masters to break his word. "I would hope your cousin understands and can release you from your vow to remain in Burmarsh. She has the support of her late husband's family, and I know the local women, my wife included, have been calling on her."

"They have, and I am grateful. I find myself with little to do – there is already a man overseeing the land, and Mr Daniel Chapman has taken it upon himself to come at least once a week. He does nothing more than strut about and hinder those who are perfectly capable of clearing the ditches and tending to animals without his advice."

Harry could see it all too well. *I wonder if it is just the farm which the Chapmans wish to keep an eye on or if this capable and decent – at least that is what I believe him to be – man also needs watching.*

"You said you were looking for me," he reminded Gerald.

"I was. You see, I don't know anyone locally but saw you in court… and Lydia speaks so highly of you that I wondered if anything has come to light through the recent investigations. I can't ask the Chapmans, of course."

They were now outside the forge, and Harry replied, "If your horse wouldn't mind being stabled here, then the best thing I can do is to take you along to see John Waller. He's both village constable and heads a team of men on the seawall. He's the man to ask and you'll get an honest answer without any drama. I wasn't on the jury, as you know, but I understand they are still seeking the killer."

"I'd appreciate that."

They busied themselves with settling the grey gelding, and Harry spoke to the men preparing for the day's work in the forge: "I'm just taking Mr Masters along to Wall End and will be back within the hour."

Already swathed in a leather apron and preparing to light the fire, Jesse turned and said, "It's all in hand here." After two days in the village, he had been lost without his usual routines and had asked Harry if he could work for him in the mornings until his return to Wissant. The arrangement eased any potential discomfort between Jesse and his cousin Matthew as they made conversation and collaborated over tasks. Privately, Harry thought that Albie and Sarah's anxiety over Jesse returning to Wissant had been pacified by

147

their son returning to the familiar routines of Dymchurch life. Yet whenever the subject was broached, Jesse remained adamant that he considered his home was now across the Channel.

"We'll make a start on those hinges and latches, as you said," Matthew responded to Harry, making his position as deputy clear. His role was undisputed, for even if Jesse were to stay in Dymchurch, he would have been given work in the new forge.

"Excellent!" Harry replied. "I'll be back soon."

With Gerald, he set off at a brisk pace. They spoke occasionally, the exertion of the walk leaving them breathless. Mostly, both men were preoccupied with gazing towards the sea, appreciating the wild beauty of the frothing tide breaking midway down the stretch of beach and the flurries of dry sand racing wildly across the surface. "It's quite a sight," Gerald remarked. "What a job to be doing – maintaining the seawall, regardless of the weather."

"It's a worthy job here in Dymchurch," Harry answered. "And quite easy to forget about if you're living out at St Mary in the Marsh or Newchurch or Burmarsh. Without this being maintained the whole area could return to saltmarsh." Turning away from the gale, he paused for a moment, catching his breath.

"You're right – I'm sure I would think nothing of it if I farmed over here or there." Gerald slowed as he too put his back to the wind, giving himself a brief reprieve, and flung out an arm to gesture towards the open countryside.

Thankfully, there was no need to battle along to Wall End, for John was spotted on the sand, studying a potential fracture near the groyne named High Knocke. Harry raised his arm, and this was acknowledged with a nod. John exchanged a few words with the men working beside him, then used wooden steps to take him to the top of the seawall. "Good morning, sir… Harry. What brings you here? Constable business, I'll be bound."

The men instinctively stood to face the east, backs to the onslaught of wind, their shoulders hunched, and thick woollen cloaks gathered tight around them. "I've brought Mr Gerald Masters to see you. He's a cousin of Mrs Lydia Chapman. Mr Masters, this is John Waller, who is both foreman for this patch of the Dymchurch Wall and village constable."

The men exchanged brief greetings before John asked, "How can I help you?"

"I'm making enquiries as to what progress has been made with finding the killer," Gerald replied. "This whole business is distressing for my cousin, and her late husband's family, of course. For myself, I was merely visiting and find myself bound to remain here while Lydia needs comforting, yet I have a home and business to attend to in Canterbury. Are you any closer to making a second arrest?"

"You will be aware that we are in the curious position of not knowing if Mr Chapman or Sir Rupert Bannerman was the intended victim," John began. "That would help us narrow down the suspects. At first, we were certain that it was the butcher who intended to kill Sir Rupert in a fit of rage having been found guilty of meddling with his weights. We now know that not to be the case, and it seems likely that Mr Chapman was the man meant to die. To put it bluntly – he was a man who made enemies, whereas Sir Rupert is well-liked and respected for his fairness both in this parish and across the wider area."

Gerald did not think to query why Aaron was disliked. *Staying in the Chapman's home, he clearly saw him as the bully I know him to be,* Harry reflected.

"It was well known that on the evening of Chapman's death, both of the men should have been attending a meal after the Michaelmas Meeting, so feasible that either could have been the intended victim," Harry advised. "And more likely that someone wanted Aaron dead, given his... his reputation locally."

"Exactly. Then there is the matter of the knife – you will recall that the weapon was found amongst some bushes in the churchyard," John continued. "We believed, at the time, that it was Mr Bushy's – and it was the same design as those he used, but all his knives could be accounted for. The knifesmith keeps no accurate records but has told us who has bought ones of the same type recently."

"Is the knife not worn? Is there some reason to believe it is new?" Gerald asked.

"There is no wear to it," John confirmed. "Unfortunately, we cannot match the names of people who have purchased this style with anyone who would have heard Mr Bushy rage about the injustice of being prevented from selling meat and utter those words we know so well – 'he said I could still go butchering'."

"I should like to know who those men were," Gerald stated.

"Those who bought knives?" John replied. "That's jury business. I've got a good team of men working on this and I trust them to make the right enquiries."

"Understood." Gerald shrugged his shoulders. "But I'm a man who keeps himself busy on one project or another and waiting about for the killer to be found is frustrating to say the least."

Harry couldn't help liking Gerald Masters. While clearly being a man of wealth who was used to getting his own way, he did not vent his frustration on John who, as village constable and wall-worker, was a decent man but with little experience of the world beyond Romney Marsh. They spoke as equals with each of them knowing this was not the case.

"I shall have to find some way around this," Gerald admitted. "There's another path to explore as far as enemies go and I'll busy myself looking into it. I'm as fond of Lydia as any cousin could be, but a man needs to have a project and if I am to stay here for a little longer then I must have something to occupy my mind."

John and Harry looked at him expectantly, but Gerald didn't meet their gaze. Instead, his eyes roamed across the wind-buffeted marshland, and it seemed that he took in every trailing waterway, every water-logged dip and every lone looker's hut between Dymchurch and St Mary in the Marsh. A frown appeared across his handsome face. Having followed a hedgerow of twisted thorns, he concentrated on a cluster of tall, upright trees, rare in this land where they usually grew with their trunks bent by the prevailing westerly winds. As for the coastline, he barely gave it a glance before saying, "Perhaps the countryside is where I'll find my answers. There are mysteries to be solved in the marshland – men are sneaking about the place, and it is nowhere near as damned lonely as it first seems. And where there are men engaged in their daily work, there will always be someone ordering them about, and perhaps that someone has made himself an enemy!"

This was digested by the other men – one Romney Marsh born and bred, the second having learned the ways of the Marsh over the past seven years. "By God!" John exclaimed, "If you seek to understand the workings of the Marsh, you'll not see Canterbury again this year, or next! But if you wish to keep yourself occupied, then I'd say you have found a task to fill your time here."

"Then that is what I shall do, but I'll do it within two weeks," Gerald stated. "This place is so sparsely populated that you are bound to find the murderer within that time. The villain cannot hide forever."

"I hope you're right," Harry replied. "At some point he will reveal himself. John, we must leave you to your work on this wretched day. I will be grateful for the warmth of my fire in the forge, and Mr Masters is eager to explore the countryside. I'll see you soon, no doubt."

With the wind behind them, Harry and Gerald were almost swept back to Dymchurch where they left the summit of the seawall for the road. "Best of luck with your investigations," Harry said.

"Thank you," Gerald responded, as they entered the yard behind the forge. "I heard nothing to give me any hope the murderer is close to being found, but I was right in thinking you were the man to ask. The constable is a sensible chap too, and I believe he is doing his best to solve this curious case." He collected his horse from the stable and bade his farewells.

The warmth from the fire engulfed Harry as he stepped into the forge, and he savoured it for a moment while appraising the work completed in his absence.

"Who was that?" Matthew asked. "A stranger hereabouts, I reckon."

"That's Mrs Lydia Chapman's cousin from Canterbury," Harry told him. "He is determined to learn the ways of the Marsh within two weeks."

Matthew's response was to emit a loud guffaw, followed by a coughing fit.

The men left the forge not long after midday, with Matthew taking a country lane leading inland to the cottage he shared with Lucy and their son. Harry and Jesse had not reached Dormers before they heard a shout carried on the wind and turned to see Owen frantically beckoning them. "Can you come with me?" Harry asked Jesse. "Something's not right – I know it."

Fear gripped him, and for a moment it was as if he was suspended in time, unable to reach Owen quickly enough, and terrified of what would be learned when he did.

"I looked out, and there you were – thank God," Owen blurted. "Something's wrong. She can't move properly. It's like she's gone weak on one side."

"Can you fetch the apothecary?" Harry turned to Jesse and managed to force the words out, despite his mouth being dry and throat constricted. "And Phoebe – please. We need her here."

Jesse didn't even reply. He merely looked towards Owen, then back to Harry before turning for the High Street in his dash for assistance.

I pray we won't need the vicar.

Owen must have read Harry's thoughts as before they entered the cottage he spoke, his voice desperate and words rushed: "I'm not having the vicar. There's no need. No need at all."

"Of course not," Harry responded as he followed Owen into the cottage.

At the table, with the bread knife still in her hand, Bess was sitting slumped. Her eyes followed them and in their grey depths Harry could see both hope and fear. "It looks like you've had a turn." Harry kept his voice calm. "Nothing that some bed rest won't help. You've been working too hard."

"Her face has fallen," Owen commented.

"It will right itself in a few days." Determined to remain positive, Harry realised that even if she couldn't speak, Bess understood their words. That fear he felt just moments before had subsided and now all he thought of was caring for the woman who was as good as a mother to him and grandmother to his children. "Shall we help you to the bed?" he asked.

In response, tears began to gather in Bess' eyes, and she shook her head, just a little but enough to show that she had some control of her body.

"It's for the best, love," Owen told her. He looked towards Harry and suggested, "I'll hold her while you move the table. Then we'll each take a side and help her through."

This was followed by a desperate whimper, and they realised why.

"She's wet herself," Owen said, his voice flat.

Harry's heart sunk towards his stomach. "We'll have to sort it out then."

Another whimper.

"Not me," Harry responded. "Phoebe will help. I'll put some sacking on the bed, or an old blanket, and she'll be along in a minute. I'm sure there's hot water in the kettle – I know how you keep it at the ready."

"No need to worry," Owen soothed. "We'll soon have you cleaned up and you'll feel a lot better then."

Harry whipped the layers of blankets from the bed, leaving just one sheet, then covered it with sacking and an old blanket. They half lifted, half pulled Bess through and lay her down. Her face expressed both relief and anxiety.

"Brandy. I'll get some brandy," Owen was saying as the apothecary rapped on the door and stepped into the home.

"What's happened?" he asked, looking around.

From the bedroom doorway, Owen replied, "We put her on the bed. There's a weakness down one side, and she can't speak."

"But she understands," Harry added. "Phoebe's coming to help. She's wet... Bess is wet, you see."

"Apoplexy," the apothecary stated before even looking at Bess. "You call it a stroke." Owen and Harry stepped aside to allow him to walk through. He knelt on

154

the floor beside the bed, and when he spoke again, there was a tenderness to his tone, "We don't understand why this happens, but it's common enough in those who reach a good age. It can happen to anyone – even those who still lead a busy and useful life. I heard mention of brandy, and while it's no cure, it may give her a lift.

"I'll go to the Ocean to get some," Harry said.

"And in a moment, I'll fetch my leeches," the apothecary continued. "It's the recommended treatment in these cases and may ease the likelihood of a repeat attack. Ah! Here's Mrs Farrers."

Harry met his wife in the main room. "It's a stroke," he said, his words rushed and voice low. "She understands what's happening but can't talk and there is a weakness in her body. We took her to the bed, but she needs cleaning... washing. I'm sorry..."

Phoebe snatched at an apron and replied, "We must do whatever is needed to bring her some comfort."

Feeling blessed with his wife, always so calm, caring and practical, Harry moved towards the door. "I'm going to the Ocean."

"The Ocean?"

"We thought a brandy might help. For Bess..."

They exchanged a brief smile, and then Harry was gone and racing down the track to the High Street. He turned back once, to see the apothecary leaving, then with his mind full of brandy and leeches, headed for the tavern.

Chapter Fifteen
Lydia

The blustery wind from the coast could only enliven Lydia's spirits as she and Rebecca scoured the hedgerows of Donkey Street, their cloaks pummelled, and hair torn from its grips. Those first months of weariness felt during early pregnancy had lifted and her skin now glowed. Besides, the person who had stamped upon and crushed any pleasure she may have previously enjoyed was now lying beneath the heavy clay soil in the churchyard. Nearby, the carved stone face of a medieval character watched the grave from his place above the tower doorway.

Mother and daughter both carried trugs – in Lydia's they collected purple sloes and in Rebecca's jewel-like rosehips lay in a small mound.

"Look, Mama!" The little girl pointed to a strand of climbing dog rose, its hips abundant and tempting, yet out of reach.

Lydia frowned, determined to take this prize for themselves. "We must look for a stick," she declared. "A good stout one. Then I can pull this stem from the hedge. These will be perfect for our cordial."

Rebecca almost leapt upon a length of wood half-buried in the hedgerow. "This one?" she shouted in triumph.

"Perfect!" Lydia took it and used the end to tug at the strong stem. Eventually it was plucked from the hedge and dragged forward. "Now you pull the berries off."

"One, two, three…" Rebecca began, soon losing momentum as there must have been twelve or more, and she usually became muddled after counting up to seven.

"Wonderful! Cook will be pleased. We have plenty of sloes for a jelly and these rose hips too."

A chill carried on the breeze and neither mother nor daughter were inclined to linger. With Lydia now carrying both trugs, they turned towards home.

For the second day in a row, Gerald had been out on what he referred to as 'Romney Marsh business'. *I wonder if he will be back yet.* It was never long before Lydia's thoughts roamed to her handsome and capable cousin. *And will he tell me where he has been or what he's been doing? He seems intent on keeping it to himself.* Gerald had informed her the day before that he had been to Dymchurch and spoken with the constable about the lack of progress in finding Aaron's killer. Lydia had voiced suitable words of concern in response, but in truth she didn't really care. *All the time the matter remains unresolved, my cousin will remain attentive.* She let out a short sigh. *Although I know I will have to release him from his promise to stay here until it is all over. He must return to Canterbury before the condition of the roads deteriorates. In a day or so, I'll speak to him about it.*

Lydia and Rebecca burst into the house, an explosion of chatter as cloaks were discarded, their spoils proudly presented to the cook, and the warmth radiating from the fires appreciated. Wearing her plain beige everyday dress, with a light shawl at her shoulders, Lydia's pregnancy was pronounced. The baby was due in the winter, probably towards the end of February. With her mind awakened and thoughts clear, she felt a small degree of shame to recall that in those early weeks of the child growing within her she had been unaware of any momentous change, thinking nothing of when her monthly bleed had last coursed from her body. Even now she could not be certain of how far the pregnancy had progressed and relied on the wisdom of the midwife recommended by Aaron's sisters. *It is different now,* she reflected. *The clouds have passed and, in time, the midwife will be able to offer soothing remedies and advice when the birth is near.* She settled Rebecca on the rug with her dolls and, while the little girl shared the stories of foraging the hedgerows with her cloth companions, Lydia's thoughts once more returned to the unborn child: *When she is born, I will be forced to remain here for my confinement, but Mama will stay with me, and we can plan for my returning home with her.* With an enthusiasm so rarely felt during the last couple of years of her marriage, Lydia gathered paper, ink, a quill and a sharp knife with an ornate silver handle. Then, sitting near the window so as to catch the best of the failing light, she set about writing to her mother.

This was how Gerald found her when he entered Rothschild Manor through the back door thirty minutes later and strode through to the parlour, bringing a gust of wind with him.

"You're back!" Lydia exclaimed. "I can't help wondering what you have found to keep you busy these past two days." Her voice was light, almost playful, and anyone who thought of Mrs Lydia Chapman as a pale, washed-out, dreary figure of a young woman would be forced to adjust their judgements if they were to see her. Her hair was almost angelic with a soft sheen, her cheeks rosy and eyes portraying an eagerness for life. The widow could not foretell what the coming months or years would bring, but she was now both master and mistress of her home and conjuring plans to put the lonely Marsh behind her.

"Yes, I'm back!" Gerald replied, "And quite mud-splattered. Let me tidy myself up, and we can have a talk."

By the time Lydia heard his step on the stairs again, her letter to her mother had been set aside and the nib cleaned. The daylight had dimmed, and she did not care to write under the glow of a guttering flame. Cook had brought afternoon tea through to the parlour and the door leading to the kitchen had been firmly closed. Gerald returned, bobbing down to avoid the low beams and slumped in the worn chair which had once been Aaron's.

"I've been wandering about the place," Gerald declared. He took a bite of shortbread then continued. "And I didn't have to go far to begin to discover what all this is about…"

"Didn't have to go far?" Lydia queried. "Where have you been?"

"Yesterday I went to see Constable John Waller, as you know," Gerald began. "It was Mr Farrers who was so kind as to take me to find him. He's a decent chap, that Mr Harry Farrers is, and you do well to further your acquaintance with his wife."

"I am." Lydia stood to fuss over the teapot and cups. "I couldn't before because…" but she allowed her words to fade away, wanting to hear more of her cousin's tale.

"The constable told me that one piece of evidence pointing them towards the butcher was the knife. It was found in the churchyard, you know. But it wasn't his."

"Wasn't his?" Lydia frowned, the pale freckles on her dainty nose wrinkling.

"It was the same, but not his because all of Mr Bushy's knives were accounted for. Besides, the knifesmith had sold several of the same type within the last few months. It had to be a new knife, or near enough. There was no sign of wear and must have been selected for being the same as a butcher's." Gerald paused and took a long gulp of hot tea. "They have worked their way through the list of men known to have knives like the murder weapon and cannot link any of them to the scene of the crime. Whoever killed Aaron must have witnessed our angry butcher bellow those words 'he said I could still go butchering'."

"Of course," Lydia agreed. "Or why else would they have been shouted at the scene? They were meant to be heard and the butcher was meant to pay for the murder."

"We also spoke about who was the intended victim," Gerald elaborated, as Lydia refilled his teacup. "At first we believed it to be Sir Rupert, but if the butcher didn't commit the crime, then for what reason would he be killed? I believe the man to be likeable, if rather haphazard in his ways. Reason tells me that I would be hard pushed to find a true enemy of Sir Rupert Bannerman."

"You are right," Lydia agreed. "Why even Aaron liked him well enough, and there are not many people I could say that about."

"And in turn, not many liked your late husband."

"True," Lydia continued, her tone unusually dark. "He had plenty of enemies."

"Tell me about them."

"What do I know of his business? I was stuck out here with only the occasional visits from his family." She reflected on this for a moment. Six years had passed since their marriage and before the first anniversary of their exchange of vows, Lydia had sensed her life was destined to be both lonely and loveless. "It isn't so much that I know who else loathed him as I did, but more of an impression that wherever we went, he was disliked. For a start, there was friction between him and Harry."

"Harry Farrers?"

"Well, yes. But it was not of Harry's doing. It was an old jealousy because he – Aaron, I mean – was in love with Phoebe. At least, he didn't like it that she married Harry."

"And Harry was there at the time of the murder," Gerald exclaimed. "As a witness! It's perfectly feasible that he did it, yet I don't believe it for a moment."

"Neither do I!" Lydia declared, rising from her chair. "I won't have it said. I just won't have it said about such a good man. I can't tell you who Aaron's enemies are, but I can tell you that you won't find a man more liked than Harry Farrers."

"Calm down!" Gerald laughed. "You forget that your daughter is here playing on the rug. She may appear to be absorbed with her dolls, but I'd wager anything that she is listening to our every word."

"Let us be sensible then." Still standing, Lydia gathered the teacups and side plates. "Here in Burmarsh, on his land and within the surrounding area, you couldn't find a man with a good word to say about my husband. He treated the workers with contempt."

"And that includes those lads who we now learn were paid to lie about the theft of the cup – what was it called?"

"The Whitsun Gallop cup," Lydia supplied. "It was for a race. Held near New Romney – at Whitsun, of course."

"That leads us to the family of the condemned man – the Alders. If Jesse Alder had returned just a couple of weeks' beforehand, I believe we would have our man – but all this business came to light after the murder, and he was safely across the Channel in some place I cannot recall."

Lydia considered this. "Would Jesse's family wait three years to murder the man they believed had caused their son to be convicted? By then they knew Jesse was happy in Wissant, albeit living in exile. That's a long time for someone's anger to simmer."

"I agree," Gerald conceded. "Like Harry Farrers, they have a motive, but I do not suspect them. It is worth airing these thoughts though, for they will lead to other ideas which we may not have considered."

"I must take these to Cook." Lydia picked up the tea tray – a mundane task, while her mind was alive to possibilities. She imagined this conversation continuing to the dinner table with Gerald confiding in her. *He needs me to give him more local detail. The people… this land… he is learning about it, but I have six years of knowledge through watching and listening. Gerald sees my worth. Might he one day see me as a woman, rather than cousin?*

"It could have been me!" Gerald announced, his voice gay, on Lydia's return.

"You? You were with me. At least I think you were… I went to bed early, but they say it happened before nine o'clock and that is when I retired. We said goodnight, and even you could not have raced to Dymchurch in time to kill your cousin by marriage."

"If I had known how it would bring such light to your life, then perhaps I would have thought of it myself!" Gerald's reply was gallant.

At this Lydia may well have swooned if she had been a younger woman, not yet assaulted by both the words and hand of her husband. But her friendship with Gerald spanned more than two decades and, as yet, she had no reason to believe his comments were any more than frivolous banter. "What if they were to think it?"

"They may well think it, but I have not only you as my alibi, but Cook and the housemaid, and even the stable lad saw me at about that time."

"The stable lad?"

"Oh, it was nothing. I just wanted to check on my horse."

While the cousins spoke, the last of the sunlight had faded and the lamps had been lit. Night-time was now upon them, and Lydia became aware of her duties to her daughter. Cook would be preparing a light supper for the little girl, and she, Lydia, always sat with Rebecca at the kitchen table. Before that, she had to light the fire in the nursery and warm a nightdress near it. Rothschild Manor ran with a live-in cook and maid, and a woman who came from the village for a few hours each morning, meaning that it was necessary for the lady of the house to undertake a few of the chores herself.

"You said that you had discovered something – that you didn't need to go far?" Lydia recalled. "I am eager to hear more, but Rebecca…"

"Things to do…" Gerald stood. "We shall speak more at suppertime. You must tend to Rebecca's needs, and I am going out for a short time."

"Going out?" Her voice was high. "It's cold and dark." These words were futile, for Gerald was perfectly aware of this.

"I've not finished my investigations!" With that Gerald was heading for the hallway and pulling on layers to keep him warm.

Lydia was left in a state of anticipation, rushing through her chores and inattentive, leading to her making mistakes and everything taking longer than usual when preparing Rebecca for bed. All thoughts were on Gerald's return and sharing confidences at the supper table.

163

The meal was a nourishing stew, but whether it was beef or mutton, Lydia couldn't say, for she gave it no attention at all. Her interest was fully upon Gerald, who had returned with his skin glowing, although clearly perplexed over something. "I shall have to go out again," he had complained, but without great rancour. "It was to be expected but frustrating nonetheless." Having discarded his outer layers of clothing, he now sat opposite her in the dining room.

After spooning stew onto his plate and offering bread, Lydia could wait no longer. "What do you mean? What do you mean by this talk of investigations? And you have discovered something – does it lead you to the killer?" And then, because these thoughts had been preying on her mind for the past two hours, she continued, her voice rising, "You must be careful, Gerald. I never feared for myself or thought I might be at risk, but if this person believes you are close to finding out, then you put yourself in danger."

"You worry without reason, cousin." All signs of puzzlement were gone, and Gerald smiled, his eyes creasing at the corners and a dimple forming to the left of his mouth. "It is the secrets of Romney Marsh I am close to discovering, just as I told John Waller and Harry Farrers that I would. What I never expected was to find the answers so close to home."

"The secrets?" Lydia echoed.

"Yes! I rode about this godforsaken place for two days, wondering what it was that had caused me to feel so ill at ease. There is always a sensation of being watched, yet no one about. I looked under bridges and in barns. I stood by the dykes and waited to see if someone – or something – might emerge from the reeds."

"But you saw nothing? You learned nothing."

"Nothing." Gerald dipped his bread in gravy and paused to chew for a moment.

"Did you meet anyone? Did you speak to people?"

He swallowed the last of the bread. "On occasions I did. There were boys and men with carts moving about the place with thatch or wood, and I even came across a chap with a wagon full of live chickens. I spoke to a few men working on the land and a looker herding sheep. I had a chat with a couple of women carrying baskets of food for their family meals, and a terrible old hag dragging a handcart of laundry. Except for a few pleasantries they were none of them eager to engage in any meaningful conversation."

"You could expect no more," Lydia pointed out. "You are a stranger to them, and they are busy with their tasks."

"But while we pass a few words, you never know what could be revealed."

"True." Lydia waited, knowing that there was news to share, for Gerald had said so. *He wants to tease me with it, to keep me waiting…*

"On my return to Burmarsh from the hills at Hurst, I recalled that it was on this date three years ago that I lost my father and so I decided to pause at the church and pray for him. I sat in the front pew on the left, and for a while I was lost in thoughts of childhood memories and the conversation I might share with him if he were here to listen. After a while, my gaze began to roam about the place, taking in the small details, and that's when I noticed one of the steps leading to the pulpit was out of place." Gerald paused, as if considering how best to express himself, then continued, lowering his voice a little. "I mean to say that the tread is removeable – it had been lifted and not put back fully. Curiosity got the better of me. I had to investigate the reason for this, and you can imagine my surprise when I discovered tea, of

165

all things, hidden within the frame of the pulpit! And that each step slid outwards to reveal a hidden compartment. All packed full of those precious leaves!"

"What did you do next?" Lydia almost squeaked.

"I set about looking for other potential hides, of course. And would you believe it – the gall of these folk who had decided to use these sacred places as a hide – bundles of lace... perhaps a dozen of them... Under the altar, they were! Covered over with the holy cloth! I must say I was astounded. Truly dumbfounded."

"There must have been a run last night," Lydia said, her tone now almost careless. "He thought I didn't know about it, but they were always talking about the trading... the French... the riding officers..."

"He? Your husband?"

She ignored this, her mind flitting to Gerald being in the church and poking about where he shouldn't. "You must put this out of your mind. It is the way of life here, but nothing to concern us. This is the secret you spoke of – I see that now – but you will return to Canterbury soon and leave the Marsh men to their unruly ways." Gerald, clearly taken aback by these revelations, was not given the opportunity to respond, as Lydia steeled herself to say the words she knew must be shared with her cousin and was not to be stopped: "I'm not sure you will find the murderer. When it happened... when he was killed, you vowed to stay here until the person responsible was found. But there is no progress, and I must allow you to return to Canterbury. It will be dull here without you, but Mother will come before the baby is due, and then I can plan to leave as well. I shall have something to look forward to as the days become bleaker."

"But don't you see that I hope to keep my promise *and* return to Canterbury?" Gerald replied. "You speak of your husband being away from home at night and now I understand that he was caught up in all this… this illegal trade, and I suggest that enemies were made through his dealings."

"Even if that were the case, it is unlikely you will ever find out who… Lips will be sealed." Lydia felt some of her old agitation growing within her. Where before her vow to release Gerald from his promise was reluctant, now Lydia became determined that he should leave. "You must not even think of remaining here. Return to Canterbury – to your home and business affairs – and think no more of the secrets to be learned hereabouts. This is enough."

"Very well," he answered. "I will stay until the end of next week and then return home. The whole business is impossible, and the constable can deal with it as best he can."

Chapter Sixteen
Toke

Throughout the year – apart from those months when freezing conditions made the tasks near-impossible – there were three reasons for Toke to be labouring in the waterways. The first of these was a job which took place in the late summer and early autumn. Armed with long, sharp knives, boys and men manoeuvred shallow-bottomed boats along the edge of the banks and sliced at the lower stems of the reeds. They took armfuls of the straw-like stalks and bound them with twine before handing them over to the farmer or his foreman who would then negotiate the selling of these to the thatchers. Midway down the banks, where the water met the sloping sides, wildlife crawled and fluttered about. Creatures raced away from the prow of the small vessel as it nudged along, escaping the assault of the blade on the already dying reeds. The weather had to be warm and dry to produce fresh thatch, and so it became one of Toke's favourite jobs – especially when he took his turn at wielding the knife. There was a satisfaction to be had at turning back to see the short, jagged stems, and knowing that before long the reeds would be topping a local cottage.

The second reason was to clear the ditches from silt and debris that created obstructions to the flow of the water. This was a truly wet and mucky task undertaken in the autumn but drew no complaints from Toke as he found a great deal of physical satisfaction in heaving spadefuls of rotting plant life and slimy mud up and out of the water. His mother, on the other hand, had plenty to say when he arrived home caked in mud with every item of his clothing needing to be dried.

The third reason to be working in the waterways suited Toke's adventurous spirit. There were pathways to be kept clear – not the tracks used by the clay carts throughout the year, but narrower routes trailing at a lower level. Hugging the banks, these paths were used by the smugglers when they needed to hide themselves and sneak about the Marsh, using local knowledge to outwit the riding officers.

It was this task Toke had on his mind when he spied a gentleman strolling along Donkey Street. Although he carried the tools for clearing away a fallen branch and was busy with this mission, Toke also had his eye on keeping a pathway clear. With a pair of leather gloves covering his calloused hands and a handsaw clasped in his palm, he set about cutting the offending branch of hawthorn.

"Hello down there!" The gentleman had paused and was peering down.

"Oh! Good morning, sir. I wasn't expecting..." Toke stopped suddenly. It didn't do any good to let down your guard.

"What are you doing?" The gentleman's tone was curious rather than accusing. "I have land myself, but not the abundance of waterways I find cutting through the fields hereabouts."

"I'm moving this broken branch out of the way before it falls and blocks the dyke," Toke replied. There seemed no harm in sharing this. Then, because the gentleman seemed friendly enough, and needed some educating about the area, he continued. "With respect, sir, I can see you're a learned man, but these ditches –

or you could call them sewers or dykes... these ditches don't cut through the land. It was the land which grew up either side of the old sea creeks."

"I'm new to the ways of Romney Marsh," the gentleman conceded.

"Sometimes they are created by hand." Toke realised he had not been entirely correct. "When the farmer needs extra drainage, then he digs another." He stopped. *I'm at it again. Talking and talking and who knows when I might say something I shouldn't.* Toke continued hacking at the hawthorn branch, gripping it with his gloved hand and expecting the stranger to continue on his way.

"Who do you work for?"

Oh! He's still here and now it's becoming a bother. "I'm my own boss, sir. I don't work for no one in particular. If someone wants a ditch cleared or reeds cut 'Toke's the man', they'll say, and I'll go along and do it. In the spring, there's the lambs to tend, and after that it's the clay carts."

"Did you work for Mr Chapman? Mr Chapman from Rothschild Manor? I believe I've seen you there?"

"I did." Toke lifted his eyes to heaven in a gesture which would please the vicar. "God rest his soul."

"Was he a fair man? Did he treat you well?"

Toke narrowed his eyes and his skin prickled. "What's Mr Chapman to you?"

"I apologise. I'm Mr Masters, and Mrs Lydia Chapman is my cousin." Now he was all smiles, and once more putting Toke at ease. "I don't think I've met a man who had a good word to say about our Mr Chapman – apart from his own family that is. A bully – that's what he was. What do you make of that?"

Now, this astounded Toke and any thoughts of the hawthorn coupled with the potential hazard it caused

170

were swept away. He proceeded with caution, "I'd say you were right."

"And would you say that he was a harsh employer? That he worked people hard without a word of thanks?"

"I'd say that's how it was."

"It would take some planning to murder him," Gerald continued. "Whoever did it was a clever man – wily, is the word I use. They not only knew of his movements that night but were astute enough to frame the butcher. And they also knew it would be believed that Sir Rupert Bannerman was the intended victim, thus no one would be looking for an enemy of Mr Chapman. It was all so simple – Sir Rupert Bannerman angers the butcher, and the butcher sets about to kill him. It appears that the wrong man was murdered. But that's not how it was, is it? Whoever killed Mr Chapman planned it to appear that way, whilst all the time knowing exactly who they wanted dead!"

Toke paled. "It wasn't me, sir. It wasn't me."

"I never thought it was." Gerald frowned as if considering the matter.

Now I've put the idea in his mind, who knows where it might lead. He'll find out – I know he will... He'll find out about the gold cup and... He'll know... The shillings Mr Chapman gave me and then the whippings... This gent will know it all by... by supper time. I've got to make him think about something else and think it quick.
"You're right, sir. No one liked him. No one liked that Mr Chapman," Toke babbled. "He was hard on us poor folk. Never had a kind word, just nasty things to say and... and whippings too..."

"I thought that's how it was," Gerald replied, his tone soothing, as if he understood.

"Even the rich folk hated him," Toke supplied.

"I hadn't considered that."

171

Noting Mr Masters' thoughtful expression, Toke paused to allow this new information to filter through the gentleman's mind. Then he continued, "There was some argument about a strip of land towards Gammon's Farm Lane – I heard Mr Chapman took it for himself, said it was his, but it wasn't. And last month there was a big fight – a proper fight with fists – with Mr Joss Bailey, him who owns land over West Hythe way."

"I wonder what that was about," Gerald replied.

He's listening to me! He's listening about those people who had reason to kill Mr Chapman and he's forgetting that he ever thought it was me who done it. "It was about something that Mr Bailey had stored in our church," Toke said, nodding towards All Saints at Burmarsh. "It was Mr Bailey's... Mr Bailey's... well – it was his, and just because it was in our church, it wasn't Mr Chapman's to take." Not wanting to be questioned about what another landowner may need to store in a church, when he had barns and sheds aplenty, Toke blundered on, "And there's Mr Farrers, him who's a jurat and blacksmith. There was always trouble between those two because Mr Chapman had a fancy for Mrs Farrers. Have you met her, sir? She's a lovely, kind lady, even though her uncle is that miserable old grocer down in the village – Dymchurch, I mean."

Toke paused for breath. Then he realised what he had done... In an attempt to befuddle this fine gentleman and distract him from considering that he, Toke, might be the killer, he had mentioned the very man who had been so good to him recently. The handsaw still rested on the hawthorn, and, for a moment, he put all his efforts into severing the broken branch from the tree. It snapped, and Toke hauled it up the bank to the roadside. Mr Masters remained there. *I hoped he'd have moved on, but he's thinking about everything I said and about all those people who could have gone murdering.*

Neither said a word after this outburst, instead they studied each other for a moment and then Gerald turned to retrace his steps towards Burmarsh. "It's all very interesting, isn't it?" he said, and without lingering for an answer, he strode off.

Toke watched the man's progress and waited until he was some distance away. Then he took a firm grip on the severed branch and dragged it along behind him as he too headed to Burmarsh.

"There's not much wood about the place and it will be seasoned before the weather turns warm," Toke explained to his mother as he hung his cloak on a hook behind the kitchen door. "I've cut it up nice and tidy."

"You're a good lad," she replied. "Always looking for ways to be helpful."

"I'm a man now, Ma," he responded, sitting down at the table. "And if you don't mind I'll have a bowl of broth and some of this here bread before the others come back. I've got some business in Dymchurch and it's important."

"Hark at you talking about business!" Mrs Spicer let out a raucous laugh. "Dymchurch today, but maybe next week you'll be off to Hythe or Dover. You've got great things coming to you, lad."

She's forgotten already about me being a man. Toke scowled but said no more about it. Instead, he continued with, "Maybe Hythe... maybe, but Dover... what fancy ideas you're getting. It's not for the likes of me to go off the Marsh and especially not all that way. Who knows what nasty characters I could meet."

The broth had been ladled into a bowl now and a hunk of bread cut. Mrs Spicer placed them both on the table and reached for the dripping. "I'd say there's

173

enough queer folk here on the Marsh that you won't find any of those Dover sorts could cause you much bother."

"Perhaps not," Toke conceded as he dunked bread amongst the gravy and vegetables. "Ta, very nice." He ate in silence then pushed his chair back and wiped his mouth with his sleeve. "I've got to go now, like I said."

"You take care, lad, with this important business," his mother responded.

"I'm a man now, Ma," Toke reminded her as he pulled on his cloak and left the cottage.

Fully prepared to face the consequences of his loose tongue, and make amends for past wrongs, Toke took the road to Dymchurch. It was a lonely route that day and he passed no one but a pair of gossipy housewives burdened with baskets laden with produce bought in the village. After a while he considered an opening onto a field and the tracks leading directly to the church, but recent rain had left the soil tacky. His boots had been brushed clean earlier that day, so he decided to take the longer but less muddy route. *When it's important business with Mr Farrers, there's no harm in being clean and respectable – in fact, it's the way it should be.*

On reaching Dymchurch, Toke passed by the properties he considered to be 'those houses where them fancy folk live' and reached the terraces and humble homes nestling together amongst shops and places where the tradesmen laboured. Without faltering, fighting the urge to flee back to Burmarsh, he rapped on the door of a cottage in the row named Dormers.

The door was opened by Mrs Alder whose ready smile immediately fell from her face as she asked, "What do you want?"

"I'm wanting to see your son Jesse," Toke replied. "Is he here?"

Mrs Alder eyed him with suspicion and said nothing but, "Haven't you caused enough trouble?"

"I'm not looking for trouble, Mrs Alder. I'm looking to say I'm sorry."

Jesse's mother was not to be softened by this. Too many years had passed with her son living across the Channel, and now he was intending to remain there. "He's up on the Wall," she said. "He walked along to High Knocke with his pa and will be on his way back."

"Ta. Ta very much." Then recalling Mr Gerald Masters and his elegant ways, Toke found himself saying, "Much obliged." With this the door was closed in his face, and Toke continued to walk along the High Street before heading for the path leading to the seawall by the Ocean Inn.

As he approached the top of the Wall, Jesse appeared and there was a pause before Toke said, "I was looking for you." There followed a few seconds of awkward silence with Jesse saying nothing in response, but merely waiting. "It's time I said that I'm sorry. I've been sorry for a long time. Years. Couldn't say it though."

Without taking the time to consider this, Jesse answered, "You did wrong, but I know what a bully Aaron Chapman was, and he was the one to blame."

"He'd never say sorry."

"He wouldn't."

"It's good of you to say that he was the one in the wrong, but I was greedy wanting those shillings," Toke admitted. "Everyone needs a bit of money, but you don't take it and put a man in gaol, or worse."

"It seems like you've done some growing up since that day, and I appreciate you coming to see me," Jesse said. "I can't say I'd want to buy you a tankard of ale, but I'm putting what's happened behind me now."

175

"Ta for that." Feeling relieved at having made amends, Toke turned to look towards the forge. "I've got business with Mr Farrers now and hoping to find him over there."

"You're in luck then. Harry was there when I passed by not long ago," Jesse replied.

They walked down the steep track, exchanging no more words, then parted ways at the bottom, with Toke crossing the road and entering the forge by the part-open double doors at the front.

"Hello Mr Farrers, can I have a word. In private," Toke asked before Harry had even turned from his position at his bench.

Glancing towards Matthew and Jack, Harry set down his ironwork scrolls, and replied, "In the yard?"

It was cosy in the forge, even with the doors ajar, and Toke resented the presence of the other men that prevented him from holding his conversation there. He had no choice but to trail behind and into the yard. No sooner was he out of earshot than Toke rushed into the reason for his being there, "There's been a gent asking about Mr Chapman and who might have stabbed him. He's not from these parts and says he's cousin to Mrs Chapman – her who was married to Mr Chapman."

"Mr Masters," Harry stated.

"That's him. You know him?" To think of Harry knowing Gerald Masters eased some of Toke's concerns. *He'll understand that he has a way of talking that turned me on my head and how he made me say things I shouldn't have.*

"He was here only a few days ago asking how the search for the killer was going," Harry told him. "Seems like a reasonable man. What did he want with you?"

"He was asking me who hated Mr Chapman and, before I knew it, he seemed to know about the trouble and how I was being bullied... and he was looking at me like he thought I was the one who done it. Then he was asking about other people who had reason to want Mr Chapman dead and I didn't want him thinking about me no more, so I was saying about that farmer over Newchurch way, and how he – Mr Chapman, I mean – had a fancy for your wife, Mrs Farrers... Then there was Mr Bailey, and they had a big fight not so long ago. There's no end to the people who didn't like him."

"You're right," Harry replied. "But why have you come here telling me?"

"I mentioned you, didn't I? It got me thinking that I needed to tell you and I needed to find Jesse Alder to say I was sorry."

"Oh, don't worry about mentioning my name," Harry said, as if it really didn't matter at all. "As you said, there's a long list of Aaron Chapman's enemies. It's no business of Mr Masters – it's for the jury and John Waller to work out. They know what's going on a lot better than some gentleman from Canterbury."

"I'd say he didn't like Mr Chapman either," Toke revealed. "He was family, but he didn't like him. I wonder even if Mrs Chapman liked her husband. Perhaps it was them who did it?"

"It's not for us to say," Harry answered. "Have you seen Jesse?"

"I have and he's a decent sort – very understanding." Toke sidled towards the gateway leading from the yard. "Well, I'll be off." He needed to return to Burmarsh now. If he set off at a good pace, then there would still be a couple of hours daylight to work in. The farmer from Abbott's Farm had asked him to cut back some hedgerow and he could make a fair start on it.

"I was thinking about you," Harry said, stopping the young man in his tracks.

"Oh, yes?" Toke replied with caution.

"Would you like me to have a word with one of the foremen working on the seawall and ask if they'd be prepared to have you working with them?" Harry asked. "Somewhere down your end of the Wall? You've said that you'd like it, and it's a shilling and sixpence a day – regular money."

The young Marshman felt himself swelling with pride. There was no job more glorious than working on the seawall, for without that great bank of stakes, thorn bundles and sticky clay-earth, there would be no fertile farmland lying behind it and no ancient villages. He pictured himself leaving Burmarsh in the morning with a hunk of bread and a thick slice of cheese or meat wrapped in paper, tied with string and nestling with an apple or pear in his canvas sack. 'There goes Toke Spicer' the villagers would say. 'We can rely on him to keep us safe. He's our man on the Wall'.

Absorbed with his imaginings, Toke forgot to respond for a moment and when he did, his words were inadequate, but Mr Farrers was a busy man and had no need to hear all that rattled about in his head. "Thank you. Thank you – I'd like that very much. An honour it would be."

"I'm glad you feel like that," Harry replied. "I liked my time there."

They parted, with Toke immediately heading for the seawall, eager to walk a section of it before dropping down and taking the Burmarsh road. The day was gloomy and the tide sluggish, but he took in every detail of the great wooden knockes, the arc of the Wall which tipped the highest waves back upon themselves, and the grassy bank on the landward side. He was alert to areas newly repaired and others appearing shabby. Any crack was surveyed, for the thinnest sliver of open bank could be worked upon by the sea until it penetrated the defence. The wall-workers received perky greetings, not yet knowing that he could soon be one of them, and he stepped aside allowing lads with carts, and women with broods of young children, to pass without risk of toppling off. The urgency to return to work on the land had passed, and he vowed that if he returned home after sunset then he would not care a jot about the pennies sacrificed.

As he sauntered, he considered the generous nature of Harry Farrers – a man who saw some good in him and would give him a chance in life. *Toke Spicer – you've known the ways of the Marsh for some time but now you're learning more about people. There's decent folk out there who will help if you're honest and hard-working. You can still move woolpacks to the beaches and lug kegs to their hides – that's different rules. But it's time to start treating people well, and in return they'll keep an eye on you and set you on the right path.*

Chapter Seventeen
Mireille

At dawn Mireille awoke to Harry's steps on the stairs and knew it was time for her to rise. The mornings of luxuriating between good linen and the warm weight of woollen blankets had ended abruptly. She could no longer allow herself the joy of waiting for the children to tumble into her room, for she was now needed and depended upon within the home of her English cousin and her Dymchurch family.

This responsibility was new to Mireille, who had lived under the domineering ways of her mother, Marie, all her life. With her brothers, Vincent and Louis, not yet at a stage of finding a wife and producing their own brood of children, she remained the youngest girl, and then woman, in the household. Grand-mère's decline had been gentle and she had remained largely independent until the end, so in Mireille's seventeen years she had never been called upon to care for either a child or an elderly person. The Bernard home ran efficiently, Marie at the helm, with her daughter at her beck and call but never giving any particular commitment. If Mireille chose to lose herself in the dunes or wander in the marketplace or sit sewing under the fruit trees while dreaming of Jesse, then she was free to do so. It was not that the young woman was irresponsible, merely that she was unburdened with day-to-day issues.

On hearing the soft thud of the kitchen door being closed behind Harry, Mireille swung her feet out of bed and into felt slippers. She smoothed her bottom sheet, folding back the top layers for the bed to air. The atmosphere was nippy, and she wrapped a shawl around her shoulders before stepping over to the washstand and plunging her hands into cold water then sloshing it over her face. Now fully awake, Mireille discarded the shawl and dressed quickly, silently thanking Phoebe for the thicker chemise and stockings she had so kindly provided the day before.

Still pulling her skirt into place, Mireille ran lightly down the stairs, and into the kitchen. "Good morning!"

"Cup of tea to warm you," Janey said as she poured.

"Thank you." Mireille drank while still standing.

"I'll be along later," Harry told her. Dressed for his work at the forge he was seated, with some papers in front of him, awaiting a bowl of porridge. "Can you tell Owen I'll call in before midday?"

"I will."

The light in the room was dim, with just one lamp and the glow from the fire. For a moment Mireille was reluctant to leave the cosy atmosphere, but she didn't allow those thoughts to develop, instead saying to Janey, "I'll be back in an hour and a more," not yet able to express her words in English as well as she would like to. Then she left the comfort of the kitchen for the darkened hallway, reached for her cloak and placed it across her shoulders before leaving.

On the street, there came a moment of hesitation – seawall road or High Street? To head towards the coast would take a little longer, but the view promised to be spectacular. Already, vibrant shades of yellow, orange and pink were glowing and spreading from the east. Mireille walked swiftly past the Ship and followed the track leading to the Wall. She was just in time, with the sun rising beyond the horizon, casting a bright pathway upon the sea, moments after she had reached the summit. This vision never failed to fill Mireille with wonder, but she didn't allow herself to pause. By the time she had reached the point where a rough track left the seawall and led to a low cottage, the intensity of the colours was already fading.

Now with her back to the sun, Mireille rounded the cottage and rapped on the door, not waiting for a reply before walking in. "Good morning," she called.

"Good morning to you," Owen replied as he walked into the living room from the bedroom which had once been Harry's.

"How is Bess?"

Owen shrugged.

Noting the kettle already suspended above the fire, Mireille pushed on the door of the main bedroom saying, "Bess. I'm here. Here to help you get ready for the day."

Bess lay on the bed, fully awake and gazing at the ceiling. Without smiling, she turned her head towards the door and worked her mouth. Slurred sounds struggled out and a bead of dribble began to roll across her cheek. Mireille dashed for the handkerchief. "I'll help you now," she said. Her words felt inadequate, but she knew them to be appreciated. "Use your strong side to help me sit you up."

With encouragement, Bess used her left arm to push on the bed, and with Mireille at her right side, she was lifted and swung around until her feet rested on the floor. Stockings and slippers were immediately provided and secured by Mireille, who was also relieved to see the bedpan had been used and there was no sign of Bess having soiled herself in the night. *Owen must have helped her.*

182

"I'll get some warm water." With a backward glance, Mireille darted through to the other room and towards the kettle.

Within twenty minutes Bess was seated near the fire with a blanket roll supporting her right side. Mireille, now wearing an apron, was preparing porridge for breakfast. Owen, clearly wanting to keep occupied, was outside beating the dust from a rug, and had mentioned that he planned to sweep through the whole cottage. "The porridge is nearly ready. Do you have cream to cool it? Yes – there it is." Mireille chatted as she bustled about but struggled with no one at hand to help with unknown words, and occasionally opened the door to call out to Owen for assistance. Before long, she was spooning small amounts into Bess' mouth. "It will help," she said, sensing a reluctance to eat. "I'm sure it will."

Not much more than an hour had passed before Mireille headed back to Walker House. Her spirits were surprisingly buoyant, given the sadness of this new situation. While dismayed to see Bess so helpless, there was a determination to both help with domestic tasks and to encourage some use of the weaker limbs. With Phoebe absorbed in the care of the three young children, it seemed clear that Mireille should do everything possible to help during her remaining days in Dymchurch.

This newfound responsibility brought with it an unexpected confidence. Heading back to Walker House, this time along the village street, Mireille greeted those she passed with a friendly 'good morning' and could almost hear their thoughts: *There goes Mrs Farrers' cousin, she's been helping out with Bess Bates and good for her!* In the time it took her to reach the front door – no more than five minutes – a plan had formed in Mireille's mind. A scheme that would free her from her mother's overbearing control and offer the opportunity for her to be truly useful. With her care, Bess *would* survive longer than the pessimistic two or three weeks suggested by the apothecary – Mireille was determined to see this happen.

"I'm not going back!" The words flew from Mireille no sooner than she entered the nursery.

They all turned, hearing the excitement in her voice but not quite understanding. Even the twins twisted towards her and stopped fussing over having their clouts changed. Mary, who had trained herself not to react to any private conversation she may hear between Harry and Phoebe, frowned and tilted her head in the direction of the now open doorway.

"I'm not going back," Mireille repeated. "You need me here to help with Bess."

"But it's your home... and Jesse is going back on Thursday," Phoebe responded. "What will the family say?"

"I would like them to say 'Mireille is not needed here. *Nous sommes fiers qu'elle va rester là pour aider son cousin.*'"

"'We are proud of her for staying to help her cousin'." Phoebe supplied. "I'm not sure..."

"I know...." Mireille felt her spirits slump a little and she held her arms out to Esther who bundled into them. "I know I am not needed there. Maman rules our home and any girl from the village could come to help with the sweeping and the washing. But here..."

"Bess only knew you for a few days before... before the..." Phoebe left the word unsaid.

"But in that short time, she accepted me as part of the family."

Daily life with three young children could not be paused for the cousins to explore Mireille's desire to be useful, or the intricacies of the Bernard family where

Marie ran home and family with efficiency. The twins were still in their chemises and fretting to go downstairs, while Esther began to question if her French cousin would be staying. Phoebe swiftly pinned James' clout and handed Mary a petticoat for him. The maid felt her way around the waistband, ensuring that she had it the correct way with the opening at the back. James was encouraged to go to be dressed, while Phoebe reached for Clara and placed her in a matching outfit.

"When the children have their nap, we can all talk about this – Janey and Mary too. This affects the whole household because when you leave – if you leave – I won't be able to cope with Bess and the children at the same time."

Satisfied, Mireille helped fasten the little boy's shoes. "Thank you," she said, wanting to explore the subject further but forcing herself to be patient.

"But first," Phoebe continued, "you and I can speak when we take the children to the beach. There is someone else to consider while you make your plans."

Some things needed discussing in private and there was no better place than the open beach. The upper sands were usually deserted, with the wall-workers congregating around the seawall and knockes, and the bait diggers closer to the waters where the sand remained wet. It came as no surprise to Mireille that as soon as the children started scampering ahead Phoebe asked, "How does Jesse fit into your plan?"

"He's not in my plan," Mireille declared, although she could hardly believe it herself. "I know he is going back in two days, and we will be apart for many months."

"You must hope that he will stay," Phoebe persisted. "And if he does, and if he loves you as you love him, then do you plan to make your home here?"

185

"No, I hope he returns to my home – to our home – because I will go back when you no longer need me."

Mireille surprised herself that she so readily accepted their separation, although her feelings for Jesse had by no means lessened in the past few days. Her desire to help Bess and in turn be a saviour to Phoebe was strong, and when considering her romantic hopes, she now wondered if to be apart from Jesse was the solution to fulfilling her dreams.

"He sees me as a girl," Mireille tried to explain. "If we are apart then, when I return, he will notice I am a woman. And if in that time he meets someone else, then that is how it must be. Perhaps he will miss me? Perhaps he will realise when he is there without me?"

"I think he already realises," Phoebe said. "But it's new to him. There is something different in the way he looks at you. I didn't see it in Wissant, but I see it now. Although you are here in my home, there is a protectiveness towards you. Perhaps it began on the boat journey here?"

"He was kind to me. I felt dreadful."

"I know." Phoebe always suffered from debilitating sea sickness. "You'll have to tell Jesse you are staying, and perhaps you'll learn how he feels."

"I will," Mireille replied as James toppled over near a puddle. She picked up her pace to help him up and turned to say just one more word, "Today."

No more confidences could be shared, for now the children demanded attention and, as it is when caring for young children, their mothers – or grown-up cousins – so often have to leave a sentence hanging and a conversation unfinished.

Late morning came and with it the daily respite from caring for the children. No sooner had the little ones settled for a sleep than Janey was pouring scalding

186

water into the teapot while Mary set out cups and saucers on the kitchen table.

"As you know, Mireille has offered to stay," Phoebe said before any niceties were exchanged about their mornings. "We need to talk about it, all four of us."

"Thank goodness!" Mary responded immediately, her face alight. "I didn't know how we would manage and hoped you hadn't changed your mind. You are so kind to me, but if I wasn't blind..."

A feeling of warmth washed over Mireille. *How unusual this family is. I love them all.*

"You are part of the family and there is so much you can do to help with the children," Phoebe assured her as they all settled in well-worn kitchen chairs.

"Maybe Mary can help with Bess too?" Mireille said as soon as the idea burst into her mind. "She needs company, not just help with washing and dressing." *It will be difficult because Bess cannot speak and Mary cannot read the expressions on Bess' face, but they will find a way of making it work.*

"She doesn't want strangers about the place," Mary added. "I'd like to help."

"That's a wonderful idea." Phoebe stood to stir then pour the tea. "But I want us to talk about the possibility of Mireille staying for a few months. What has happened to Bess affects us all because if I have to go there more, then how will we manage with the three children? I don't want to have to bring someone else here to look after them and it is too much to ask you both to do any more. Until a few days ago, we were relying on Bess to help in the mornings so are already one person less."

"Her family won't be happy," Janey said, recalling the time when Phoebe's Tante Marie had swept into their lives.

"They won't." Mary, usually so quiet, offered her opinion. "Mireille must be a great help to them."

"I wouldn't leave if Grand-mère was still alive." For a moment Mireille almost forgot she was in the kitchen of her cousin's home as her mind wandered and she saw herself once more under the fruit trees in the garden at home. She could smell the richness of the damp soil and the sweetness of rotting fruit. But Grand-mère's chair remained empty, her blanket of Romney Marsh wool now folded upon Mireille's own bed in her room under the eaves. "But Maman doesn't need me."

"They'll still miss you," Janey responded.

"I hope they will understand that Mireille is doing a great kindness in staying," Phoebe answered. "I can't think of any other way that we can manage, can you?"

The housekeeper and maid, so much a part of the family, both shook their heads and agreed. Then Mary surprised them all by asking, "Will Jesse mind?"

"Jesse?" Mireille repeated, her voice high while her eyes darted from one face to the next.

"I thought..." Mary began. "I thought that you and he... I can't see how he looks at you, but I thought there was something in the way he speaks to you. Is there an ...?"

"An understanding," Janey supplied.

"Oh no. No. Not at all." The words rushed from Mireille.

"Best go and see him," Janey suggested, as she seamlessly moved from role as cook and cleaner to motherly figure. "You are due to leave on Thursday."

"When should I go?" Mireille asked. "I was going to..." She looked at Phoebe.

"Go now. To the forge," Phoebe suggested. "It will be no bother if you interrupt his work there, and best to avoid his family. They'll be looking for a reason as to why he insists on returning to Wissant."

Queasy with nerves, Mireille walked briskly through the village. The cool breeze became her ally, giving her reason to pull her hood up and hide away from those she passed. This wasn't how it was meant to be between herself and Jesse – her staying in Dymchurch and him returning. *I thought that perhaps on the boat back... He was so caring when I was ill... Maybe he would have said something... Now he won't – he can't.* Her thoughts flashed to another possible outcome: *It could have been him staying... Staying here with a Dymchurch woman. That would have been worse.*

She passed Aunt Peggy's and Uncle Giles' shop – *Not my aunt and uncle but I can't help calling them that!* The forge came into view and Mireille pondered, *what will they think of me asking to see him. It's nearly time for their midday break. It will be better if I wait and then when he sees me... that's when I'll tell him.* She slowed down.

There was time to spare now. Mireille lingered and gazed through the windows of the shoe mender's workshop and the drapery store with disinterest, having no purchase in mind. Crossing the road, she stood before William Parris' shop and looked at the displays of groceries, without being tempted to make a purchase. Turning away, she was alerted to movement at the doorway of the forge and her heart leapt as Jesse and Matthew walked out together. *Now what am I to do?* At that moment, Jesse glanced across the road and grinned at her; he turned to say something to his cousin, and they parted, Jesse darting across the road before a cart lumbered by.

"Hello! How are you?"

"I've decided not to go home," Mireille said without preamble.

"You're staying?" he asked. "Staying here?"

Noting his shock, she replied, "I have to. How can Phoebe look after Bess *and* the children? And she must – there is no one else."

"But I'm going back. In two days."

"I know."

They remained standing on the street, Mireille willing Jesse to declare that she must return with him... that he needed her to be there with him. But Jesse was too decent, she knew that, so instead he said, "I understand. You want to help."

"I have to. I need you to explain that I will come home, but not yet." Mireille paused to consider the winter months ahead, then continued, "It will be in the spring. I don't know if Bess will get better or... But whatever happens, I won't stay here. I'll come home."

"I'll tell them the best I can," Jesse responded. "It won't seem right without you, but the time will pass."

"Thank you."

"Your family must understand this is a good thing you're doing." Then he glanced down the street and looked back at Mireille. "I need to go now. Ma is expecting me."

They walked together to the family home at Dormers, speaking no more of Mireille's plans. Then, on the street, brief, awkward goodbyes were exchanged, and they parted, neither of them looking back.

Chapter Eighteen
Harry

Returning to work after dinner, Harry walked along the High Street and mused on the changes in his home. The day before, Mireille had announced her determination to remain in Dymchurch. Despite some unease about the family in Wissant being upset by her choice, Harry could think of no better solution to his family's need to support Owen in his care of Bess. He was mulling over the details when William Payne bounded into view.

"Ah! Just who I was hoping to see."

"Oh?" Harry eyed his friend, certain he was about to be prevented from returning to the forge. "Am I right to feel cautious?"

"Not at all." William grinned, and continued, "I've been to see the butcher's sons and Mrs Bushy – Anthony Bushy is a bully and I wondered if the sons set their father up. We've been before, me and John Waller, but there's no evidence. Remind me again – what did you hear on the morning of the trial?"

"That was a while ago now," Harry said. For some reason he felt uncomfortable about going over it all again. "It's a dreadful plan to murder someone and make it appear as if your father did it."

"But possible," William persisted.

"Of course. They had the knife – or at least one the same – and they knew those words we all recognise now."

"He said I could still go butchering!"

"Exactly." Harry stopped and flashed a grin at his friend. "Hey, I knew you were about to drag me into something. I've got work to do and there's nothing to tell."

"Come and have an ale with me?" William suggested, looking towards the City of London. "I saw your assistant just now and told him I needed you for a while."

"I might be too busy," Harry hinted.

"Not at all. Jack said it was fine." William waited for a horse and cart to trundle by, then began to cross the road towards the tavern – an unusual place with one entrance on the High Street and the other on the elevated Seawall Road.

"Just the one," Harry said, following William into the bar, then up to the higher level. Here the door was open towards the coast and the fresh breeze brushed away tobacco smoke and the aroma of ale spills that rose from the plank flooring.

"Good afternoon, Mr Payne, Mr Farrers. What takes your fancy today?" No sooner had the chirpy wench greeted them and reached for the tankards than steps were heard pounding on the stairs and a gentleman entered the bar, causing her to pause and stare. "I don't think we know you here, sir," she uttered, eyeing him with appreciation.

"I'm visiting the area," Gerald Masters replied, giving her a friendly smile. "A brandy please and I'll pay for these drinks too. I was hoping to see you, Harry. Lucky to spot you both crossing the road."

Hiding his despair, for Gerald's determination to learn about the mysteries of the Marsh had not been forgotten, Harry attempted a welcoming response, "Mr Masters, you were fortunate to find me then, for I don't usually frequent taverns during the day – or at any other time!"

"It's this damned murder that brings me here," Gerald replied. "I've come up with some ideas."

Aware of the wench's open-mouthed interest, Harry answered, "How interesting. Let's sit over there." He gestured towards a table and benches at the far end of the room. "Could you bring the drinks to us?" he asked the girl.

"Very well, sir." She smiled prettily but couldn't hold back a pout from settling on her lips.

The men moved to the far side of the room, but before they were seated, William aired his discomfort that they were now three. "Mr Masters, I know how this affects you, but Harry and I need to talk about the case. I'm one of the jury and need to speak with him about something he witnessed. I'm not quite sure how you come into it." Known for airing his thoughts, William stood with a hand resting on the tabletop, unwilling to sit before the interloper was dealt with. "If you wouldn't mind waiting – perhaps over there," he nodded towards a table by the fire, "then we'll soon be done, and I don't object to you joining us."

Gerald, raised to be a gentleman, appeared to consider this before replying, "Mr...?" he looked at Harry who apologised for not making an introduction and swiftly supplied the name, "Mr Payne, I am here with information and if you are a member of the jury then I am glad to meet you." His tone was smooth, and he spoke with ease, clearly not wanting to rile William. "But I have intruded and am happy to wait, if you would kindly spare me some time afterwards."

Pacified, William looked at Harry, "If my friend here is happy, then I have no objection."

"I'm happy for Mr Masters to sit with us afterwards," Harry confirmed. "But it will do no harm if he joins us now. He is Mrs Lydia Chapman's cousin and was staying in Burmarsh during the night of the murder."

"The cook and Lydia can vouch for my being safely ensconced at Rothschild Manor at the time Aaron was killed," Gerald added.

William couldn't help but grin at this and retorted, "I know! You didn't escape our initial list of suspects!"

"I'm glad of it," Gerald declared. "If I had been absolved from the start, then I would have little faith in the jury."

With the mood lightened between the men, William said, "Let us sit." His own bench scraped across the floor as he pulled it free from the table and seated himself. "I'll begin with what I wanted to speak to Harry about: We can't help wondering if Mr Bushy was set-up by his sons or one of them. John Waller has reported the butcher's words to his wife on the morning he was arrested. 'I told them I've not been out killing no one, not even you and I've a mind to sometimes' – that's quite a thing to say when you are being accused of murder. He's a man who doesn't have a good word to say to anyone and we have numerous reports of his foul behaviour towards his wife and sons. Harry, can you remind me what you heard on the morning of the trial. The jury were wanting to add this to our report."

"It was early, and I wanted to get some work done before the trial," Harry began. "There was no one about and, as I walked past the butcher's shop, I heard someone shout 'It's for the best Ma. Leave it be'. There was a reply, but I couldn't make it out."

"One of the sons," William said.

"It had to be."

"But it doesn't mean that they planned it," William acknowledged. "Just that it would be a blessing if a bully were to be gone from their lives."

"I wonder if it would be," Harry pondered. "Gone – maybe – but because he killed someone... The family would never be free of it."

"Perhaps it would be worth it," William suggested, narrowing his eyes. At that moment the serving wench neared with a tray holding two tankards brimming with ale and slopping dangerously close to the brandy. The men paused, knowing that she was eager to pick up any interesting snippet of their conversation.

"There you go, gents," she said, serving them each with a smile.

"Thank you." Harry pushed tuppence across the table towards her, giving a clear message that they required no more from her. She dipped a curtsy and left.

"If he were that much trouble to them," William continued, "perhaps they would be grateful to have him gone even if it meant that he swung from the gallows."

"It sounds like they were pleased, whether that was because they killed Aaron and framed their father, or because someone else did it," Gerald said. "But there is one thing that makes no sense – if the sons did it and wanted their father to be blamed, then why not use his knife? I believe the weapon found in the churchyard was the same as Anthony Bushy's, but not his own. The sons would have no difficulty in obtaining the knife."

"You're right," William admitted, "and it is the strongest thing in their favour. If it wasn't for this knife business, then I think we would have made an arrest by now. That's why I wanted to speak to Harry again."

"They remain suspects, but you continue the search," Gerald concluded.

"That's correct," William agreed. He took a swig of ale, and cautioned, "This is between us, please remember that."

"Indeed, that goes without saying," Gerald replied. "Now you may be interested in what I found out. There are some discoveries which I suspect will hold no surprise: for a start our little church at Burmarsh is – or was, because it's been moved on now – holding secrets in the form of packets of tea and lace." He noticed the feigned looks of surprise on his companions' faces and continued, "Now I believe our murdered friend was in the thick of this business of trading with the French, and I wonder if that is in some way connected? I have been provided with a name – Joss Bailey – and been subtly asking a few questions about him. It would appear that he was involved as well, and I know there was a disagreement between the two men very recently. It is common knowledge hereabouts that this Mr Bailey has a bit of a temper..."

"Joss Bailey," Harry repeated. Memories of himself being a newcomer to Dymchurch flashed through his mind – a stranger who had walked down from the hills with no connections to vouch for him as a decent law-abiding fellow. Harry had been twenty-one years of age with a head injury and he had offended Joss Bailey. The result of his words blurted in haste was a clout to the head from Joss' fist. Harry recalled waking on a damp clay bed at the base of the seawall, head pounding and confused. That was when he first met Owen Bates and John Waller with who he had become firm friends over the years. It was also Harry's introduction to the Dymchurch Wall, having arrived on the night it breached at an area known as Willop.

The next time he had seen Joss Bailey was in the courtroom. After a night in gaol, Harry had stood to face Sir Rupert, having been accused of theft. Sir Rupert

196

must have asked for anyone who could give an account of Harry's character – good or bad – to be there, because Joss Bailey sat at the edge of the courtroom, his stance menacing. He had relished giving his opinion of Harry – painting a picture of a young fool who impeded the urgent repairs to the seawall by wandering in front of a clay cart, seemingly with no awareness of the important task in hand. As magistrate, Sir Rupert had been lenient. Harry left the gaol bound over to remain in the village and labour on seawall repairs for the next six months. With Joss living near Butlers Bridge at West Hythe and Harry working at Wall End, the two rarely met and over the years an uneasy truce hung between them.

"Where was Joss Bailey on the night of the Michaelmas meal?" Harry wondered. "And, before that, I know he was not in the courtroom when the butcher was convicted, but was he in Dymchurch later that day when Anthony Bushy was shouting those words we know so well?"

"I'll look into it," William replied. "We have a man with a foul temper, likely to be in the thick of the smuggling and known to have argued with the victim recently."

"'A fight with fists' according to the lad who told me," Gerald elaborated. He took a sip of his brandy.

A clatter of hooves and a shout distracted the men. From their place by the window, they could look down on the street but stood to gain a better view. A pair of riding officers were moving at a fair pace through the village, scattering a small group of women and children. The sight was not uncommon, and without commenting on the scene Gerald returned to his seat and continued, "I have also been told about an argument involving a strip of land in the area of Gammon's Farm Lane." He frowned. "Odd sort of name – have I got it right?"

"You have," Harry confirmed. "And it makes sense because it's Newchurch and Aaron's land lies in that direction." He turned to William, who as a landowner would be more familiar with the ownership of fields, "Have you heard anything?"

"Oh yes!" William rolled his eyes. "I had to spend an afternoon at New Hall with Sir Rupert, George Bannerman and the bailiff over this. Waste of time. It was only a strip, as you said, and was proved to belong to Gammon's Farm. I don't see that there would have been any further bother over it, but I'll ride over and have a word with the farmer involved."

"And Mr Bailey?" Gerald asked, keeping his voice low and an eye on the serving wench who was nearing with an empty tray. "He seems like a more likely killer?"

"Any more drinks?" the girl asked. "Shall I fill those tankards?" She looked at Gerald and gave a dimpled smile, "Not you, sir. But a tot of brandy to warm you?"

"Maybe?" William glanced at his companions.

"No," Harry responded immediately. "I have things to do." He stood, aware the conversation was unfinished. To the girl, he said, "No more, thank you," in a clear indication that there was no need for her to loiter. She shrugged and gathered the empty vessels, then moved away, hips swaying suggestively.

"I have to leave on Friday," Gerald said. "You'll follow this up? My cousin seems oddly unconcerned about who the murderer is, but I would be more settled to know that he is snug in your gaol. Canterbury isn't far away, but when the weather worsens, as it is bound to, then it will be harder for her to get word to me if needed, and the journey for me will be arduous – although if needed, I will be here."

"I understand," Harry said, as he walked to the doorway and stood on the threshold to the seawall. "Your cousin has no family of her own here and feels

198

no connection to her husband's. If it were me, I would want to know the matter was in hand."

They stood, gazing past the fish sellers' shacks to the sea. "So... Mr Joss Bailey?" Gerald asked, "You'll look into his movements?"

"I'll speak to John Waller now, and ride over to West Hythe tomorrow," William confirmed. "Harry, will you come with me in the morning? It's not your business, I know, but I'd appreciate the company."

"You know we are not on the best of terms?"

"Oh, those troubles are in the past," William declared. "I could ask every jurat and landowner between Ivychurch and Hythe and none would be on good terms with Mr Bailey. Come with me? I'll go to Gammon's Farm alone, but not Butlers."

"Very well." Harry turned and began to walk towards the forge, forcing the others to move on. "Jesse leaves in the afternoon and I want to see him off, but I'll go with you to see Joss Bailey. I won't like it, but I'll meet you by New Hall at ten o'clock."

Chapter Nineteen
Harry

Despite their agreement to meet at New Hall, William Payne was rapping on the back door of Walker House by half-past nine that morning and minutes later he was settled at the kitchen table with a cup of tea provided by Janey.

"Marianne insisted I came with a message for Phoebe," he told Harry. "Janey and Mary have promised to pass it on – my wife and daughters are coming to Dymchurch later and plan to call here."

"I'm sure Phoebe will be pleased. She has already spoken of introducing Mireille," Harry responded. "But you've caught me in the middle of my accounts. I suppose if we leave now then I'll have time later this morning..." *Why must William always descend upon me without warning? I'd have liked another fifteen minutes to myself.* "I see you have made yourself comfortable!"

Raising his cup of tea towards Harry, William said, "They treat me well here. If I could lure Janey and Mary away to St Mary in the Marsh, then I'd be well cared for!"

Harry laughed. "I wouldn't allow it!"

"Tea before you go?" Janey asked Harry.

"Not for me, thank you. I'll get my jacket and boots, then we can be on our way." The chestnut had already been fetched from the stable at the forge earlier that morning. Then to William, he said, "Let's set off to Butlers. I can't say I'm looking forward to this, but there are affairs that need settling before I can get back to work here in Dymchurch. I'd like to get this over and done with."

Astride their horses, the men soon left the coastal village behind, taking the road towards Burmarsh. On their way they passed several donkey carts laden with clay, each of them led by a local lad gripping the halter. The road was littered with clods of sticky earth, and it covered the hands and breeches of those who walked to and from the seawall, loading and unloading at either end.

"Busy time for them," William commented.

"They found a crack near Beacon Knocke," Harry responded. There was no need to give a further explanation. All the locals knew that November brought the stormiest weather and in the coming weeks the wall-workers had to be extra vigilant for any sign of a weakening in the seawall. The water which seeped in at this time would freeze and swell in the coming months, causing further deterioration in the usual robustness of the structure.

Before reaching Burmarsh, they turned the horses into Donkey Street and rode directly towards the steep hills bordering Romney Marsh. With the tree branches now bare, the castle and church were prominent atop the hill and, below, the slumped walls of an ancient Roman fort lay bathed in weak autumnal sunshine.

"Did you go to Gammon's?" Harry asked, suddenly recalling the recent tension between Aaron and a neighbouring farmer.

"Yes, and I was told there had been no further problems," William told him. "He reminded me that, at the time, all Aaron did was move some sheep over the bridge and onto his field. It was nothing as serious as ploughing the land or fencing it off. When we met at New Hall, there was no denying the field was Gammon's Farm land and it seemed that Aaron accepted this." He looked back across the acres of almost flat land, bleached of colour by the summer sun and brisk winds. "He's removed the bridge, the farmer has. Stops any nonsense but... well, you know it's damned inconvenient."

While pondering the removal of a bridge, the friends found themselves nearing Butlers Farm, a place midway between Burmarsh and the hillside marking the edge of the Marsh.

They knew, of course, that seeking Mr Joss Bailey could involve further riding – as a farmer, it was unlikely he would be found at home. However, they were in luck to find his wife tending the last of her summer roses which took pride of place in front of a rambling house of indeterminate age. With a frown on her face, and knife raised, she appeared to be considering lopping a withering bloom. On hearing the horses' hooves come to a halt, Mrs Bailey turned, and gave a nod of recognition. "You'll be looking for him, I suppose."

"Good morning, Mrs Bailey." William's tone contrasted with that of the sour-faced woman. "Is your husband at home, or nearby?"

"He's out on business at the tavern under the hill." She jerked her head in the direction of the escarpment.

"Thank you," William replied. "We'll head in that direction."

"If we miss him, perhaps you could tell Mr Bailey that we were looking for him," Harry suggested.

"I can tell him," she responded, implying that it would make no difference.

"We'll call back if we don't meet up with him," William suggested.

"Maybe I'll see you then." Mrs Bailey returned to her roses, deciding to allow the bloom to live another day.

The men urged their horses to walk on and soon reached a collection of no more than half a dozen cottages scattered on the very edge of Romney Marsh. Not even a chapel served this settlement but, in a small plot, skeletal remains of a Norman church rose from their foundations.

Dismounting at the base of the escarpment, they spotted the tavern squatting in the shadows of ancient oak and beech trees. Harry could only surmise that being on this road from Canterbury to Romney Marsh was the reason for it receiving any trade, for it looked to be a miserable place, unkempt and pokey. However, in contrast, it boasted a row of smart stables, and for a moment he thought of Gerald Masters, who would be passing this very spot the following day. *No doubt he will be eager to leave Burmarsh behind him – he is leading an idle life here, and I believe it does not suit him.*

But I am not here to consider Gerald Masters. Harry shook himself back to the present as he approached the tavern.

"Can I take your horses, sirs?" A stablehand appeared.

I don't know that we need them taken anywhere," William replied. "We are looking for a Mr Bailey. Is he here? Have you seen him?"

"Mr Bailey from Butlers?" the boy asked. "He's here. I've got his horse."

"Well then, Harry here can take my reins and I'll seek out Joss Bailey," William responded.

The boy grunted and turned away, no doubt feeling he had been cheated out of a tip.

By the time the horses had snatched at some lush grass, William had returned with Joss Bailey. "He'll ride back with us," he announced.

Mr Bailey paused on the step of the tavern, his stocky frame filling the doorway. Despite the chill in the air, he wore no cloak over his tunic, so the breadth of his chest and thickness of his neck was pronounced, reminding Harry of the bull they had passed on the road to West Hythe. He ran a hand through greying waves of pale ginger hair and snarled, "What's he doing here?"

"Harry came along with me because this is important, Mr Bailey, and I don't want to be blamed if I mishear anything. He's a sensible chap, as you know, so you'd do well to be friendly." William shrugged off the animosity and took the reins of his horse while they waited for the stablehand to bring Joss' beast.

"Good morning, Joss. This is jury business, and it will be William asking the questions, not me," Harry offered. "I hope you and your wife are keeping well," he added. An unnecessary nicety which was ignored by the farmer.

There was an awkward silence, thankfully broken by Joss' gelding being returned to him, and the boy receiving a penny. Soon the men turned their backs to the hillside and headed towards Butlers Farm, keeping the horses on a loose rein.

"What's this about?" Joss asked before they had taken no more than a dozen steps.

"We'll start with you storing goods in Burmarsh church," William began.

"It's as good a place as any," Joss responded. "So, this is smuggler business? You're wanting to be more involved? You already make good money for your fleeces, William, and your labourers earn well."

"I said it was jury business," William reminded him.

"You did."

204

"What led you to use the church as a hide?"

With no immediate response, they walked on in silence for a moment, the farmer's temper clearly smouldering. Harry noticed how his fists, as square as mallets, clenched on the reins. A twisted branch of blackthorn lay in the road and Joss pointed towards it with the tow of his boot. "Wasteful!" he snapped. "I'd give whoever dropped that a good whipping."

Ignoring this, William persevered, "Why was there trouble over you storing something in All Saints? We're all on the same side – us against the customs officers. We all understand you can hardly go putting kegs of brandy or bolts of material in your own barns."

"I wouldn't usually put it there," Joss replied. "You're right about us all being on the same side, but it was placed so close to Chapman that he thought he could take it as his own. My place – my usual hide – was flooded and I had to act fast. He had nothing to store that night, so it made no difference to him."

Now the three men hardly saw the sun on the browning leaves or how it lent that last golden glow to the withered reeds. They were all in a different time – a summer's night when the call of an owl signalled movement of men and packhorses around the twisting rural tracks, and French boats came as close as they dared to the shallow beach at Dymchurch for the exchange of untaxed goods.

"What did he do with it?" William asked.

"He moved it on before I had a chance to get back to it," Joss replied. His voice could not have held more bitterness. "He was closer, wasn't he? It was nothing for him to keep an eye on it and pay a few of his men to snatch it."

"That's all wrong," William responded. "It's not how we do things."

"It's not how you do it and," Joss jerked his head in Harry's direction, "it's not how he'd do it if he were one of us. It wasn't just me who he cheated that night, but my men who were due to be earning. It was going off the Marsh to Tenterden and they'd have done well from it."

"Did you go after Aaron's men?" William asked.

"That's exactly what we did." Now there was approval in Joss' tone. He knew that William understood the way the Marshmen traded, and that those who had been thwarted would have known the routes due to be taken. Without the burden of carrying contraband, it should have been no trouble for Joss' men to catch up and demand their brandy and lace was returned to them.

Through his years of living in Dymchurch, Harry did not have to be actively involved to understand the process. He could imagine a trail of men and packhorses following a track by night, alert to any danger from the riding officers, listening for the call to warn of troubles ahead or to the rear. On their tails, he imagined a group able to move swiftly. It would take no time at all for them to catch up with the thieves. Sickened to think of the bloody battle bound to follow the two groups meeting, Harry feared Joss' next words.

"But they weren't using the usual route. They knew we'd be after them – hell's teeth, they did – so they chose another way. My men searched for hours but they were too bloody late."

Harry felt his body relax. *Thank God there was no blood lost between these men who should be allies.*

"You and your men returned with nothing, and Aaron became richer that night," William stated. "You must have been angry – hated him for it."

Joss let out a guffaw. "Blazes! I see your game! No need to kill the scoundrel – I'd have got my own back

206

sooner or later. There was another run within a week, and I did handsomely out of it."

"Where were you on that night when the Lords and jurats met?" William asked.

"Home by the fireside with my wife," Joss responded. "Where else would I have been?"

William ignored this. "I guess you know the butcher, Anthony Bushy? Did you hear about him being in court for dabbling with his weights?"

"I do business with the butchers in Hythe," the farmer responded. "Never dealt with a Dymchurch butcher in my life, nor my father before me. Hythe is the place for us."

"But did you hear about a Dymchurch butcher cheating with his weights?"

Joss was slow in his response, "I can't say that I did."

By now the men had passed a junction where two narrow lanes wended their way to the coast. The farmer had been open in his dislike for Aaron and his account of the smuggled goods being taken and moved seemed credible – there was no need for further questioning. No evidence placed Joss Bailey at the scene of the crime, and his name had not been linked with the purchase of a knife identical to the butcher's one. Harry pondered this as they approached Butlers Farm and saw no further line of questioning. William fell silent and it seemed that he had no more to ask. *Or has he reached the point where what we have discovered must be shared with the jury? This man has a temper, and we would be wise not to rile him.*

They parted without exchanging pleasantries and, as soon as the two friends had left Butlers behind them, they encouraged their horses to break into a trot. Minutes later they eased to a walk. With a distance between themselves and Joss, they were able to speak freely.

"I can't help agreeing with him," William said. "Aaron did wrong, but Joss could have outwitted him soon enough. He's been working in the smuggling business for ten years longer than Aaron and is wily enough."

"But was he so angry that he plotted this greater revenge?" Harry wondered.

"Joss is a man who reacts instantly. When did this happen – this incident with the stolen goods?" William asked. "I believe it to be a month or so before the murder."

"Not long before," Harry pointed out.

"Long enough to simmer down," William countered.

They rode in silence along Donkey Street, both glancing at Rothschild Manor on the outskirts of Burmarsh before turning their horses towards Dymchurch. Harry relived Joss' words in his mind and considered the times when he had heard of the man's temper. On nearing the coast, William spoke again, "How would he know what type of knife the butcher had?"

Startled from his thoughts, Harry frowned and asked, "Type of knife?"

"If Joss Bailey killed Aaron, then he had to know what was said at the time of the murder *and* what type of knife the butcher used. These were the details which led us to accuse the wrong man."

"You're right," Harry agreed. Bringing himself back to the present, he allowed his gaze to linger on the buildings at Slodden Farm, then across the field to the seawall. "The knife," he continued. "Of course, Joss would have to know. Did he tell the truth about never dealing with Dymchurch butchers? Was there a reason for him going there and discovering what kind of knife was used?"

"I'll ask Mr Bushy myself!" William declared.

"Ask him?"

"Why not? If we can't place Joss as being somewhere he could have heard those words we know so well…"

"I can still go butchering," Harry added.

"Exactly! …then perhaps we could find out if he knew what knife was used to do the butchering."

"It's worth covering everything. At least then Joss Bailey can be ruled out – or not." They were now nearing the Ship, and Harry's home was almost in sight. Hoping to return to work, he asked, "Can I leave you to it now? It doesn't take two of us to update the constable."

"That's fine," William agreed. "I'll see the butcher, then John Waller, and be back at St Mary in the Marsh as my dinner is dished up."

Harry couldn't help but smile at his friend's optimism – certain that midday had passed and knowing William would enjoy a lengthy discussion with John Waller. It was unlikely he would reach his kitchen table before his family had eaten. Not that William would grumble about eating a meal kept covered and warm by the fire. Recalling that Marianne and the girls were planning a trip to Dymchurch that afternoon, Harry imagined them all meeting on the road between St Mary in the Marsh and Dymchurch.

"I'll help you out with something," Harry suggested. "I hoped to go to work but it's too late for me to focus on anything in the forge, so I'd like to see the knifesmith. Perhaps he will recollect Joss Bailey buying a knife similar to the murder weapon. It's no trouble for me to ask as I already have some business with him."

"I'd appreciate that," William responded as they slowed outside Walker House.

"If there's any news, I'll tell John Waller, and pass on a message through Marianne," Harry told him as he dismounted. "Although I know he's been asked more than once. I'll see you soon, my friend."

"Thanks for your company," William replied, tightening the reins and pressing on the flanks of his horse.

Ned Dugman, silver-haired knifesmith, practised his trade in the front parlour of his home which shared the same terrace as the Rose Inn. Harry tethered the chestnut to a post outside and noted the front door was ajar. Rapping on it, he walked in. "Good day, Ned. Do you have a moment?"

The men were well known to each other, both practising the skill of metalwork. Today the knifesmith was seated on a stool shaping a wooden handle. Shavings and sawdust trailed down his coarse apron and littered the floor at his feet. On a bench, placed to benefit from the light pouring through the window, pots of nails in various sizes pressed against small hammers, pliers and clamps. A broom and pan rested against a set of drawers with a cupboard above, home to more tools, pieces of wood, metal blades and fixings.

"Good afternoon to you, Harry." Ned continued to smooth the wood but offered a welcoming nod. "How can I help you? Sit down, won't you?"

Harry perched on an armchair covered in a sheet of hessian. On a Saturday afternoon, both chairs would be revealed as the cloth was removed, shaken out, and folded before being stored in one of the drawers. The floor would be thoroughly swept by Mrs Dugman, and the bench cleared by Mr Dugman. The knifesmith and his wife would then eat their Sunday dinner in the front room before it was once more transformed to a workshop.

"I'm asking about the knife," Harry began. "The one that was used to kill Aaron Chapman but didn't belong to Anthony Bushy. You know the type?"

"I make them every so often," Ned replied, his fingers still busy with the sandpaper and wood. "The constable told me it was a new knife, or at least one that had been kept as new."

"Do you ever see Joss Bailey about the village?" Harry asked. "You've got a good spot here. You see people passing by."

"I see him every now and then, but half the time I'm looking down at my work or out by the fire." Ned had a small forge in a brick shed at the end of his back yard.

Harry didn't probe any further. The mention of Joss would have created a reaction if Ned had sold him a knife in the past few months. Conversation moved onto other matters, and the men spoke amicably for a few minutes before Harry left.

Back on the High Street, he untied his horse and headed towards the forge. The skies above New Romney were grey, and it was likely Dymchurch would receive a soaking before dinner time.

"I'll be here this afternoon, but out again to see Jesse off," he assured Matthew and Jack from the doorway of the forge, but with half an eye on the ominous clouds.

"You just missed him," Jack said. "He came to say his goodbyes."

As he walked home, Harry spotted Mireille at the doorway of Bess and Owen's cottage and waved. *I'm certain that Jesse is in love with her, and she is part, if not all, of the reason why he plans to stay in Wissant, and there's no doubting her feelings for him. Now he is going, and she is staying here. Has anything been said… anything been declared before he goes?*

Chapter Twenty
Jesse

"You're really going back then? Back to stay?" Jack asked while washing his hands at a deep sink. "It's been good to meet you and thanks for coming to say goodbye. There's often been talk about what happened."

"I'm going back," Jesse confirmed. "It's become my home."

Over the past few days Jesse had found that he could speak openly with Jack as they worked side-by-side in the forge. Unlike Jesse's family, Harry's employee had no particular interest in the outcome of this visit from Wissant. Instead, Jack showed a curiosity about the village – its customs, trades and people – without seeking opportunities to prove Dymchurch was the better place to be.

"Good luck to you then. I'd have liked you to stay because there's work here for us all now Harry's buying that old forge over by the Ship, but if Wissant's the place for you then I'm pleased." Jack dried his hands and glanced through the open doorway towards Matthew who was in the yard shovelling charcoal into a small handcart. "I wondered how it would be with you and him and well... you know... But it's been all right."

"It's in the past now."

From a distance Jesse had seen Lucy a few times during the week he had been back in Dymchurch. She had been spotted walking into a village shop, gossiping with other women on the corner where Mill Road met the High Street and even stepping into her cottage along Eastbridge Road.

This last sighting had been when Harry asked him to ride out to deliver some hinges to a farmer. It had been strange to see her at the home she had made with his cousin, Matthew, and he had pondered as to why she had married within a few months of him leaving Dymchurch. Where would he and Lucy have settled if life had continued as expected? Before Aaron Chapman had interfered with his plans.

At that moment, a couple of days ago, when she had stood on the threshold of her home, Lucy had turned, her changed figure in full view, albeit swathed in a woollen cloak. Her second child was due within days. For some reason he couldn't quite fathom, this had caught him off guard. The pregnancy had not been obvious before, hidden by a shopping basket or her first child held in her arms. She was no longer the young woman on the brink of marriage with him, but a woman with a family and home. No longer *his* Lucy. Jesse had not, in the seven days he had now been in Dymchurch, considered going to see her, and Matthew had not invited him to their home.

"All in the past," Jack repeated, bringing Jesse to the present. "Thanks for coming to say goodbye."

"Well, I'll be off. It's been good meeting you and no doubt I'll be back one summer," Jesse said before turning towards Matthew, "See you, Matt." Absorbed in his work the other man offered a half-hearted wave.

Jesse had intended to go home and spend time with his mother, but his mind was so full of memories that he wandered, lost in thought, away from the High Street. It took a moment for him to realise that rather than

213

approaching the family home at Dormers Cottages, he was passing Mackett's Cottages and then the school. He paused, momentarily bewildered as to why he had taken the wrong turning. After all, to walk from the forge to Dormers was as natural to him as putting his shirt on after his vest.

"Hello Jesse." A soft voice came from behind him, and there she was – looking older and a little weary, but still Lucy. "You're looking lost."

"I was!"

"Shall we walk together?" she asked.

"I will for a moment."

In her arms there was a small child – a boy, Jesse had heard, although they looked much the same to him at that young age. His gaze fixed on the young boy who, in response, stared back intently. Aware that the child's weight pushing the basket against her swollen belly was making Lucy uncomfortable and tired, Jesse's next words came in a rush, "I'm sorry, can I help? The basket?"

"Thank you." Lucy extracted it from the crook of her arm.

They took a few steps before Jesse spoke again, "It must have been a shock when you heard I might be coming back."

"I was pleased for you, but it brought back memories of… of… well, you know."

"I know. They thought I would have asked you to come to Wissant, but I couldn't provide for you there," Jesse explained. "Anyway, you found a better man."

"Not better," Lucy corrected him, "but someone who was here. And you found a reason to stay in Wissant."

"A reason?"

"A woman. Mrs Farrers' cousin."

Jesse should not have been surprised that in a small place such as Dymchurch, and with a young

French woman in their midst, the villagers would have come to such an obvious conclusion. Yet to hear those words from Lucy startled him. "No! No, Mireille is just..." But now he was being unfair and knew it because Mireille was not *just* a member of Phoebe's family. She was someone quite special. Very special. "She welcomed me and taught me French," he said, knowing that his words sounded awkward.

"You were lucky then," Lucy acknowledged. "I often thought of you and wondered what it was like to move to a foreign land and to have to start again. I've heard you speak it – French, I mean – like you belong there, and you look different too."

"It's been a while."

They stopped outside her home, one of four cottages and, having stood her son on the step, she reached for the door handle. "Did you want to come in?" she asked. "You're Matthew's cousin, after all," she added, in an attempt to justify the invitation.

Jesse made his excuses, "Thank you, but I have to get back to Ma. I'm leaving this afternoon." He had spoken to Lucy and that was enough to lay any ghosts to rest. He wouldn't say this to her, but she was now just another woman in Dymchurch and one of many people he had known through the years of growing up in the village. They had spent many a pleasant time together, but he felt no urge to linger. "Good to see you and I'm pleased for you and Matthew with your home and your little boy, and... and I'll see you again sometime."

"Safe journey home."

Home. The word stayed in his mind longer than the image of Lucy with her son on her hip. *I'll be back there soon.* He envisaged those prolonged stretches at sea, comforting Mireille if she were to suffer from sickness

215

again, and the time when all sign of land had disappeared. It would be during those uneventful hours that they would scour the horizon, welcoming the sight of another vessel, and would give an unseen nod in its direction. Then the white sands and the rambling dunes would come into view, and the family there on the beach to welcome them back. Later, at the table, how the questions would flow with everyone speaking at once, battling to be heard over each other. *But she won't be there!* Realisation came to him with a jolt. *It won't be like that at all. Yes, there will be questions, but they won't be pleased. Will I be so welcome once they realise their daughter… their sister… their niece is staying behind? It won't be the same at all.*

I must find her. Jesse realised that he had been standing in the street outside Lucy and Matthew's cottage. The day, which had promised to be bright, had changed and a light rain now fell upon him. It obliterated the view of distant fields and threatened to seep through his cloak. *I must find her.* He began to walk at a brisk pace, striding along, determined not to pause and exchange pleasantries with anyone he passed. *She'll be with Bess. I'll wait outside for her. Or on the Wall – perhaps that would be better?* Crossing the High Street, he then weaved his way past cottages and up the seawall, only stopping when he reached the top. He pulled his cloak tighter and turned his back to the sea, watching Bates Cottage so as to ensure he wouldn't miss Mireille leaving. Not certain whether she would take the route on to the top of the seawall or the main road home, he knew from this vantage point he could easily spot her and catch up with her whichever way she went.

There she is! If I'd lingered, I'd have missed her. His stomach churned at the thought of it. As Mireille walked along the High Street, Jesse trailed her and waited to see if she chose to turn off towards the seawall. The Wall obviously beckoned – he saw her turn but then lost her amongst the shacks where the fishermen sold their catch. Within moments, their paths met, and he noticed her pause in her tracks then offer a wide smile.

"Jesse! Have you come to see me?" Mireille asked, her voice soft and face sweet.

Now as she stood before him, Jesse froze and all thoughts of expressing his newfound feelings were lost. Flowing sentences, previously formed in his mind, became a mix of rambling words. He opened his mouth... and closed it again. *Why did I never notice how perfect she is? Why did I never see that she is more than Phoebe's cousin?* He glanced out to sea. It was grey, echoing the colour of the sky. The intensity of the rain increased and as he opened his mouth to speak his voice failed. A sudden gust of rain-laden wind struck his throat. He felt wretched, embarrassed, and the words he desperately wanted to say remained unsaid.

"You are leaving today," Mireille prompted, breaking an awkward silence. "You'll tell them that I am needed here? Phoebe needs me."

"I'll tell them," he managed to splutter.

Footsteps closed in on them and Jesse received a slap on the back. "Come on. Ma will have the dinner ready and won't be best pleased if you're up here."

"Bye then," Jesse continued, the moment for confidences now hopelessly lost. "I'll see you when you come back home. Soon, I hope..." But his brother had no time for Jesse or the French girl who, regardless of the fact she was staying in Dymchurch, was believed to be the reason for him choosing to make Wissant his home.

"Think of Ma," Joe persisted. "And the rest of us. It's not easy seeing you going off again."

Jesse shrugged.

"Safe journey. *Bon voyage*," Mireille said as she moved away.

He could see the sadness in her dark eyes and the slight downturn of her perfectly formed lips. "I'll see you soon," Jesse repeated, but perhaps she hadn't heard him. He had hesitated before speaking and Mireille had already stepped away.

"It's probably for the best that she stays here," Joe muttered.

"Why?" Jesse frowned. *It's best for Harry and Phoebe, but that's not what he means. Why's it best for Mireille? And what does it have to do with Joe?* "What difference does it make to you where she is?"

The brothers were striding to the High Street now. Jesse looked back towards the seawall before facing Dormers and the last meal with his family. There was no sign of Mireille.

"Because she's French from that place over there and you're Romney Marsh from here." Joe didn't look at his brother as he spoke, and Jesse was shocked by the bitterness in his tone. "You're going back over there and maybe if she's not there, it won't seem so special. You've come here with your new ways – your clothes and your new fancy words – and you don't care to think what it's like for Ma and Pa to be losing you all over again. All you think about is that Mi-ray... that cousin of Mrs Farrers. She's not for you. I don't know why you even bothered to come back."

The outburst shocked and sickened Jesse. All this from his brother who wasn't known to be much of a talker. This wasn't an argument to be taken into the home, so Jesse stopped and began his response. "There's no understanding between me and Mireille. She's just part of the family who took care of me. Would you have wanted me to be transported to the Americas?

218

Because that's what Sir Julian had planned. It's been three years. Three years, Joe. I had to make a life for myself and be grateful for the friendship offered by the Bernards."

"You didn't have to change. Change your ways."

"I had to fit in. Do you think Phoebe's father would have lived here in Dymchurch and not taken the trouble to learn English?"

"He had the sense to go back," Joe spat at him.

The subject of Jacques Bernard was complicated and not one to be aired at this time, so Jesse ignored it and said, "Mireille is staying because Phoebe and Harry need her help. It's nothing to do with me and her. I'll miss her, but she's doing a great thing." He paused to consider his next words. "Look, Joe, I do understand how this has come as a shock to everyone. I had to make a choice back in Wissant when the letter came. I felt it was my home now. There's work for me here if I want, and the family, but it still feels like home is over there, across the Channel."

Joe could only mutter, "It doesn't seem right, and it won't seem right when Ma's in tears and Pa's in a dark mood."

"You've done all right over the past few years and now you'll know I can come back to see you."

"We'll remember you decided to make your home there." Joe moved away and walked briskly to Dormers, opening the front door and leaving it ajar for Jesse.

Mopping his plate with a chunk of bread, Jesse knew it would lie heavy, but his mother was watching his every move. The slightest wrong word would cause more offence during this last family meal. Both brothers were there, although why Philip came, Jesse could not fathom. *He's barely said a thing to me, and if that's the way he wants to be, then he should be at home with his*

219

wife and child. Sarah and Albie spoke in bursts, recalling memories of happier occasions and encouraging their sons to join in. No one mentioned Wissant.

"You don't ask about it," Jesse spoke before he could contain the words. "You don't ask about what the village is like with its marketplace, or about the fishing boats, or the beach. It's got sands that are almost white – imagine that!"

Philip rose suddenly from the table, causing his chair to scrape across the brick floor. He dropped a kiss on Sarah's head and left, the door slamming behind him.

"We don't ask because we know all about it," Sarah stated. She leaned forward and reached for the plates, her movements slow as if a leaden cloak covered her body.

Jesse pushed his plate towards her. "You know about it?"

"When we heard where you were, Harry told us all about the place and the people who were looking out for you," Albie told him.

"And you didn't want to find out more? To ask me about it?"

"I didn't think about needing to," Sarah responded as she stood and lifted the stack of plates, then turned away from the table.

"It's just a village the other side of the Channel, isn't it?" Albie shrugged and he too got up from the table. Reaching for his cloak, he continued with, "It will be the same as here or near enough. Just different people, speaking different." Then he handed Joe his jacket and said, "Here you go, son. We mustn't be late."

"I'll see you when I go along to Wall End then," Jesse reminded them.

"That's right," Albie replied. Without a hug or a pat on the arm, he was gone, Joe trailing behind him.

Sarah now removed a kettle of hot water from the fire and headed towards the scullery, tipping it into a large bowl. From the open doorway, Jesse reached out and said, "Let me fill it for you, Ma." He took the kettle and topped it up from a jug on the floor, then settled it back onto the trivet over the smouldering embers. "By the time it's boiling, I'll have packed my bag and then we can have a cup of tea. If you like?"

His mother didn't answer, so he opened a door to the side of the chimney breast and took the stairs two at a time, ducking as he entered the bedroom which was now Joe's. Having checked the trunk at the bottom of the bed, and the clothes on the pegs, Jesse found nothing of his. A bag lay part open on the floor; he pulled the ties, knotted them and stood by the low window framed with thatch, peering on to the street below. It was quiet, most people having returned home or dropped into the local pubs for their midday break.

This time staring out of the window gave Jesse an opportunity to reflect on his time at home. *I can't blame them for being upset when I said I was going back to Wissant, but I wish they would try to understand. I wish they would show some interest in my home and the people there.* He glanced back at the room, his gaze roaming across the two beds, around the beamed ceiling and up to the apex in the roof, then back to the window. *Dymchurch isn't a bad place, and I could make a room like this my home. But not here. Not here sharing with Joe. I'd have to get a room somewhere, like I have back in Wissant. I'd get used to working for Harry again and be happy enough.* Yet there was something that stopped him doing what was, in many ways, the right thing. *It's not my home anymore. It's as simple as that. Mireille will return to France. I'm sure*

221

she will, but I don't know if there's a chance for me... for me and her.

Back downstairs, the kettle was boiling, and Jesse made the tea, then sat near the fire in an armchair. At his feet, the canvas bag slumped. His mother joined him, and they spoke a little, both skirting around what they really wanted to express. He could tell she was resisting the urge to beg him to stay – or to at least think about returning to make a life in Dymchurch the next summer. In turn, Jesse wanted to tell her about the small aspects of life in Wissant. Had she allowed him to, maybe Sarah would have been interested in the domestic details, but he knew her mind was closed to such things.

"Time to make a move," he said when the mug was drained. His mother made no reply as Jesse reached for his thick cloak and then for the bag.

Finally, as he waited for Sarah to wrap herself up for the walk to the fishing boats, she said, "I'll say my goodbyes here, Jesse."

Shocked, he couldn't think of how to reply, but instead wrapped his arms around her so her head tucked under his chin. He held his mother tightly for a moment, his reaction perhaps better than any words. Then he merely said, "I'll miss you, Ma. See you next year."

By the time Jesse reached the seawall, he was dashing tears away with the back of his hand.

Harry caught up as Jesse left Dymchurch behind him, heading for Wall End. They exchanged few words, but his company was appreciated. He didn't need to be told that there was friction within the Alder family, and although Jesse's father and brothers left their work packing clay into the landward side of the seawall to see him off, they too barely spoke.

It was a relief to join Walter and Joshua with *Louisa-Ann,* and to help them push her down the skids until she was ready to catch the tide. Then Jesse gave each of his family a brief hug, and they made polite sounds about wishing him a safe journey. Harry grasped his hand firmly and said, "She won't be staying here, you know. She'll be back with you in the spring." There was no time for Jesse to explore or expand on these words, but they lingered in his mind throughout those long hours at sea.

Dusk came and the sky darkened until stars shone as best they could through wispy clouds. An hour or so after most of the people of Wissant had retired to bed, *Louisa-Ann's* bow rested on the pale sands, and Jesse prepared to tell Mireille's parents that she had remained with her cousin in Dymchurch.

Chapter Twenty-One
Harry

"I've invited Lydia here this afternoon," Phoebe told Harry as the family gathered at the kitchen table for their midday meal. "I fear she was far too attached to Gerald – she seemed to depend on him for everything – and now he has returned to Canterbury."

"Yes, he left the day after Jesse," Harry replied. He looked up at Janey as she placed a large pot of mutton stew in the centre of the table. "Thank you. It looks delicious." Then back to Phoebe. "It's been three days and I am sure she must be missing his support. Perhaps another member of the family will visit?"

"I worry that while her sister or mother would be welcome, her feelings for Gerald go... go beyond that of cousin." Phoebe stood to dish two small servings for the twins. Janey immediately added a slosh of milk, and the bowls were handed to Mireille to cut and mash the meat and vegetables. All this was completed with no words exchanged and none needed.

"I sensed nothing of that in Gerald, but we were not speaking of such things," Harry said before thanking Phoebe for his own serving. He reached forward and took a hunk of bread.

"It's not something men talk about," Phoebe suggested. "Unless there is a particular friendship." She helped Esther load her spoon. All the children were swathed in aprons, and she adjusted her elder daughter's a little to ensure Esther's skirt was fully covered. Satisfied, she continued with, "I can only hope that the friendship offered by myself and Marianne will help ease Lydia's loneliness."

"Will Lydia go to the *fête du feu de joie*?" Mireille asked, her eyes lighting up at the thought of a planned evening adventure which would take them by horse and cart to the home of William and Marianne Payne.

"Bonfire," Phoebe supplied. "Bonfire party – or Gunpowder Treason Day. I don't know. We'll go as a family group, the three of us. I'm not sure if there is anyone for her to travel with."

James dropped his spoon, causing a clatter on the floor and a squeal of glee from him, while Clara let out a wail then dropped her spoon. This was followed by the inevitable fuss: scrambling about to secure the spoons, inspecting them for dirt and a quick rinse in the scullery. Then Clara's apron had to be re-tied and all was peaceful, now with both Janey and Mireille feeding the twins.

"I've never seen fire... fireworks," Mireille told them.

"What's fireworks?" Esther asked.

"Pretty lights in the sky," Harry replied. "At night when it's dark and cold. Like the sparks that fly from my metalwork!"

"Pretty lights," Esther repeated as she mulled over the idea. "Like stars?"

"Like orange stars," he told her. Then he looked at Phoebe, "Do you think...?"

"That would be lovely!" she responded. "Esther, you can come with us."

The little girl beamed her pleasure, although not quite understanding what she was to be a part of.

"Mrs Chapman is in mourning," Janey commented in between mouthfuls.

"Both Mrs Chapmans. All the Chapmans," Mary supplied.

"Of course they are." Phoebe scraped the last of the stew from Esther's bowl to her spoon. "Mireille, we must not say a word about it if we see Lydia."

"It is forgotten!" Mireille pursed her lips but couldn't contain a smile. "Now I'll help Janey and you will go to see Bess?"

Mary was already finding the apron ties and releasing the twins from their highchairs. "We'll go and look at some story books." Once Esther had told her what was on the cover of the book, Mary was able to relay the story from memory, something which never failed to impress Harry and Phoebe. After their midday meal, she usually took Esther, and now James and Clara, to the parlour where they all soon became absorbed in the pleasure of retelling a favourite story. The younger children would prod at the pictures with chubby fingers and babble away, while Esther showed a curiosity about the story and characters, frequently interjecting in the storytelling.

"I'll be at my desk and then I'm off to New Hall," Harry reminded Phoebe.

"Oh? Oh, yes! Of course, you are," she said while wiping Esther's hands. "There's always so much going on. I hope... I hope this is the end of it all."

Harry left Walker House not long after and walked briskly to New Hall. November was now upon them and, other than the yew in the nearby churchyard, the tree branches stretched out bare towards the grey sky. Leaves, so recently crisp and golden brown, now made sludgy piles against the churchyard walls and clung firmly to the strong upright post of the gallows. This was not the case on the gravel forecourt of the Bannermans' home, seat of law and order on the Marsh. Tended daily, sometimes twice daily, by Brown or some boy servant instructed by him, this area was immaculate. Nothing the manservant considered to be unsightly was allowed to soil his domain.

Before Harry had lifted his hand to the knocker, the door was opening, and Brown revealed himself. "Good afternoon, Mr Farrers," he said, offering a brief nod of respect.

"Good afternoon, Brown. I hope you are keeping well?"

"I am, sir. Thank you."

With this Harry strode across the flagstones and took the stairs two at a time. Here he almost collided with Sir Rupert who was entering the courtroom from his private entrance to the house. "Blazes, Harry. Must you rush about so?"

"I wish I didn't have to, sir."

"Serious stuff today," Sir Rupert reminded him as they walked through the empty courtroom. "Mr Payne must refrain from speaking of Gunpowder Treason Day, or any other such nonsense. I rely on you to keep him in check."

"Will you and Lady Charlotte be at the bonfire party?" Harry enquired.

"Wouldn't miss it! We're taking both coaches as the vicar is travelling with us as well as George, Eleanor and Gabriel."

"Excellent!"

Stepping through into the jury room, they came into an airy space, boasting an ornate fireplace and, in the recesses, cupboards reaching from floor to ceiling. A long table, set out to seat eight on each side with ease, took centre stage and already it was filling with members of the jury entrusted with solving the murder of Aaron Chapman. John Waller was making himself comfortable as they arrived, and William shot into the room as Harry pulled out a chair to sit in.

Sir Rupert placed himself in an empty chair at the head of the table. Clearly in no mood to linger or engage in idle chatter, he scanned the faces at the table and stated, "There's enough of us here to begin. Plenty to get through, so I suggest we proceed."

At this moment there came a discrete cough and they all turned to see Brown at the doorway. "Mr Chapman senior," he announced.

Mr Chapman, a man who had aged ten years in the past weeks since his son's untimely death, stepped forward. "Can I join you?" he asked, his voice wavering. All the confidence he was known for had disappeared. He had never been a large man in height or girth, but now his face hollowed beneath his cheekbones and his shoulders slumped forward.

"Come in, Andrew," Sir Rupert stood and gestured to an empty chair opposite Harry. "You're welcome, of course."

No one spoke as Mr Chapman, bereaved parent, landowner and jurat, walked around the table and seated himself. There was a murmur of welcome... of support, along with nods and brief smiles, but none of it seemed to touch the newcomer in the room. Harry noted that he made no eye contact with any other man at the table and settled with his gaze upon the oak surface before him.

"This will be painful," Sir Rupert acknowledged. "I ask that everyone keeps to the point, and we spare no time speculating. Today I wish to deal in the facts and only the facts."

Nearly all those assembled had their attention fully upon Sir Rupert. Only Andrew Chapman kept his gaze averted, as if the patterns in the wood grain were of the utmost interest.

"On Thursday 10th October, Mr Anthony Bushy was acquitted of the murder of Mr Aaron Chapman. Despite there being strong evidence to place Mr Bushy at the scene, his alibi was strong: our schoolmaster, the well-respected Mr Dickens, told the court that he had been teaching the accused at the time of the murder. There is no doubt this was the case." Sir Rupert paused, and he looked about the table. No one spoke, and he continued, "The evidence against Mr Bushy was purely based on the words we now know so well: 'You said I was welcome to go butchering' and the fact that a butcher's knife was found in the churchyard. Those remarks led us to believe that I was the intended victim, for it was I who had uttered the very same words in our courtroom. Indeed, Aaron had not been there that day when Mr Bushy was accused and convicted of meddling with his weights. However, it was not the butcher who shouted that phrase not once, but three times over as he killed a man. Who was it?" At this point, Sir Rupert's voice had risen dramatically, yet a glance at Mr Chapman sobered him and he continued at a lower pitch, "Were these words uttered by someone who wanted to place Mr Bushy as prime suspect? It seems likely."

Murmurs of agreement hummed about the table. Sir Rupert continued. "Furthermore, all Mr Bushy's knives were accounted for. The one used was new. Although in the style of our butcher's, it suffered none of the wear you would expect to find with a tool used daily.

"The jury were left to seek out the cunning individual responsible for this heinous crime. A person who would use another man's words and the tool of his trade to frame him for a crime he didn't commit. A person who planned the deed with care. Did that person plan to end my life, or that of Aaron Chapman? It appeared I was the one meant to die, but I am a much larger man, not easily confused with a slim figure, much younger in age, and..." Sir Rupert glanced at the father of the victim and lowered his voice, "...and I am a man with fewer enemies. However, without our killer, we cannot be sure who was meant to die.

"John Waller, can you please tell us what has been done to find the villain."

"We thought about those sons of his," John stood as he began talking. Although a well-respected constable in Dymchurch, his purpose in life was primarily that of wall-worker. To address a room of landowners and businessmen did not come easily to him. "Those two sons..."

Harry smiled his encouragement to his friend, knowing that once he started, the words would begin to flow.

"You see Mr Bushy isn't a man who treats his family nicely and perhaps it suited them to have him gone," John continued. "Did one of them do it and let their pa take the blame? We looked at it all ways, but they were in the Ocean that evening until past nine-thirty, and the knife wasn't worn as a true butcher's would be. I can't say they would be sorry to see him gone from their lives, but to set him up for murder... That takes cunning and we didn't think they had it in them.

"So, we started looking at who might be the enemy of either you, Sir Rupert, or Mr Aaron Chapman. But whoever that enemy was, they had to know about those words, didn't they? And they had to be able to plan and act on them quickly."

Sir Rupert raised his hand, indicating he wished to speak. "Just to remind everyone, the court hearing where Mr Bushy was convicted of cheating with his weights was on Friday 27th September and the murder was on Monday 30th. Three days later. Three days to plan a devious crime."

"That's right, sir." John paused for a moment, clearly gathering his thoughts. "Ah, yes: the knife. We went to the knifesmith – him who works along by the Rose Tavern on the High Street – and no one had bought a knife like the murder weapon recently. But he gave us a list of who had bought one in the last few months.

"But try as we may, we couldn't match it with a likely suspect. Then this lad Toke Spicer came forward wanting to speak to Harry Farrers..."

Sensing that his friend needed support, Harry offered, "Shall I say about this part, John?" The constable gave a smile and, with a small sigh of relief, he lowered himself back into his chair.

"Toke is a young man from Burmarsh. Alongside another man, both boys at the time, he lied about seeing Jesse Alder take the Whitsun Gallop cup." Harry looked directly at Mr Andrew Chapman who remained gazing down at the tabletop, and said, "I'm sorry this has to be said, Mr Chapman." There came a nod of acknowledgement, and Harry continued, "It has long been believed by myself and the Alder family that Jesse was innocent of theft, and it has now been proved. The boys were paid by Aaron and the purpose of these lies was to cause trouble for myself, for he had no grudge against my assistant. Was the killer one of the aggrieved Alder family, or even myself who, as you know, was there at the scene? The Alder family would not know of those notorious words 'you said I was welcome to go butchering', and if they, or I, wanted to take revenge, would we wait over three years? I doubt it.

"But now Mr Gerald Masters, cousin of Mrs Lydia Chapman, begins his investigations which are separate to our own." Harry looked towards his friend, "William, would you like to?"

231

William now stood, his manner easy, "Yes, Mr Masters from Canterbury, who happened to be staying at Burmarsh when Aaron lost his life, was eager to have this solved. He started prowling about and speaking to the locals, and he came across young Toke who seems to be free with his tongue.

"We met Mr Masters, Harry and I, and he repeated Toke's tales of there being friction between Aaron and a couple of local farmers."

"Mr Payne!" Sir Rupert raised his voice. "Mr Payne, I object to the word 'tales' – were these fictitious stories or true accounts?"

"True, Your Worship," William responded, then, "Sorry, sir. I forgot we weren't in court." A snigger ran about those sitting at the table, excepting the grieving father. "Toke reported the recent troubles when a patch of land at Gammon's Farm was used as pasture for Aaron's sheep. I recall the matter being dealt with here at New Hall and believed it to be resolved with no ill-feeling. However, I called on the farmer and was pleased to hear that there had been no further difficulties. The farmer had removed the bridge between the adjoining land, which is not ideal but gave him peace of mind. I could see no reason for any nastiness from his side.

"The second person who Toke mentioned was Mr Joss Bailey from Butlers Farm. This needed further investigation. He claimed Aaron took something of Joss' which happened to be stored in Burmarsh, then moved it on as his own." William paused, glanced around the table, and said, "No need to say any more about that. Anyway, Harry and I rode out to see Joss. He was more than happy to share his contempt for the man who had cheated him out of money that night. That man has got a temper, and there's no denying it."

"He knew what we were up to, of course," Harry added. "Knew we were looking for the killer. He said within a week he had earned handsomely out of the next run and that he would have got his own back on Aaron soon enough."

"We just can't place Mr Bailey in a place where he would know what words to use to frame the butcher," William continued. "He doesn't even use Anthony Bushy and Sons. The Butlers Farm animals are slaughtered in Hythe. I went to see Mr Bushy and he says he has no dealings with the man. Harry went to see Ned Dugman, the knifesmith, and he's not seen him recently."

"I didn't ask outright," Harry added. "Just said enough to see if Ned suddenly recalled anything."

Sir Rupert ran his gaze slowly around the table. "I have spoken to every one of you over the past few weeks and understand this case has been thoroughly investigated. Whoever murdered on the night of our Michaelmas Meeting must have known those ill-fated words and they planned... by God, they planned this meticulously. This was no chance killing. He was cunning and clever – too clever for us, I am saddened to admit. You have followed every possible lead to no avail. I pray that one day a slip of the tongue may scupper this villain who lives amongst us, or a new piece of evidence will make itself known. Much as it grieves me, I am ready to ask you all to leave this crime unsolved and to continue with your usual business and duties to the Corporation of Romney Marsh."

"No!" The word came from Mr Andrew Chapman. It stretched out long and low as he faced Sir Rupert for the first time since entering the room. "There must be something... some lead you have not followed. A good man died and he must be avenged."

"I've had men on this for five weeks," Sir Rupert pointed out. "And all the time they keep searching and questioning, they are putting their own work aside. The search is over Mr Chapman."

"It must never be over." Standing abruptly, so his chair almost toppled backwards, the father of the dead man, left the room. They all heard his footsteps pounding across the courtroom next door and down the stairs.

"In my experience," Sir Rupert stated after a moment of shocked silence, followed by whispers and murmurings around the table, "these mysteries have a habit of untangling themselves sooner or later. Thank you all for your time." He stood and left the room, leaving everyone else to trail in his wake.

Chapter Twenty-Two
Phoebe

Towards the end of the day, the sun hung just above the hills at Rye, casting orange and yellow across the sky, as Harry and Phoebe, with Mireille and Esther, left Dymchurch for the village of St Mary in the Marsh. Huddled in the open cart, with their thickest cloaks and rough blankets to protect them from the sharp chill in the air, they admired the sunset and relished the adventure ahead of them.

While Harry occasionally enjoyed the company of the menfolk at the Ship Inn of an evening, there was rarely any attraction for Phoebe to venture out for as the day drew to a close. Any visiting took place during the day and, besides, she had the children to care for. To go out at night for no good reason was unwise, for you never knew what unsavoury people may be lurking in the shadows along the roads and tracks. The Marsh was known to abound with dangerous characters who claimed the place as their own from sunset to sunrise. However, Gunpowder Treason Day was an exception to the unspoken rule of not going out after dusk. Many of the farmers and landowners invited their friends, neighbours and workers to marvel at the spectacle of their bonfire, to enjoy a feast and make merry with ale.

Excited to show her cousin the Marsh countryside, Phoebe pointed out isolated farmhouses and cottages, relating the history and stories of the people who lived there. The deep ditch alongside the road to St Mary in the Marsh had been freshly cleared and they clambered out of the cart to stand on a bridge, four sturdy planks wide, to watch the darkening water flow slowly to the coast. An eel swam towards them, no more than a featureless shadow, and, fascinated, they turned to look at it emerge from the other side of the bridge. "It's too dark," Mireille exclaimed. "I can't see it."

"There! There!" Esther, her hand held firmly by her father, aimed a chubby finger towards the water, but they couldn't spot the creature.

"We can make a stick eel," Mireille suggested, carefully extracting a whippy branch of willow from the roadside and stripping it of withered leaves. "Here's our eel, Esther." She dropped it into the water, and they all waited for it to appear after floating under the bridge. Satisfied, the little girl allowed herself to be lifted back into the cart where she settled on her mother's lap.

The chestnut pulled contentedly at wayside grass, but soon he was encouraged to walk on, and everyone's attention focused on the spire of St Mary's Church. By the time they were approaching the village, the sun had set, leaving a weak glow in the sky. Harry and Mireille now walked at the horse's head, each carrying a lantern to guide the way.

Turning back, Phoebe became aware of another vehicle on the road behind them. "There's a cart, or coach catching up with us," she called out. Twisting to study the dark shape and dancing lights, she continued, "Perhaps two? I'm sure one is a coach. They are still some distance away."

"Sir Rupert and Lady Charlotte, I expect." Harry picked up his pace and Phoebe could see that Mireille followed suit as both their lamps bobbed about in front.

The small group passed a couple of wayside cottages then St Mary's Church, a solid ragstone building with a neat porch and plain tower, topped with a spire, loomed to the right. *When we visit Marianne in the daytime, I must take Mireille to see the faces in there,* Phoebe thought, recalling the carved stone images. While it was on her mind, she called to her cousin, "Mireille, I'll bring you here another time. There are three sculptures you must see – three faces and each one different." She looked down at her daughter, snuggled close, and pulled back a strand of hair to kiss her cheek. "And you too, Esther, although they are the oddest things and I hope you won't find them scary. The twins will think nothing of them – they are too young."

"I'd like that!" Mireille answered. If darkness had not fully descended, then Phoebe would have noticed how her cheeks glowed in the cold, and her eyes gleamed bright with anticipation for the evening's entertainment.

While the church stood majestically and serenely on its mound of raised earth, dark and silent, the Star Inn opposite created a stark contrast. Through the lamp-lit windows much frivolity could be seen, accompanied by faint strains of a tin whistle and much raucous laughter. They glanced towards the rambling stone building, but Harry led his horse to the right and rounded the churchyard, putting the inn behind them.

Now they faced William Payne's land. In a field they could see a few dozen dark figures already jostling around a smouldering fire. However, Phoebe knew that sacks of bone-dry kindling had been stored under cover and within seconds the fire would be brought to life and flames leaping through thin, dusty sticks. The last time Marianne had visited Dymchurch, their talk had been of Gunpowder Treason Day as they planned the details of the feast. Phoebe's contribution, individual minced lamb pies and slices of honeyed pear cake, were safely packed away under the bench in the cart.

"Come on, Esther. Time to get down." Phoebe lifted her daughter off her lap. "There's Mireille. She'll help you."

"Where's Georgina? Where's Joanna?" Esther wriggled in an attempt to spot the two older girls who she admired so much. "It's too dark!"

"It has to be dark so we can enjoy the fireworks in the sky," Phoebe explained, and not for the first time during the journey. "I don't know where Georgina and Joanna are, but I am sure we can find them." She scrambled down, feeling the soft soil and damp grass of the roadside under the soles of her boots, then reached for the dishes of food.

"I'll see you in a minute," Harry called, and the cart lurched forward. As it moved away, the two coaches bringing the party from New Hall came to a halt nearby. Doors opened filling the air with a combination of excited chatter and cautionary words, while the Bannerman family and guests left their cocoon and ventured down the steps to gather by the roadside.

Phoebe, with Mireille and Esther, walked through a gateway and stood for a moment, their eyes searching for familiar faces through the darkness. Their host, William Payne, was a popular figure locally, generous with his time and to those who worked on his land. Confident and cheerful, he was just as much at home at the bar of the Star with a pewter tankard to hand as dining at New Hall with a cut glass goblet held between his rough fingers. The locals were eager to leave their firesides to be a part of the traditional celebrations and upward of a hundred figures milled about.

Weighed down by the heavy dishes in her hands, Phoebe suggested that they head towards the tables. "Marianne is sure to be there." Appreciating that Mireille had scooped Esther up into her arms, Phoebe took the lead, cautiously negotiating the rough ground.

"Over here!" Marianne could be heard calling, and Phoebe picked out her friend amongst a group of three women presiding over a line of tables. Nearby, planks balanced on logs served as low, makeshift benches. "How lovely that you brought Esther!"

"It's quite an adventure," Phoebe responded. "She hasn't stopped chattering about this all day. The twins are out of sorts, knowing their sister has been included in something while they stay at home, but they are far too young. Can I put the food here?"

"That's perfect." Marianne moved a couple of dishes to make space for Phoebe's offering. "Mireille, do you have bonfire parties in Wissant?"

"We have them in the autumn, when we celebrate the harvest," Mireille told her.

Phoebe glanced towards the flames which had not yet reached what she believed to be a stuffed effigy of the pope and felt a twinge of unease while she waited for her Catholic cousin's response. They had already discussed the history of Bonfire Treason Day when forming their plans for the evening.

Following her friend's gaze, Marianne spoke quickly, "Oh! It's not the pope this time," the merriment in her voice giving a hint of a story to come. "William found out that it's not how we do it now. At least times are changing... and he said that to make a Guido Fawkes for the fire was more appropriate."

"It will cause less offence," Phoebe suggested while eyeing the hay-stuffed figure. Then, aware of Esther, still in Mireille's arms, she attempted to reassure her daughter, "Don't worry, Esther. Don't be scared. It's not a real person, just a pretend one."

"Like my dolls?" Esther queried.

"Just like your dolls," Phoebe responded. "But this one isn't very nice."

239

At that moment, the flames began to lick at the legs, and they stood in silence watching the figure being engulfed before collapsing into the fire.

"Not very nice," Esther repeated. Her arms wrapped firmly around Mireille's neck.

"I must stay here with the food," Marianne said. "No doubt you'll spot the children and I see the Bannermans are here. William said we must eat first and then he'll set off the fireworks."

"Thank you," Phoebe replied. "Thank you for all of this and inviting us." Then to Esther, "Shall we walk around the fire and look for Georgina and Joanna?"

The little girl wriggled free from Mireille's arms but submitted to both her mother and cousin holding a hand while they crossed the tussocky field. Having circled the fire, pausing frequently to admire its splendour and to pass fleeting comments with others gathered for the evening, Phoebe spotted William and Marianne's daughters by the food tables. "There they are!" Lifting Esther onto her hip, she pointed, "Look! Over there!"

"And Papa!"

"Oh yes! Papa is there too." Once more, they took a meandering path, stepping carefully over hillocks and moving around the flow of well-wrapped figures heading towards the bonfire, now fully ablaze.

The heat could be felt on their backs and, not for the first time, Phoebe reflected on the frivolity of burning wood in an area where its scarcity made it precious. *It is no more than scraps,* she told herself and tried to believe it. *Besides, the whole village are here, and it gives them something to look forward to before the worst of the winter descends on us.* "Hello Lady Bannerman, we are lucky with the weather this evening…" Phoebe pushed the worrying thoughts away to exchange a few words with Sir Rupert's wife. Then

Esther was released and able to run into her father's arms, as Georgina and Joanna came to join their party.

It was agreed that the older girls would join them to eat, and three benches were claimed, then moved into a triangular shape. Planks were rebalanced on logs, and the whole arrangement approved of, before Phoebe produced a set of pewter plates and some plain earthenware beakers. Wide eyed, and unusually silent, Esther looked on and waited for the moment when she could choose her food, under the guidance of her mama and Mireille. "I'm glad we decided to take her with us," Phoebe said to Harry, as she placed a plate in Esther's hands. "It's such fun for her."

"Maybe next year we can bring the twins?" he responded.

"Maybe the year after," Phoebe laughed. They both knew that the company of all three children would be chaotic. "Let's go and choose our food."

There were no servants on hand, and the Bannermans were called to fill their own plates, then neighbouring landowners followed. Next Harry led his family group to the tempting spread. Choosing food from a table in half-darkness, with lamps offering pools of flickering yellow light, was fun. Marianne's plan was for everything to be easily eaten with fingers, and most of the offerings were encased in pastry, although many oozed their contents. This was accompanied by bread rolls, slices of ham, and chunks of cheese. They ate with thick napkins on their laps and tankards of ale or beakers of wine at their feet, resting precariously against the plank and log seats.

"I said to Marianne that we should have fireworks before the sweet puddings," William announced as he appeared amongst them and squatted on the end of a low bench. "We've set them up over there," he continued, waving a hand in the direction of the fire.

241

"The other side of the fire?" Phoebe asked. "We'll stay over here."

"Of course. Best keep your distance." Then as he walked away, William looked back to call, "They're mini explosives, you know!"

"Looking forward to it!" Harry called, then to Phoebe, "As long as we stay this side of the fire, then we'll be safe."

"I'm cold!" Esther suddenly wailed, and all attention turned to her. Occupied with the thrill of choosing her food and eating outside in the dark, she now allowed her empty plate to fall to the ground, knocking a beaker as it landed.

"We'll go back to the fire," Phoebe suggested. She leaned down to pick up the plate. "I know it's cold, but such fun!" James and Clara will be in bed soon, and we have fireworks to watch and cake or sweet pies to eat!" Turning to Harry, she said, "It's much safer by the fire now; most of it is just smouldering. Let's go and watch from over there."

Momentarily they busied themselves with brushing crumbs off plates and folding napkins, then meandered towards the bonfire just as the first explosion of orange sparks shot into the air. Mesmerised, all thoughts of warming themselves were lost as they stood gazing upwards. A further eruption of bright flashes burst through the night sky and, in quick succession, another and another. Phoebe glanced at Esther in Harry's arms – a wave of love and contentment washed over her. She thought of Jesse now back in Wissant while Mireille stayed on Romney Marsh and knew that one day soon her cousin would be as satisfied with her marriage and children as she was.

"Look!" Esther shrieked, bringing Phoebe back to the present.

A lone orange light streaked skywards before exploding into thousands of tiny fires high in the sky. The display lasted only minutes but thrilled grown-ups and children alike. Then, having watched in near silence, the onlookers' chatter now filled the air as everyone descended on the supper tables once more to choose between apple or cherry pie, or spiced pear cake.

Afterwards, no one could agree on which was the highlight of the evening – the fireworks or the fun of eating outdoors.

"No one mentioned the murder this evening," Harry commented as they walked back to the cart, a sleepy daughter in his arms. "I'm tired of hearing how the killer has not been found yet."

"It is at the forefront of everyone's thoughts," she agreed. "In another month or so, there will be other matters to occupy our minds, and his death will just be a small part of Dymchurch's history."

"I hope so," he responded. "I hope this is the end of it."

Chapter Twenty-Three
Phoebe
Early Spring 1766

The winter weeks and months had passed with the majority of the Dymchurch folk reluctant to stray from their places of work or the firesides in their homes. They filled their bellies with hot, thick stews and broths, and fretted over the diminishing stocks in woodpiles. Within the shops on the High Street, on the stalls where the fishermen displayed their varied catch, and in their own store cupboards, the villagers had found all they needed for survival. Many of them remained within the parish boundaries for several months.

When the days were grey, and damp penetrated their homes, the villagers soon forgot the moments when the sky offered a beautiful, deep blue colour and a light wind whipped at their washing. During the times when rain fell unceasingly, they claimed there was no place more miserable than Romney Marsh.

It had been a mid-February afternoon, when the evening sky was ablaze and Bates Cottage bathed in its golden light, that Bess was taken from this earth. Phoebe and Mireille had hoped – in fact, Mireille had been adamant – that there were signs of recovery since the stroke. After all, Bess had lived for longer than the apothecary had predicted, with no notable deterioration during the days before she passed away. Feelings were mixed. Alongside the sorrow there came a sense of relief and of it's being for the best. Without full control of her body and unable to speak clearly, Bess' life was lonely and one of suffering daily frustrations. "Apoplexy," the apothecary had stated. "Another stroke."

By the time the aconites and snowdrops had opened their fragile blooms, Bess Bates, had been laid to rest in the churchyard. Her husband, Owen, with his swollen knees and gnarled fingers, declined the offer to live with Harry and Phoebe, but had accepted their invitation to eat his daily midday meal at their kitchen table.

A couple of weeks later, Harry came across Toke Spicer, now happily part of a team of six workers tending a middle section of the Dymchurch Wall. The lad was ending his shift and about to hasten to the Ship for an ale and a chance to warm through before walking home to Burmarsh.

"How are you liking it here on the Wall?" Harry asked.

"I can't say it's not cold with them winds coming at me all day," Toke exaggerated, "but it's a fine place to be nonetheless."

"You're doing your part to keep us all safe," Harry stated.

"His wife – Mrs Chapman..." Toke began. "She had a baby, or so I heard. A few days ago, maybe a week."

"Oh! That is good news," Harry replied. "My wife will be glad to know, and she'll ask me if it's a boy or a girl?"

"There's a question." Toke frowned and then gazed upwards as if searching for an answer. "I can't rightly say."

"Never mind. We'll find out soon enough."

"It's a girl!" Phoebe announced as she and Esther entered the kitchen, having discarded stout boots in the scullery. "Susanna, Lydia called her. All is well!" Then to Mireille, who was helping the twins with beakers of milk, "Thank you for looking after James and Clara."

"She wanted a girl," Janey remarked from where she presided over the teapot, immediately pouring a cup for Phoebe. "She'll be thinking of leaving then?"

"And good luck to her," Mary added. "It's a lonely life living out there in Burmarsh."

"Did she say anything… anything about leaving?" Mireille asked.

"Goodness! Too many questions! Let us settle down first." Phoebe leaned down to help Esther remove her cloak and accepted the tiny slippers offered by Mireille. "Up you get." She helped her eldest daughter onto a chair. "Look, there's a drink of milk, and some delicious biscuits." After the outer garments had been removed, Phoebe was finally able to sit down with the tea.

The walk to Burmarsh and back had been tiresome, the tracks rutted, yet frozen hard. Each step had to be managed with care and the bridges cautiously negotiated. She could have taken the road and would have done so if the weather had been milder and the earth soft underfoot, but that route was further and came with its own difficulties. "I'm glad it's over," Phoebe said with feeling. "If we go again, then it will be by cart. I just didn't want to be a bother."

"You know Harry wouldn't have minded," Janey remarked.

"I know." Phoebe took a long sip of tea. "Thank you for this. You were asking after Lydia… She looked well and happy, and the baby is placid."

"How old is she, Susanna, now?" Mireille queried while supporting the beaker between James' hands. "Two weeks?"

"Two weeks and five days," Phoebe answered. "Lydia's mother is still there and will be for another month. I didn't ask... didn't like to ask if Lydia still hopes to return to Canterbury. She was absorbed with caring for the baby. But I'm sure it will be on her mind, and plans will be made as soon as Susanna is a little older."

"Perhaps in three or four months," Janey suggested.

"By then I will have gone," Mireille said. They all looked towards her, aware that, much as she was a great help at Walker House, the time was nearing when their visitor must return to Wissant.

She has been a little lost since Bess died, Phoebe reflected. *I imagine she is thinking of her reunion with Jesse and wanting matters to be settled between them. It won't be long now.* Harry had been to speak to Walter, and it was agreed that if the weather was fair at the end of March, then he and Joshua would take *Louisa-Ann* across the Channel. After five months of living in Dymchurch Mireille would be reunited with her family. Phoebe imagined herself and Harry following the same route in the small fishing vessel three months later. It would be fraught with difficulties with the children, and part of her wanted to beg Mireille to remain in Dymchurch for longer so they could travel together. *But I would never ask it of her. It is time for my cousin to return to her family and her love.*

"I will miss you," Mary said. Her response simple, but heartfelt.

"I'll miss you all," Mireille responded, "but it is time for me to go."

"You'll come back?" Janey asked.

"Oh yes! I will visit again, maybe next year?"

247

Phoebe tried to imagine her cousin arriving once more and being a part of their household for a week or two. *But time does not stand still. In another year she will have married and may even be expecting a child of her own. Perhaps another year will pass, or more, before they can travel here. And when they do... will they stay here or with Jesse's family?* Much as Mireille worried over there being no agreement between her and Jesse, in Phoebe's mind the matter would be fully resolved within a day of them meeting again. *I will hear all about it in the summer.*

"I'll be pleased to see Lydia leave," Phoebe declared, returning to the topic of Aaron's widow. "She's been utterly miserable here. In fact, I believe her only time of happiness has been the past few months since his death, although I only say this here amongst ourselves."

"It sounds like she was happy enough when her cousin was here," Janey added. "My! He was a handsome man and charming too."

Smiling to herself, Phoebe replied, "I didn't know you had ever met him?"

"I saw him a few times when I was in the village," Janey told her. "Once he was with Mr Harry. Gave me a lovely smile *and* doffed his hat, he did. Can you believe it! A real gent, he is."

"He certainly did seem very pleasant."

"Wouldn't it be a happy ending if he and Mrs Lydia Chapman were to marry?" Mary suggested. Despite her not being able to see people's expressions, the young woman had an uncanny ability to know their true feelings when not a word on the matter was uttered.

"I don't think..." Phoebe began. "At least, it would be a happy ending, but he is most eligible, and she is... well, she is much happier now... far livelier... but has

248

two daughters..." She feared heartache for Lydia if her hopes were fixed upon Gerald.

The teapot was empty, and Esther clamoured for the biscuit crumbs on the plate. Mireille unfastened Clara's apron, while Mary wiped James' mouth then untied his apron. They wriggled, eager to be released, then raced through the doorway, heading for the parlour.

"Chamber pots!" Mary called, following in their wake.

"Thank you, Janey. I needed this after the walk," Phoebe gestured to the teapot alongside and empty cups and plates. "James! Clara! Upstairs now."

Thoughts of the newborn baby at Rothschild Manor played upon Phoebe's mind, causing her to dwell on packed-away memories of Saturday afternoons spent in the company of Mrs Chapman, Susanna's grandmother. At that time, Aaron's mother had been lonely, her daughters newly-married and living in the Hythe area. To see them involved careful planning over several days and notes passing back and forth by groom. Meanwhile, as part of the courtship ritual with Aaron, he had expected Phoebe to offer a sympathetic ear to Mrs Chapman's twittering about her daughters while sharing a pot of tea and nibbling slices of cake. This arrangement had ended abruptly when Phoebe resolved to end the relationship with Aaron. The last time she had visited the Chapman home, she had returned a book of poetry and fled, relieved to be free of the stifling commitment to both mother and son.

Seven years have passed, Phoebe reflected. *Whereas my life is filled with the company of good people, I am happily married and kept busy all day, Mrs Chapman must be lonelier than ever. I can only assume that her daughters visit, but does she have any other company beside her cook and maid? They are not a family who extend warmth to others and, in turn, the local women will not be inclined to give her any thought, even at this time when she must still mourn for her son."*

"I shall go!" she said aloud, while smoothing and folding clean laundry on her bed. "I shall go to see her."

That same afternoon, having left the children in the capable hands of Mireille, with Janey and Mary close to hand, Phoebe put on her best woollen cloak – the one without the snags from countryside walks or the inevitable smearing of dirt from boots when she carried the twins. Her shoes were newly polished, although bound to be spoiled a little during the walk, and her dress was a soft green, trimmed with a modest amount of French lace. She wore no additional adornments, other than her wedding band, favouring a plainer style of dress but knowing the cut and quality of her outfit was as fine as that worn by any other wife of a well-to-do businessman.

"I don't know how long I'll be," Phoebe said as she stood at the parlour doorway, ready to leave. "She may not be wanting a visitor. She may not want to see me."

These same words had been running through her mind and voiced several times already since the decision had been made. *I'll just have to go and see.*

Walking through the village, Phoebe avoided any more than a brief greeting or passing comment with anyone. She noted Aunt Peggy's beady eyes watching her from the doorway of the grocery shop and acknowledged her with a wave and cheery 'good afternoon' but refused to be drawn into any explanation as to where she was heading. From the High Street, Phoebe turned into the lane that eventually led to St Mary in the Marsh. Crossing a wide sewer, she noted the waters were brown and sluggish, the banks ugly with debris and the hollow, broken-down stubs of last years' reeds. *It will change soon,* she thought, knowing that new growth would soon be pushing through the wet mud and fresh, green reeds forging upwards.

The clusters of cottages were now behind her, and scattered houses stood in large plots of land, one of those being the Chapman home. With some trepidation, Phoebe approached the house, a pleasant looking property, flat-fronted with windows spaced evenly, one either side of the door and a matching pair above. In the gable end, a smaller window gave light to an attic room belonging to the maid.

"Good afternoon, Annie. Is Mrs Chapman at home to receive a visitor?" Phoebe offered an encouraging smile.

The maid returned the smile and replied, "I'll find out, Mrs Farrers. Would you like to wait here?" She gestured to a heavily carved, oak chair in the hallway.

"Thank you." Phoebe stepped into the house but chose to stand and study an oil painting of rolling pastures, preferring this to sitting. Annie moved almost noiselessly up the stairs; a light knock could be heard, then muffled voices. Distracted by a slight creak, Phoebe turned from the rural scene depicted with bold sweeps of olive greens and soft browns. The kitchen door was ajar, and she sensed someone was peeping at her through the gap.

Movement at the top of the stairs alerted her to the maid's return, and Phoebe watched her careful progress to the hall. *This is a house where everyone must creep about quietly,* she surmised.

"Mrs Chapman would like to see you," the maid said, her tone barely more than a whisper. "I'll stoke the fire," she continued, opening the door to the parlour and inviting Phoebe to enter. "It's a bit chilly. The room hasn't been used today."

251

"It will soon warm," Phoebe responded. "Besides, the sun has helped nicely." Her words were optimistic, for although the sun was shining through the front windows of the house, they were heavily draped. She eyed the curtains, longing to pull them back.

Annie must have read her thoughts for she was about to attend to the fire, but instead turned to approach the windows, tugging at the sumptuous green curtains, immediately releasing light and warmth into the room. A couple of logs were then added to the fire and the glowing embers stoked. "I'll take your cloak," she offered. "And make some tea."

"Thank you." Phoebe seated herself on a delicate upright chair positioned so her back and shoulders could benefit from the sun's rays. The maid left, her feet tapping lightly on the wooden floors, pulling the door to a close behind her. Other than the gentle crackling of the logs in the grate, silence reigned.

The parlour clearly remained the domain of Mrs Caroline Chapman. A room familiar to Phoebe, she noted the changes which had occurred since her last visit seven years ago. The panelled lower part of the wall had been repainted, pictures rearranged on the wall, and ornaments added to those already decorating the mantelpiece. However, the most recent addition was an oil painting of the late Aaron Chapman, encased in an oval frame of polished elm and currently residing on a side table facing his mother's armchair. *Perhaps, in time, it will be hung on the wall.* Phoebe looked about for a suitable place.

No sounds could be heard from the rest of the house, and as it seemed unlikely that Mrs Chapman would burst into the room to catch Phoebe unawares. She took a couple of steps towards the portrait, curious to observe his likeness. The image was of Aaron's head and shoulders – *he was not that broad; this is the breadth of figure he aspired to* – and although his head was turned to the left, his eyes looked directly at her. Repelled, Phoebe couldn't help stepping back. Yet she could not resist studying the painting further: the subtle twist to his lips, the tilt of his chin and the slight bump in an otherwise good nose were all just as they should be. *His hair had thinned over recent years.* Phoebe could only approve of the unknown artist for pandering to Mrs Chapman's grief as he enhanced her son's features.

Upon hearing movement in the hallway, Phoebe moved back to her chair and smiled at Annie who entered with a tray. The girl proceeded to set out the teapot, crockery and a plate of biscuits while saying, "I'm sure Mrs Chapman will be here shortly." Her expression revealed the uncertainty in her words.

"I'm sure she will," Phoebe replied, not believing it.

"She was pleased to know you are here," the maid told her. "I hope the tea stays warm."

"If there are any… any delays, then perhaps you could bring a pot of hot water to add to the pot," Phoebe suggested.

"Thank you. Yes. Yes, I will." The maid seemed to perk up and left with a smile on her face.

How difficult it must be trying to please a grieving mother. The minutes passed and Phoebe decided to pour her own tea. Then she rose to study the scene behind Aaron's image, recognising it as being the flat lands of Romney Marsh, but unsure if it was intended to depict a particular view. Just as she returned to the chair and took her first sip of tea, Phoebe heard steps in the hall, hurriedly returned her cup to the side table, then rose to greet Caroline Chapman.

"Mrs Chapman, I hope you don't mind…"

"Phoebe, my dear, I am delighted… How very kind of you to think of… Do sit back down. The tea… it's not cold, is it?" Aaron's mother, withered and stooped,

253

paused and gazed at the portrait of her dead son. She gazed at it for a moment. "The likeness is remarkable, don't you think?"

"I do," Phoebe agreed, while thinking that Mrs Chapman was rather distracted. Her sentences were short. Unfinished. *That's how I remember her – always kind to me, but rather foolish.* "I'll pour, shall I?"

"We would have preferred a boy, of course," the baby's grandmother replied. "The family line, you know... Although I could see the resemblance." With this she nodded towards the portrait, indicating to where the likeness lay.

"Oh yes!" Phoebe responded with well-meaning, if insincere, enthusiasm.

By the time the second cup of tea had been consumed Mrs Chapman had recalled hearing a young woman from France was visiting the Farrer's home. "A family member?" she enquired.

"My cousin, Mireille." Phoebe proceeded to recount Mireille's impressions of Dymchurch, the evening visit to St Mary in the Marsh, and how she had been helping with Bess and the children. "She'll be leaving soon. In a few weeks."

By now Mrs Chapman's attention had wandered, and her next words were entirely unconnected: "I was sure it was the butcher," she announced. "They say otherwise, Sir Rupert Bannerman and the jury, but I am still certain of it."

"Oh?" was all that Phoebe could muster, not certain how to respond.

"I heard him you see."

"Heard him?"

"I was there taking a walk through the village and heard him making that terrible fuss outside the Ocean Inn. It was rather unsettling – all that shouting about slaughtering and butchering – and in the street too. I moved away rather more quickly than I ought at my age. Around the corner I went and ended up tripping into Mr Bailey. He was terribly kind and listened to my concerns as to how disturbing it all was, then walked me up to the seawall. Mr Chapman says he can't take to the man, but, on that occasion, I found him to be most kind."

Phoebe could envisage the scene: the butcher shouting in the street outside the pub; a flustered woman not concentrating on her step and hurrying away; the farmer, Bailey, in the village on some business, and keen to hear of the gossip.

"You know who I mean, don't you, dear?" Mrs Chapman chirped. "Mr Joss Bailey from Butlers Farm."

"Mr Bailey?" Phoebe repeated. "Yes. Yes, I know him. He hadn't seen or heard it for himself? But you told him all about it."

"Such a comfort." Mrs Chapman glanced toward the painting of her son, as if to ask for his approval. "I felt so foolish, but he told me there was no need. No need at all."

"How kind of him," Phoebe responded whilst reimagining the scene, with Mrs Chapman babbling away, repeating those fateful words over and over. And while she gushed her appreciation to the farmer, he would be absorbing the words shouted by the furious butcher.

Chapter Twenty-Four
Harry

Since the new year, Harry had worked between the two forges. His new business kept him fully occupied and he was thankful that he was no longer called upon by William Payne, Sir Rupert or even Gerald Masters to assist in solving the mystery of who murdered Aaron Chapman. It was not forgotten. From his new forge beside the Ship, he saw the gallows, straight and strong, with the solid, comforting presence of the church behind them. The carefully transcribed records of the killing in the churchyard would remain in a heavy, leather-bound book, and stored in a cupboard in New Hall for decades, perhaps centuries, revealing the story to anyone who cared to look. Over the years, it would become a tale to be told in the taverns or around supper tables, and with opinions being freshly aired.

Harry held no particular judgements on the matter. Sometimes he thought the initial response had been right – Anthony Bushy had intended to murder Sir Rupert Bannerman, and it was a simple case of mistaken identity on the night. After all, it was only the word of the schoolmaster which had freed the angry butcher from the gallows. Any other suggestion of possible suspects had always seemed far too complicated, especially with it being only a matter of days between those well-known words uttered and the death. Not long enough to plot such a complicated scheme – the murder, and the framing of an innocent man. Other times he pondered over the likelihood that Aaron was stabbed by someone he had cheated or bullied, probably during the course of a smuggling run. Mostly, the events following the Michaelmas meeting had settled in the back of Harry's mind and he concerned himself with his family and work.

On this day in early March, Harry's focus was on the decorative details making up a length of railing, and this took all his attention as he worked alongside Jack in the new forge. When Phoebe walked into the building, he started, having not spotted her through the misted windows or the part-open doorway. "Is everyone all right?" he asked immediately.

"Yes – the children, Mireille... Owen... everyone else, but..." Phoebe darted a look towards Jack who had turned away but would, no doubt, be curious. "There is something."

"Did you see Mrs Chapman?"

"I've just come from there..."

It's something to do with the Chapmans then, or at least something serious because Phoebe wouldn't come here unless she really had to. "You're fine with this, Jack," Harry spoke to his assistant. "I'm just going outside, but I'll be back for the heavy part. If not, wait for me." Still wearing his leather apron, Harry gestured to the doorway and followed his wife outside.

"It's something Mrs Chapman said," Phoebe began as soon as they had stepped clear of the forge. There was no one about, but she kept her voice low – the stables for the Ship Inn were nearby and there was likely to be a stablehand about. "She was there in the village that day when the butcher was shouting in the street outside the Ocean. She heard what he said."

"I know," Harry responded. "The jury did a good job of finding out not only who was in the Ocean, but also who heard him ranting in the road."

"But there's something they didn't know. They didn't know that she found it... found it threatening, I assume. Although she didn't use that word. She wanted to move away from the unpleasant scene... and she tripped – tripped into the farmer, Joss Bailey."

"Joss Bailey?" Harry repeated.

"You know how she twitters, like a little bird, fussing about everything. Can you imagine how she told him, over and over, about the butcher and those words he was shouting?"

"I can."

"He was very kind to her. That's what she told me, and that is strange in itself as he is not a man known for his pleasantries."

"We need to see John Waller," Harry said. "Will they manage at home without you?"

"Oh yes, they expect me to be out for some time."

Harry turned back to the forge and spoke to Jack, "I've got to go – urgent business with the constable. We'll move these railings, and if you can tidy up, make everything safe, then you can finish for the day."

They worked together, swiftly moving the ironwork into place, then Harry exchanged his apron for a jacket and left.

Phoebe had wandered a short distance and stood gazing up at the gallows. "What horrible things these are," she said, before turning to look directly at Harry. "Let's find John."

If Joss Bailey is convicted, then he'll end up here, Harry reflected. *I don't like the man. Never did like him. But I don't want to watch him hanging there while I'm going about my work.* "Yes, let's find John," he replied to Phoebe as they began to walk towards the village.

But Phoebe, who knew him so well, responded to his unsaid words, "If he is condemned, it will draw quite a crowd, won't it? You and Jack, if you don't want to be a part of it, then go to the other forge that day and any other when the gallows are used."

"I'll see how Jack feels if it comes to it." Harry picked up his pace, taking a track leading to the seawall.

They walked in silence for a while, each of them absorbed in their own thoughts, knowing it was hardly the time for idle chatter about the children or household matters. The track was muddy and took careful negotiation, then they were on the summit and heading towards Wall End. "Tide's high and it will be dark in a couple of hours," Harry remarked. "The men will have packed up for the day, so we should come across him walking home."

He was right: along the length of the Wall, men strolled in groups of two or three, then dropped down to the landward side as they reached a track leading towards either their homes or the tavern of their choice. Some pushed their barrows filled with tools to be shut away securely for the night.

"I had hoped it was all over," Phoebe said. "That we could forget about it all."

Understanding how those innocent words spoken by Mrs Chapman would have repercussions on their lives for the weeks to come, Harry agreed, "I thought it was."

"And do you know the worst of it? His mother was pleased to see me... grateful to see me... Now she'll have the constable or Sir Rupert wanting to ask her questions and it will bring it all back." Phoebe paused, as if to consider her words. "Not that it ever went away."

"How could it?" Harry changed the subject slightly. "Did she say anything about Lydia? Is there any word of her leaving for Canterbury?"

"I don't think it has been spoken of yet. At least not to Aaron's family – I am sure Lydia would have talked to her own mother about it. I imagine it is going to be very difficult to broach the subject with her mother-in-law."

"I'm sure plans have been made." Harry spotted a familiar figure not far from the High Knocke area of the seawall, and once more changed the subject: "There he is – John." Waving, he caught the attention of the village constable who separated himself from his small group of workers.

"I'd like to say I'm pleased to see you," John said as they drew close, "but I fear this is constable business."

"You're right," Harry replied. "Would it be rude to ask if we could talk in your home? Or you are welcome at ours."

"Ann is with her sister in Newchurch for a couple of days. Come to my place, if you don't mind the chill while I stoke the fire into life."

They left the seawall for the village centre and the terrace of cottages known as Mackett's. Walking through the front room and into the kitchen, John immediately dropped to his knees before the fire. "This one is still warm, and I know you're not too proud to sit in the kitchen," he said. "There's water in the kettle; shall we warm ourselves with tea?"

"Lovely," Phoebe replied. "Let me get it ready." She took cups and saucers from the dresser.

"There's fresh milk in the scullery – I'll get it – and Ann left me with some boiled fruit cake." John removed his jacket and hung it on some hooks fashioned by Harry several years beforehand. "Yours can go there, Harry, it's no cleaner than mine! But Phoebe – put yours over the chair. Strange to see you without the children…"

260

For a few minutes they crowded together in the small kitchen. Then, while the tea brewed in the pot, Phoebe began her story. "You mentioned me not having the children with me, and there is a reason – I decided to visit Mrs Caroline Chapman. I've not been before, not in many years at least, but I went this afternoon."

"I rarely see her about the village," John observed. "Not anymore."

"I believe she's become a bit of a recluse, but she was pleased to see me," Phoebe told him. "We were speaking about Mireille visiting from France, and suddenly Mrs Chapman mentioned the butcher. She was certain he killed Aaron and said that she had heard him ranting outside the Ocean on the day he had been in court over the weights and measures business."

"Yes, we had her on our list of someone who witnessed the scene, but it hardly seemed right to question her." John reached forward to stir the tea, then added milk to the cups before Phoebe poured.

"I understand that, but no one knew what happened next. She was upset and hurried away, around the corner and bumped straight into Joss Bailey."

"Joss Bailey?" John echoed. "I knew you weren't wasting my time, but I don't like the sound of that name."

"I didn't either," Harry added.

Phoebe repeated Mrs Chapman's words the best she could and added her own impressions of the woman's distress on the day. "Caroline Chapman is a person who seems unable to control her outpourings once she gets going," she told them. "It appears that Joss Bailey, known to be bad-tempered and unfriendly, offered her an extraordinary amount of attention. It quite perked her up to speak of it."

261

"So, Joss Bailey knew about the words said by our butcher, and knew them well." John paused and his eyes narrowed as if he saw the scene between the burly farmer and flustered woman. "The knife..."

"He has his animals slaughtered in Hythe," Harry recalled. "He wouldn't be familiar with Mr Bushy's knife but may well be aware of the tools used by a butcher or slaughterman. In fact, he would also kill his own animals, and would have a variety of knives to hand."

"The knife used was newly crafted... Damn, I've let the fire go out." John leapt up with unnecessary haste to tend the fire. His chair clattered across the brick floor. "Sorry about that."

"Yes, it was new, but perhaps that was a co-incidence. Our killer had very little time to go out and have a knife made," Harry observed. "Most likely he already had a new one to hand and it was the perfect choice, having no tell-tale marks to link it to anyone."

"I've often thought," John confessed, "that it was hardly believable how our killer could hear of those words, hatch a plan *and* procure a suitable knife within such a short amount of time."

"Yet somehow he did," Phoebe murmured.

"I was happy enough with it all being over," John admitted. "We tried our best, but nothing led to the culprit."

"Until now," Harry added.

"Yes, four months after we decided no more could be done." John raised his eyes to the ceiling and let out a long sigh. "I'll speak to Sir Rupert tomorrow, and the jury will have to meet immediately."

"I just wish it didn't involve Aaron's mother," Phoebe said. "That poor woman still suffers and will feel so foolish... even responsible. It was her who repeated those unfortunate words to the man who possibly went on to kill her son. Tomorrow, or the day after, she will have to live with that. It will haunt her for the rest of her life."

"It's a real shame," John agreed.

"But we have no choice." Harry reached out, placing his hand on Phoebe's arm. "We should go now."

"We must," she agreed. "I'm needed at home."

They both stood, thanking John for his time. He walked them to the doorway.

"How long is Ann away for?" Phoebe asked. "Join us for supper tomorrow? You'd be welcome."

"Thank you. I'd like that," John replied. With the door now open, he glanced up at the sky "It's not too late. I've changed my mind – I'm going to New Hall now."

That's what I would do, Harry realised. *No point in sitting at home with this weighing upon him. Sir Rupert won't appreciate hearing this new twist any more than John did, but we have to do the right thing by Aaron and the Chapman family, much as we would prefer to let it lie.* "Would you like me to come with you?" he offered.

"Thank you, but no. I'll smarten myself up a bit and go along shortly," John responded.

They parted now, with Harry and Phoebe walking the few steps to the main road in silence before pausing at the junction.

"Did you know...?" Harry asked, "that Joss had goods stored in Burmarsh Church and Aaron took them?"

"No?"

"It was a couple of weeks before the murder."

"He must have been furious," Phoebe responded as she considered this revelation. But they could linger no more. "We can talk more of it later."

Now they went their separate ways, he to his original forge and she to the family home, their minds full of the unfolding events.

That evening, while Harry sat on the couch reading a story to Esther, and Phoebe settled the twins, there came a tap at the front door. "Wait there," Harry said to his daughter, as he stood and reluctantly moved from the warmth of the fireside.

Sir Rupert Bannerman's manservant stood on the doorstep. "Good evening." He doffed his hat and gave a sharp nod.

"Good evening, Brown," Harry responded. "Come in."

"Thank you." Brown stepped into the hallway and closed the door behind him. "Sir Rupert asks that you and Mrs Farrers kindly call upon him at ten o'clock tomorrow morning. He wishes me to convey his wishes that Mrs Farrers is not inconvenienced by this."

"No, we still have Mireille here for a couple more weeks," Harry replied. "She helps with the children."

"Very well." Brown turned to the closed door behind him.

"Thank you," Harry said, moving forward to open the door. "Thank you for bringing the message." His words were insincere. *It has all started again. The questions. The running about at Sir Rupert's beck and call.*

He returned to Esther and her storybook but now Harry's attention wandered.

Seated in Sir Rupert's study with a cup of coffee cradled in her hands, Phoebe retold the conversation between herself and Mrs Chapman. Without embellishment, it made a short account, yet those words confided while the women shared a pot of tea were compelling evidence.

"I repeated it to Harry and then John Waller," Phoebe explained to Sir Rupert, "so I am sure I remember it just as she told me. Mrs Chapman said that she had heard Mr Bushy ranting in the street and how she found it unsettling. She rushed away, around the corner, and bumped into Mr Bailey." Phoebe paused and glanced at Harry. He offered a brief smile, trusting her to repeat Caroline Chapman's words accurately, and she continued, "Then she said... Aaron's mother said, 'He was terribly kind and listened to my complaints about how disturbing it all was, then we walked up to the seawall. Mr Chapman says he doesn't take to the man, but on that occasion, I found him to be most kind'. I'm sure that's exactly what she said, or very close."

"So you see, sir, we can now be sure of Joss Bailey knowing those fateful words," Harry concluded. "He has motive and a temper. It's just the knife..."

"Our constable is in Hythe as we speak. He met the groom at my stables at some ungodly hour and will have been in the town for the past hour. If he has no joy with the knifesmiths there, he will ride to Lympne. I understand Mr Bailey does more business in Hythe than Dymchurch, and Lympne is no distance from Butlers Farm."

Momentarily stunned by Sir Rupert responding so swiftly, Harry thanked him for taking Phoebe's account seriously and acting upon it as soon as John told him.

"And Mrs Chapman?" Phoebe asked. "Will you speak to her?"

"Only if the murder weapon can be connected with Joss Bailey," Sir Rupert admitted. "Without that, I fear the evidence would not be strong enough and it would be unlikely a conviction could be made."

"That poor woman." The distress could be heard in Phoebe's voice. "First, she loses her beloved son, then the family are told that it was he who stole the Whitsun Gallop cup, and now – and this is the worst – she may learn that it was her folly in speaking of the butcher's fury that led to Aaron's death. I don't know how she will bear it."

"Which is why this will go no further if the knife cannot be linked with our bad-tempered farmer," Sir Rupert responded with uncharacteristic sensitivity.

They spoke half-heartedly of other matters for a few minutes before leaving the comfort of Sir Rupert's study. Brown, who always timed his duties to perfection, arrived in the hallway to escort them to the front door. Before it was fully open, there came the sound of hooves upon the gravelled forecourt and John Waller appeared astride a grey mare.

"By God!" Sir Rupert exclaimed. "I didn't expect… There must be news!"

They walked towards John who dismounted and joined them, the horse on a loose rein.

"Sir, Harry… Phoebe…" John nodded towards each one of them. "There was no searching to be done. The information I sought was found just before I reached Hythe High Street, when I happened upon a knifesmith opening his workshop for the day. He sold Mr Bailey a knife like the murder weapon just a week or so before the crime took place."

"I'd say it *was* the knife," Sir Rupert responded. "Fine work, John! Fine work indeed."

"I was lucky," John admitted. "So, now we know Mr Bailey already had the knife before he plotted to kill."

"Enabling him to act quickly once the idea came to mind," Harry surmised. He glanced at Phoebe. Whereas Sir Rupert and John were clearly exhilarated by the revelation, her expression was serious, and he understood why. "We have found our killer," he said, "but Mrs Chapman will suffer all the more when his name is revealed."

"It must be handled carefully." Sir Rupert lowered his voice. "No one can get wind of this before the Chapmans are told and an arrest made. I see no reason for the whole jury to be called. This will raise gossip and

266

speculation amongst those who hear of our meeting – the wives, the maids... they will all have opinions and before the end of the day, the whole village will know that the case has been reopened. We keep this amongst ourselves."

Harry glanced towards Brown who remained at the doorway of New Hall.

"Brown hears nothing," Sir Rupert told him. "Now, let's return to my study." He glanced at Phoebe, "You are as much a part of this as us men, but I know you have duties at home. Do you prefer to stay or leave?"

"I'll go home, sir," Phoebe answered immediately. "My thoughts are with Mrs Chapman, but I can do no more than pray she finds a way to come to terms with the shocking news she'll hear today or very soon."

Chapter Twenty-Five
Toke

There's something odd going on in the village today. I can't say what. If I could, then perhaps it would make some sense. And if it made sense then it wouldn't be odd.

Sitting atop the Dymchurch Wall, with his legs dangling down towards the sand, Toke took a swig of weak ale, then returned to his packet of bread and cheese. With his eyes narrowed, he twisted to watch Sir Rupert and Phoebe pass by.

I can't say I've seen the pair of them out walking before today. First, they went one way and now the other. She looks… she looks… Sad. Yes, that's exactly what it is. Not like she's suffering over something terrible, but just sad.

As he followed their progress, Toke saw Sir Rupert and Phoebe moving from the seawall to take a landward track.

There's the pair of them going back to their homes, no doubt. I see a lot from up here on this old Wall, but I don't see it all. All sorts can happen in the village, and it goes unseen by us when we are here or down on the beach. But today I feel it – I feel there's plotting and scheming and secrets being whispered about the place. I won't say nothing to the others working though – they think about the wooden stakes and about not getting splinters in their hands, and if their wives have got a nice bit of dinner waiting for them. They don't know there's something brewing.

We'll all know about it soon enough, whatever it is. It's the sort of news that won't stay quiet for long.

Toke put the last piece of bread in his mouth and chewed slowly. Then he took a long swig of ale and secured the bung in his flask.

"Come on, Toke," the foreman bellowed at the end of the working day. "Get your tools packed up. The expenditor won't wait for you."

"I don't plan for him to be waiting," Toke called back. "You know me – I'll be there in a flash and away off home for me supper."

He bounded up the ladder from the beach to the Wall, darting past a pair of older and slower wall-workers, then carefully placed a heavy mallet in the bottom of a handcart. A wizened old man gave a nod to acknowledge the tool being returned. Toke picked up his bag, feeling the weight of his flask shift within it, and slung his woollen cloak across his shoulders.

The workers travelled the length of the Wall to receive the shillings doled out by the expenditor who had left his comfortable office at New Hall, as he did at the end of each working day. Usually, the men took their pay and left. This was not the place to stand and gossip like the women of the village. The tavern or their own fireside beckoned and, even though the primroses and crocuses were in bloom, there was a definite chill in the air. On this day, for some reason, as yet unknown by Toke, they lingered.

Why aren't they moving on? Toke wondered. He hadn't managed to shake off that feeling of there being secrets to be learned. *There's news to be told. I'm sure of it. And it will have something to do with Mrs Farrers going walking on the Wall with Sir Rupert himself.* Toke picked up his already swift pace and was soon pushing his way into the gathering of about two dozen men.

They all spoke amongst themselves, expressing their disbelief and opinions:

"Who'd have thought it."

"I never liked the man."

"He had a temper, and there's no denying it."

"They took him this afternoon – to the gaol."

For a couple of minutes Toke felt as if he was drowning in a sea of words. They swept over him: broken sentences, reports of an arrest, speculation. Yet he heard no name – perhaps they dare not mention it. Nor could Toke fathom the reason for the arrest, although it was clear this was no petty crime but an event to rock Dymchurch and the wider area.

"Excuse me, but who's been arrested and why?" Toke asked the man who stood beside him, someone who worked along the next stretch of seawall and generally had a friendly word to say when they passed each other or met to collect their pay.

"Joss Bailey!" came the response. He lowered his voice. "For the murder of… Aaron Chapman."

Good for him! Toke had the sense to keep his initial reaction to himself, and instead he responded with a vague, "In the churchyard?"

"Of course. He didn't get himself stabbed anywhere else, did he?"

"I knew something was happening," Toke replied. "I saw Sir Rupert with Mrs Farrers and they were up to something important." But the other man had turned away and Toke was left rather deflated. "What were they doing?" he continued, his words trailing to a whisper.

A lad who worked on the eastern stretch of the seawall joined the gathering. "Is there a problem with getting our money?" he asked no one in particular.

Pleased to oblige, Toke responded, "Not at all. The money is there for the taking, but we're all here talking about the latest news." He paused in anticipation of relaying the shocking revelation.

"That's all right, then. Ma won't be best pleased if I go home with nothing but torn breeches and mucky hands." He started to push through the crowd.

"Hey, don't you want to know?" Toke called out. "Don't you want to know about..." But the lad was focussed on his shilling and getting home. So, Toke elbowed his way through. *I'll get my money and head back home as fast as I can. There's news to be told at Burmarsh, and I reckon I'll be the first to tell it.*

"What's wrong with you, boy?" Ma Spicer snapped. "Don't come rushing in here like the devil is at your backside. You're raising all the dust."

"I'm a man now, Ma," Toke reminded her. "There's news from Dymchurch and I thought you and Pa would want to hear it."

From his armchair by the fire, Pa Spicer turned to watch his son progress from the doorway to the fireside. "That Joss Bailey's been arrested," he stated. "Had a temper on him, but who would have thought..."

Deflated, Toke turned and slumped on a chair at the kitchen table. "They're all talking about it," he said. "Up on the Wall."

"They'll be talking about it all over Romney Marsh by sunset tomorrow," Pa Spicer responded. "Them jury, they won't want no one making fools of them again. He's heading for the gallows, and I won't be sorry."

"He's a nasty one. But I don't want talk of the gallows, not here in our cottage." Ma cut a thick slice of bread, spread a generous portion of dripping over it, and passed it to Toke, who bit into it with relish.

"You heard her, boy. No more talk of him over at Rothschild and him who's in the gaol now," Pa ordered. "It's upsetting your ma."

Toke gave no reply but ploughed steadily though his bread. *I'll be off to the tavern. There won't be no women in there, bossing me about.*

Over the coming weeks, speculation flew about the place. Stories of Mrs Bailey casting aside her dour expression and taking a lover from Hythe were passed from one eager ear to the next and embellished beyond recognition from the original whisper of gossip. Joss Bailey's nephews came, two of them from Sellindge, to tend the sheep and continue the spring ploughing. Said to be likeable chaps, they met with approval from those who happened to meet them – although no one ever shared a first-hand report of the pair.

Then there came stories from New Hall and even the gaol. It was claimed that the stablehand heard Joss Bailey demanding Romney Marsh mutton for his dinner, and that he bellowed his fury long into the night. Brown manned the front door, his expressions unreadable as the village constable and members of the jury came and went.

Such was the attention upon the intimate triangle of church, gallows and New Hall, that those good folk of Dymchurch barely noticed the young Frenchwoman leave from the beach at Wall End. Having caused such interest on her arrival, hardly a murmur passed their lips when she departed upon *Louisa-Ann* at the end of March.

Toke, who had long been an admirer of Mireille's gentle beauty, noted and mourned her departure. From his place working on the Wall, he had spotted her daily, and lately, when there came an opportunity, he had been bold enough to offer a simple greeting: 'Good morning, Miss Bernard'. Her response – a smile or a brief 'Good day' had cast a glow within him for the coming hours.

One April morning, which would never be remembered for a glorious sunrise, or tempestuous winds, for it was merely a day of misty drizzle from dusk to dawn, Mr Joss Bailey of Butlers Farm was led from the gaol to the courtroom. A couple of hours later, for he vehemently denied killing Aaron Chapman, he stood in the dock to hear the outcome. Guilty. The following day, Joss Bailey's life ended at the noose. The people of Dymchurch gathered on the land between the gallows and Ship Inn, and the landlord smiled to himself, knowing his coffers would be filled that day.

Epilogue
Early June 1766

"I wonder who will be on the beach to meet us," Phoebe forced herself to keep up with the patter of excited chatter coming from Esther. Exhausted from the boat journey across the Channel, she continued, "Do you recognise anyone?"

"It's too soon," Esther complained. "I can't see them properly." She looked towards her brother and sister who lay together, arms and legs entwined with a bundle of rough blankets. "Shall we wake them?"

"No!" Phoebe's response came swiftly.

Esther fell silent for a moment, all her concentration on the white sands of Wissant beach. Phoebe glanced towards Harry who was with Joshua at the helm.

"Mama! I can see the donkeys!" Esther screeched.

"The twins…" Phoebe reminded her. They slept on, oblivious to their sister's excitement.

"There's Mireille and a man. Is it Grand-père? Is it?"

Phoebe studied the person standing close to Mireille. "No, it's not. This is a younger man, perhaps…"

"It's Jesse!" Esther announced. "Can you see, Mama? It's Jesse! Why does he have his arm around Mireille? Is she sad?"

"It is Jesse!" Phoebe felt the fatigue lift. "No, she's not sad. She looks happy, don't you think? Very happy."

The End

About the Author

Romney Marsh writer, Emma Batten, loves to combine her interest in local history with creative writing. It is important to her that historical details are accurate in order to give readers an authentic insight into life on Romney Marsh. She enjoys giving author talks about her journey as a writer, planning unique writing workshops and meeting her local readers.

The Dymchurch Reckoning is Emma's twelfth novel.

Books
Reading order and publication dates

The Dungeness Saga (also featuring Lydd and Ashford) set in late Victorian times through to WW2:

Still Shining Bright* (2020): Cora and her daughter, Emily, are brought ashore to Dungeness by lifeboat. With no home or possessions, they rely on the kindness of strangers, and Cora must use her wit to survive.

Reckless Choices* (2021): A chance meeting on a train upsets Emily, while on the streets of Ashford someone lurks waiting to make trouble. As tensions brew within a close family, the young woman makes a rash choice.

Secrets of the Shingle (2016 & 2020): A mystery set on the wild, windswept wastes of the Dungeness peninsula in the 19th century and seen through the eyes of a naive young teacher.

Stranger on the Point (2018): Lily sets off to discover the remote coastal village her mother called home. A wrong turning takes her to a place where her arrival brings hope. The story of a determined young woman's quest to fulfil her worth, as shadows of WW1 live on.

The Artist's Gift (2019): This tells the story of a fictional young woman, widowed through the war and living amongst real life events during the Second World War. Inspired by the bombing of Lydd Church.

*Prequels to *Secrets of the Shingle*

Stand-alone novels:

A Place Called Hope (2005, reworked 2019): Set in the 16th century, this tells the story of two young women living through the decline of a remote settlement named Hope on Romney Marsh.

What the Monk Didn't See (2017 & 2021): The story of New Romney and the 1287 storm, which changed the fortunes of the town forever. As the storm breaks out, a monk climbs to the roof of the church tower. It is a superb vantage point, but what doesn't he see?

The Saxon Series introduces West Hythe, Lyminge and Aldington in 7th- century Anglo-Saxon times:

The Pendant Cross (2020): For a few days a year, the Sandtun (West Hythe) is used as a seasonal trading settlement. While they await the boats from Francia, friendships are made and hatred brews. Meanwhile, four monks travel by night carrying a precious secret.

The Sacred Stone (2021): An earthquake uncovers a Roman altar buried in the foundations of an old fort. An ambitious thane and his priest are determined to secure this prize, and their actions have repercussions on the people of Aldington.

The Dymchurch Series is set in Georgian times.

But First Maintain the Wall (2018): Harry is passing through the village when the seawall breaches and events force him to stay. As an outsider, he struggles to be accepted and a tentative friendship is forged with a young woman who seeks answers to her past.

The Whitsun Gallop (2022): On the day of the annual Whitsun Gallop, the people of Romney Marsh gather. It is a day to parade their best outfits, make merry, and wager on which gentleman jockey will glory. When the prize cup is stolen under the eyes of local dignitaries, a chain of events is set in place, rocking the secure world of Harry and Phoebe Farrers.

The Dymchurch Reckoning (2023):
A brutal encounter in the churchyard raises shockwaves beyond Dymchurch as the hunt for the killer begins and Harry Farrers finds himself in the midst of troubles caused by an old enemy.

For more details take a look at Emma's website:
www.emmabattenauthor.com